The start of something big...

Mac's gaze flitted with studied nonchalance around the room, returning every few seconds to the door. A feeling of taut excitement hummed through his body as he waited for Juliet to arrive.

He could still see her striding up and down the pier, the curves of her body molded by the stretchy fabric of her suit, a sea nymph as graceful on land as she was in the water. He hadn't been able to take his eyes off her.

It's the case that's so intriguing, not the woman, he reminded himself. It was always this way at the beginning of the chase. Every cell in his body was tuned for battle, his senses heightened, his mind focused. Adrenaline pumped through his veins in an exhilarating rush as he prepared to face the enemy.

Then he sent another glance to the door, where Juliet stood framed in the entrance as if summoned by his thought.

Could this woman ever be his enemy?

Dear Reader,

The editorial staff of Silhouette Intimate Moments is always striving to bring new and exciting things your way: new authors, new concepts in romantic fiction and new ideas from favorite authors. This month we have once again come up with something special.

Emilie Richards is one of your favorite authors, as your letters have made clear, and this month she embarks on a project that will delight her current fans and undoubtedly win her new ones. Tales of the Pacific is a four-book miniseries set in Hawaii, Australia and New Zealand, and the cast of characters who fill the pages of these books will make you laugh, make you cry and make you fall in love—over and over again. Of course, each book stands alone as it presents one very special story, and in *From Glowing Embers*, the first book of the series, Julianna Mason and Gray Sheridan will capture your heart as they strive to mend the hurts of the past and rebuild their marriage. Theirs is a love story that will truly leave you breathless.

Also this month, look for delightful treats from Paula Detmer Riggs, whose first book was part of our March Madness promotion, Marion Smith Collins, and an author who's new to Silhouette Books but not to fans of romance, Andrea Parnell.

As always, Silhouette Intimate Moments is the place to find love stories *for* today's women *by* today's women. We hope you'll enjoy them as much as we do.

Leslie J. Wainger
Senior Editor

Paula Detmer Riggs

Suspicious Minds

Silhouette Intimate Moments

Published by Silhouette Books New York

America's Publisher of Contemporary Romance

SILHOUETTE BOOKS
300 East 42nd St., New York, N.Y. 10017

ISBN: 0-373-07250-3

First Silhouette Books printing August 1988

Printed in the U.S.A.

PAULA DETMER RIGGS

discovers material for her writing in her varied life experiences. During her first five years of marriage to a naval officer, she lived in nineteen different locations on the West Coast, gaining familiarity with places as diverse as San Diego and Seattle. While working at a historical site in San Diego she wrote, directed and narrated fashion shows and became fascinated with the early history of California.

She writes romances because "I think we all need an escape from the high-tech pressures that face us every day, and I believe in happy endings. Isn't that why we keep trying in spite of all the roadblocks and disappointments along the way?"

To Pat Adams-Manson, Kathy Austin and
Diane Dunaway, three terrific ladies
who've helped me
more than they can ever know.

And to Carl, who's always there.

Chapter 1

Captain Roarke McKinley walked alone, his footsteps echoing in uneven cadence along the deserted corridors of the Pentagon maze.

He was a tall man, lean and hard, with a flat belly and shoulders so broad they had taxed the skills of Navy tailors for over twenty years.

His eyes were deep blue and intense below arrogant chestnut brows. The weathered skin of his cheeks stretched tautly over the prominent bones of his face, giving him a spare, almost hawklike look, and he walked with a cane, a sturdy walking stick of ebony and silver that seemed a part of him.

It was a few minutes before midnight, eastern time. Typewriters were silent, and computer screens were dark, except here in the heart of the huge building where the senior members of Naval Intelligence had their offices.

The call had come at eleven. He'd been home alone, reading in front of a fire in the book-lined den of his Alexandria town house.

The man on the other end of the line had been Admiral Hendricks himself, his voice clipped and cold, and the captain had known then that his plans for a rare quiet evening had just been changed.

The admiral's aide stood instantly to attention as McKinley entered the sparsely furnished anteroom and closed the door behind him.

The aide saluted smartly. "Good evening, sir," he said crisply.

"Hell of a blizzard out there, Lieutenant," Captain McKinley said in a baritone rumble. A brief smile deepened the harsh lines bracketing his mouth as he returned the salute.

"Yes, sir," Lieutenant Blake agreed with alacrity. "It's a wild one, all right." He remained standing, waiting while the captain removed his gold-encrusted cap and shrugged out of his heavy coat.

"I'll take those, sir," the lieutenant said with formal courtesy, his tone respectful as he stepped forward to take the coat and hat.

McKinley nodded his thanks and smoothed a large hand over his wiry chestnut hair before rapping sharply on the heavy walnut door leading to the admiral's private office. Without waiting for an answer, he opened the door and stepped inside.

The office seemed more like a room in a private club, with warm pecan paneling and tastefully framed naval prints providing a deceptively serene backdrop for the hard-faced man behind the desk.

Vice Admiral Carter Hendricks looked up from the file he was reading and watched in brooding silence as McKinley closed the door behind him.

"Evening, admiral," McKinley said in a dry voice. "Or should I say good morning?"

The older man scowled and muttered a terse greeting. He was in his shirt-sleeves, his tie loosened and his gray hair disheveled. His craggy face was lined with fatigue, and his pale blue eyes were bloodshot.

His desk, framed by the American flag and the blue-and-gold ensign of the U.S. Navy, was piled high with papers and folders, and there was a sophisticated phone console with a built-in scrambler at his elbow.

"Have a seat, Mac," he growled in a voice turned to gravel by a two-pack-a-day cigarette habit. "I have a hell of a problem."

"Yeah, so I gathered, Carter," Mac said with a quick grin, his eyes warming several degrees. "Otherwise, why would you be spending Friday night sitting behind that desk?"

Using the polished black cane in his left hand with the ease of long practice, Mac moved across the spacious room and eased into the leather-bound chair in front of the massive mahogany desk.

The grimace of pain that crossed his face as he extended his long legs out in front of him was fleeting, but the admiral, in the process of lighting a cigarette, noticed.

"Is that bum knee of yours giving you trouble again?" he asked brusquely.

"No more than usual." Mac kept his expression carefully neutral. He knew that the admiral's concern was genuine; they'd been friends for a long time. But he hated to talk about his leg, hated even to think about it.

Eight years ago he'd been rescued, battered and unconscious, from a small country in the Middle East, gravely injured in a covert action gone sour.

Hendricks had been at his bedside through more rough operations and sleepless nights than Mac wanted to remember.

Mac propped his cane against the desk and methodically rubbed the knotted muscle in his left thigh. He was lucky that he could walk at all.

His slightly halting gait was a major triumph for the Navy orthopedists at Bethesda, who'd spent sixteen months putting his shattered leg back together again. Now he wore a heavy brace of leather and steel on his knee and walked with a cane.

Mac glanced across the desk and grinned sardonically. "It's these frigid winters, Carter," he said in the lazy Virginia drawl he'd never quite managed to shed in spite of all the years spent away from the state of his birth. "Days like this when the snow is up to my butt, I swear I'm going to retire and buy myself an island in the South Seas someplace where I can sit on the lanai and sip rum. Maybe even write a book—after a few years or so.''

"Actually," Hendricks replied with a grim smile, "you're going to be seeing sunshine and sandy beaches a lot sooner than you might think. I'm sending you to San Diego on a matter of highest priority. We have a nasty leak in one of our underwater research projects out there, and I want it plugged, A.S.A.P.''

The amused glint in Mac's deep blue eyes disappeared, replaced by a look of deadly intensity.

"Which project?" he asked, shifting his weight. His knee throbbed with a dull ache that he'd accepted long ago.

"The dolphin project for the Naval Research Center," Hendricks amplified. "Code name Ping Pong."

Mac frowned. As a senior agent he was privy to most of the vital and sensitive projects being undertaken by the Navy and its private contractors, but it took him a minute to place this one. "Ping Pong? The one linked to the submarine detection network?"

Hendricks nodded soberly. "The same. As I understand it, dolphins have this built-in ability to locate and identify objects by the use of echo-sounding, something that we're just beginning to understand." He grimaced self-consciously. "The experts at the Defense Department tell me that someday we'll be able to string a line of these electronic detecting devices along both coasts that will be so sensitive we'll know everything about a passing sub except the name of her captain."

Mac chuckled. "Sounds like a hell of an idea to me. Especially if the other side doesn't know we have it."

"They know we're working with the dolphins. Anyone steaming the channel on San Diego Bay can see the tanks. But so far as we know, the Soviets don't know what kinds of tests we're running."

"And you want me to make sure they don't find out, is that it?"

"Exactly." The admiral's brows swooped into a dark scowl. "Naturally it's complex as hell, but fortunately, you and I don't have to understand what the technical types are doing. We just have to make sure that *our* technical types don't spill the beans to *their* technical types, and it looks as though that's exactly what's been happening."

"You've heard about this leak from a reliable source, I gather?"

"The information came straight from Hydra," Hendricks replied, his eyes narrowing at the mention of the CIA's most valuable double agent. "Two days ago he was ordered by Moscow to contact an agent in San Diego, code-named Alexey, who gave him a roll of film to deliver to the KGB."

Mac rubbed the stout cane with his thumb in silent reflection. "You've seen the text?"

Hendricks nodded toward a red folder lying on the corner of his desk. Top Secret was stamped in white on the front. He lit another cigarette from the butt of the last one and blew the smoke toward the ceiling.

Mac reached for the folder and paged through the photocopies with a grim expression that hardened into steel as he read.

"Damn!" he exclaimed in dismay. "I'm no expert, but it looks like it's all here. Facts, figures, projections, theories, even detailed speculation on how to use the findings." He closed the folder and tossed it onto the blotter in front of him.

Excitement was beginning to snake through him, honing his senses and tensing his muscles. This wasn't an ordinary case. He could feel it.

"Yeah, it's all there, all right," Hendricks said in a sour tone. "About twelve years' work, according to the Defense Department." The admiral ran one hand agitatedly through his thick gray mane. "Thank God Hydra intercepted it. I hate to think what kind of damage this could do in the wrong hands."

Hydra had never been wrong. Mac didn't know his name or his face, but he knew that the men had proven invaluable as an informant, especially in matters concerning the KGB.

Mac smoothed the dark blue wool of his uniform trousers over his knee. "So what's the problem? If Hydra knows the identity of the agent, it should be easy enough to trace the leak."

The admiral shook his head. "Alexey is a go-between. The real threat is the person inside Ping Pong. That's the man—or woman—I want you to find, and you only have three weeks to do it."

Mac's brows drew together over the pronounced hump at the bridge of his nose. "Why three weeks?" He could already feel the exhilaration of the chase heating the marrow of his bones.

"In three weeks Hydra will be attending a conference in Vienna on grain exporting. He's supposed to turn the information over to the KGB courier who's a member of the Russian delegation." The admiral took a deep pull on his cigarette, narrowing his eyes against the smoke as he exhaled. "This material is so vital to the Russians that they're not taking any chances with their normal channels."

"So fake the information."

Hendricks shook his head. "Too risky. We have no guarantee they'll use Hydra the next time they have material to send. You know how paranoid they are, switching couriers to keep their agents on their toes."

He took another deep drag. "If we fake the test results and they get hold of the real thing through another source, they'll know something is wrong. We can't put Hydra at risk."

He coughed in hacking spasms, excusing himself with an impatient wave of his hand. "The KGB trusts Hydra. That's why they're letting him bring the information." His voice took on an added urgency. "Three weeks, Mac. The boys over in Langley are adamant. We can't risk blowing Hydra's cover. He's too valuable."

Mac gave his superior a thoughtful look. "So I plug the leak for you from the inside, the KGB thinks it's a routine security check that got lucky, and the CIA sends phony facts and figures with Hydra."

Admiration shone in the admiral's wintry eyes for an instant before he nodded curtly. "Exactly. We're already working on a harmless substitute for Hydra to pass on. It'll be a one-shot deal, leading the Russians to think our research is a total bust, and as long as the leak is plugged at this end, there's a good chance they'll buy it. But Hydra has to know that his back is covered when he's all alone over there. One hint that something's not right, and he's history."

"I understand." Hydra was a man who'd chosen to betray the country of his birth. Why, Mac didn't know, but he preferred to believe that it was for honorable reasons that the man believed the U.S. stood for things the USSR didn't.

His eyes slid to the American flag to the right of the admiral's desk. In every generation since 1776 there had been a member of his family who'd served that flag as an officer in the military. "Duty, Honor, Country" was more than a slogan to the descents of Edward Roarke, an indentured servant who'd come from England in search of freedom in 1642. To Mac and those who'd gone before him, it was a way of life, even though it was one that had almost killed him.

The admiral sighed heavily and stubbed out his cigarette. His voice assumed a hard edge. "Here are the facts as I see them, Mac. Someone has access to the test data virtually as soon as it's compiled. My best guess is that it's one of the four marine biologists involved in this particular project. But which one?"

Mac shrugged. "Ask me in three weeks."

A grim smile brushed the admiral's lips. "You're the best investigator I have, Mac. And this is just about the toughest assignment I've ever handed you. I'm not exaggerating when I say that it would do tremendous damage to our counterintelligence force if Hydra is compromised."

Mac shrugged out of his uniform jacket and draped it carelessly over the back of the chair. For the past six years, since his release from the naval hospital, his highest priority had been his work, and he was eager to get started.

"What kind of support can you give me on this one?"

"Whatever you need. Top priority all the way. I've already made arrangements for an F-14 to be standing by to take you to the coast when you're ready, and I've ordered the head of Naval Investigative Services in San Diego, Phil Cahill, to give you anything you want as soon as you ask for it."

"Right," Mac replied grimly. "If Blake can scare up some black coffee, I'll get started." He loosened his plain black tie and unbuttoned his starched collar.

The admiral buzzed his aide and asked for a pot of coffee, and Mac opened the bulging manila folder on top of the pile. His weekend plans to spend time at the family estate in southern Virginia were already far from his mind.

Three hours and four cups of coffee later, Mac sat back and rubbed his stinging eyes. Hendricks was still reading the last of the four dossiers, absently rubbing the bridge of his nose with his thumb and forefinger as he concentrated. The ashtray at his elbow was full, and the air was thick with smoke.

It was past 3:00 a.m., and Hendricks looked years older than the fifty-two Mac knew him to be. Mac himself was feeling bone weary, and he was nearly ten years younger than his superior.

He slumped against the back of the padded seat and rested his hands on his thighs. The blue stone in his Naval Academy ring caught the light from the desk lamp, forcefully reminding him that he'd spent exactly half of his life in the United States Navy, most of them on twenty-four-hour alert.

The admiral looked up and grimaced as he fumbled for another cigarette. "So, what do you think?" He nodded toward the folders.

"I'll need an airtight cover," Mac began. "Something that won't make the project team suspicious. Maybe something to do with the computer system they're using, so I can have access to their files. I'll check with Information Systems, see if they're due for an update."

"I'm glad you understand that gobbledygook well enough to fake it. I sure as hell couldn't."

"Spend a year flat on your back with nothing else to do and you can learn to understand anything," Mac said with a dismissive shrug.

The admiral grunted. "Investigative Services is pretty sure this woman Prentice is the guilty party. Do you agree?" He regarded the glowing tip of his cigarette with hard eyes.

Mac glanced at the thick folder in front of him. The red flag affixed to the name tab indicated the highest possible clearance for a civilian employee of the government.

"On the basis of the evidence we have to date, she appears to be the *only* logical suspect," he said with slow deliberation. "The other two biologists, Kurtz and Feldman, are so clean they squeak. Still, that doesn't necessarily rule them out."

"What about her assistant, Handleman? The FBI background check shows a juvenile arrest for possession."

Mac shrugged. "The kid was caught with less than an ounce of grass when he was fourteen. I'll check him out, of course, but first I intend to make the acquaintance of Dr. Prentice."

He opened the folder and flipped through the pages until he reached the back of the file. "The first thing I have to check out is this unexplained income that's detailed in Investigative Services' preliminary report." His voice thinned as he read aloud. "'Fifteen thousand dollars was paid by subject over a period of eight months, in cash, to Mar Vista Rehabilitation Center, where subject's younger brother is a patient.'"

Mac thumbed to a copy of a computer printout. "Here's her pay record to date, and from what I can see, she hasn't been making the kind of money that would allow such a huge extra expense. Also, there's no record of a loan from the credit union or any other lending institution. In fact, there's no paper trail of any kind."

Hendricks lifted an eyebrow. "Looks fairly conclusive to me."

"Maybe," Mac conceded, a cautious undertone softening his drawl. He glanced down at the photograph lying on top of the file folder in front of him. It was a color picture of a leggy, deeply tanned blond woman taken in front of the oceanographic research vessel, *Neptune*.

The photo had been taken by a good camera using a telephoto lens. The subject had been caught in the act of speaking to a young sandy-haired man in brief swimming trunks who was perched on the prow of the ship.

The woman's attire was almost puritanical by comparison. Her shiny green swimsuit was severe in cut, reminding Mac of the tank suits worn by Olympic swimmers. Her shoulders were covered by a man's blue cotton shirt, unbuttoned and tied in a knot below her generous breasts.

A thick wavy mane of honey-colored hair was blowing around her face, framing classically high cheekbones with tawny color. Her small chin sported a saucy cleft and was lifted almost defiantly, as though she were making a point.

Her skin was clear and glowing, tanned the color of a ripe peach, and tiny golden freckles dusted the bridge of her up-turned nose.

She was smiling—no, that was too tame a description, Mac decided, his eyes narrowing. Her coral lips were slightly parted, as though for a kiss, with the sensuous curve of her full bottom lip promising tantalizing delights.

He turned the photo over. "Juliet Forsythe Prentice, Ph.D." The name rolled off his tongue in a poetic cadence. "Pretty name for a pretty lady," he mused with an involuntary glance at Hendricks.

"We both know that's no guarantee of innocence, Mac. Don't we?" The admiral gazed back at him impassively, his fingers forming a steeple in front of his face.

Mac nodded. "Yes, we know," he replied, a cynical edge crisping his drawl. Carter was the only one who knew the full story of the incident in the Middle East, the only one who knew what a damned fool he'd been.

Mac stirred restlessly in his chair. He didn't want to think about the past. "I saw her father on stage once," he said with a slight smile. "Justin Forsythe Prentice. Hell of an actor."

Hendricks nodded. "Hell of a lover, too, if I remember correctly. Didn't he leave his family to run off with some starlet or something?"

"Model, I think." Mac frowned. "Middle America never forgave him for leaving a sick wife and two kids. His career was pretty much shot." He paged through the file, then glanced up at the admiral. "He's been dead, what? Ten, twelve years now?"

"God knows. I can't even remember what happened yesterday." Hendrick's grin flashed suddenly, then disappeared just as abruptly. "Could be the daughter is just as shallow and selfish."

"Paying her brother's medical expenses doesn't sound selfish to me," Mac said evenly, watching his superior with veiled eyes.

"Selling out is still selling out, Mac. No matter what the reason is. On paper this woman looks guilty, and if she is, I want her nailed." There was an edge of command in the admiral's voice that brought a wash of dusky color to Mac's cheeks.

"Understood, sir," he said with just the right amount of military sharpness, his eyes locking with his superior's.

Hendricks scowled. "Forget I said that, Mac. You don't need me to tell you how to do your job." He crushed out his cigarette in the overflowing ashtray with jerky, agitated fingers.

Mac's fist closed around the photo, curling the glossy paper into a tight tube. Carter was being diplomatic, but they both remembered a time when Mac had disregarded Carter's warning, a time when he'd allowed his personal feelings to overrule his professional judgment.

There had been a photograph then, too. A fuzzy snapshot, taken by a hidden camera, of Misrani meeting with Colonel Hashemi of the secret police of Beshtar, a man she'd professed to abhor.

Mac had defended her, had fought to keep her from being eliminated. Using every scrap of influence he'd possessed, he'd won her a brief reprieve, then gone back to confront her personally. And walked straight into a trap.

As Mac watched Carter pour two more cups of coffee, piercingly vivid images from the past marched through his mind. He'd been thirty-four and recently promoted to commander when he'd been assigned to Beshtar.

There had been several glowing commendations for bravery and skill in his service record. Hendricks had just made him a senior agent, and he had felt as invincible as the flag he served when he'd been assigned to recruit covert agents in a clutch of oil rich sheikdoms in the Middle East. He'd already achieved a creditable amount of success by the time he'd arrived in Beshtar.

He'd been introduced to Misrani the second day, at an embassy reception where he was posing as a trade expert. From the first he'd been enchanted by her eyes. Soft, innocent eyes that had called to a man's soul. By the time he'd convinced her to go out with him, he was already half in love with her. Several months after she'd agreed to spy on the Marxist elements infiltrating her country, Mac had asked her to marry him. And she'd accepted.

Mac shifted in his chair, trying without success to ease the discomfort in his leg. He could feel the familiar black thoughts beginning to push against the edges of his conscious mind, thoughts of despair and self-loathing, thoughts that had tormented him through countless sleepless nights before he'd been able to master them.

He could still see her. Misrani. A woman with a beautiful name and a beautiful face. A woman who'd won his trust and his love, only to betray him, callously and without remorse.

He'd almost died in that arid, strife-ridden country. As it was, he'd been tortured into unconsciousness while Misrani had watched in silence, her face a mask of vicious satisfaction.

Mac took a deep breath and forced his rigid muscles to relax. He'd made a bad mistake in Beshtar, a mistake that had left him a cripple for the rest of his life. Never again would he allow his emotions to overrule his intellect. Never again would he allow himself to be vulnerable.

He opened his fist, and the photo of Juliet Prentice slowly uncurled. His eyes shone with bleak determination as he stared into the woman's piquant face. Her beauty was like a beacon calling to the unwary, but Mac was immune. He had no personal feelings for her one way or another. If she was innocent, he would simply move on to the next likely suspect. But if she was guilty, he would follow his orders to the letter. He would nail her to the wall.

A storm was headed her way. She could feel it, and so could the dolphins in the bayside tanks.

Juliet Prentice gritted her teeth in rising frustration as she scanned the darkening sky above her. "Damn," she muttered, drawing her silky blond brows together in a worried frown.

The wind had shifted suddenly and a stiff breeze, moisture-laden and heavy with the scent of salt, was blowing in from the Pacific, reddening her smooth cheeks and ruffling the thick ponytail of honey-blond curls that brushed the neckline of her pale blue wet suit.

A puffy canopy of rain-swollen clouds blocked the warming rays of the mild winter sun, casting a chilly shadow over the peninsula of Point Loma, where the Naval Research Center was located. Home for a variety of top-secret projects, the base was composed largely of squat boxlike buildings erected during World War II to accommodate the swelling ranks of raw recruits passing through San Diego on the way overseas.

Here, on the north shore of San Diego Bay, the water had been divided by boardwalks and low chain-link fences into six pools of various sizes and depths where the dolphins were housed and tested.

Juliet was working in Alpha tank, the deepest of the six, using Poseidon, the largest of the four adult dolphins, as her primary test subject.

"Give me a break, okay?" she yelled at the gray clouds overhead. "All I need is one more hour." The wind pulled the words away from her mouth as soon as she uttered them, leaving her breathless and edgy.

Lightning flashed to the southeast, splitting a towering black cloud hovering over the jagged mountain peaks of northern Mexico.

"Thanks a lot," Juliet muttered in disgust, stalking down the pier toward the monitor board that contained the specially designed instruments used to record the complex sounds emitted by the dolphins during each test.

The sound of muffled thunder reverberated across the bay, and Juliet scowled. She and Greg would be extremely vulnerable standing over the water during a violent electrical storm. Was it worth the risk?

Her heart began to pound, and the fine hairs on the back of her neck stiffened. How many times had she asked herself that question during the past nine months?

Gnawing absently on the inside of her cheek, she stared across the wide bay, trying to decide what to do. She could feel the charged particles of dense air swirling around her slim body as the high-pitched chatter of the impatient dolphins filled her ears.

"What do you think, Dr. Prentice? Should we quit for the day?" Greg Handleman, the project's only research assistant, climbed out of the tank and glanced toward the clouds over their heads. His tall, reed-thin body swayed with nervous energy as he wiped the water from his angular face with a ragged beach towel.

"I think it'll hold off long enough for us to complete these last two tests," Juliet said with more assurance than she felt. Tension thinned her delicate upper lip into a determined line. "We're already behind schedule as it is, and if we stop now, we'll have to rerun the entire series."

Greg's face flamed with chagrin. "I'm really sorry about the foul-up, Dr. Prentice. I know you're under a lot of pressure, what with your brother being in the hospital and all, and—"

Juliet cut him short. "Mistakes happen, Greg," she said with a generous smile that smoothed some of the apprehension from his sunburned brow.

They'd lost almost an hour while Greg had driven to the other side of the base to fetch an underwater microphone he'd forgotten to pick up at the repair shop.

"From now on I'm gonna make a list of things to do each day, just like you do. I promise." He rubbed the top of his crew cut as though for luck, and Juliet managed to stifle a laugh.

"Let's go, guys," she shouted at the two male dolphins in the tank.

Poseidon, always the opportunist, swerved to the edge of the pier and began asking for a treat.

Juliet laughed through her anxiety. "Beggar," she said with a fond lilt. "You know better than that." During a formal training session the dolphins received food only as a reward.

Poseidon chattered a scolding rebuttal, then slipped head first beneath the rippling surface. Choppy waves broke against the pier, shaking the pilings beneath Juliet's wet sneakers.

"Ready when you are, Dr. Prentice." Greg crossed the pier to stand next to the tank, a bucket of raw fish by his rubber boots. In his hand he held three sealed squares of clear plastic, each one weighted at the corners and attached by a short cord to a red nose ring. Two of the stiff squares contained silver quarters, while the third contained a brass coin. At Juliet's command, Greg would fling the squares into the water, and it was Poseidon's task to find the odd one and return it as quickly as possible.

Variations of the same test would be run until the statistics clearly indicated whether or not the dolphins could distinguish size, shape, composition or all three with their built-in sonar.

Juliet slipped the headphones over her ears and switched on the hydrophone. "Poseidon, pay attention," she commanded in a calm voice, raising her right hand.

The dolphin eyed her attentively for an instant before suddenly turning his head toward the shore. Water sheeted from his slick charcoal skin as he began racing around the perimeter of the tank, clicking excitedly as he swam, the frantic sounds signaling a refusal to participate.

Juliet and Greg exchanged puzzled looks.

"What the hell?" Greg exclaimed in exasperation. "Do you know what's wrong?"

Juliet removed the headphones and rested her hands against the flaring curve of her hips. A worried frown drew her finely etched brows together in a faint V above the freckled bridge of her nose as she shook her head. "I've seen this happen sometimes during mating season, or when a stranger comes near the tank, but—" Her mouth closed abruptly as she jerked her head to the side. A man stood at the end of the stubby pier, clearly in the line of sight of the tank.

He was as tall as Greg, but older and heavier, with the shoulders of a wrestler and the long legs of a distance runner. His large frame was trim beneath the navy blue blazer, with hard muscle packed solidly across his chest, his midriff flat, his waist narrow.

His hair, wiry and thick and very curly, was a deep chestnut brown, with a wash of gray at the temples. His face was burnt the color of teak, and the lean planes of his cheeks seemed fashioned from that same hard wood.

An aura of rugged male insolence surrounded him as he leaned with rakish nonchalance on a black cane, legs wide apart, the cane more a signature than a support.

His head was tilted to one side, as though in question, and he was watching her with eyes the color of the sky at dusk. Watching *her*. Not the dolphins, or even Greg. His eyes were riveted on her with the intense focus of an X-ray camera, and there was a look on his dark face that she couldn't decipher.

Juliet's pulse fluttered as she stared at the intruder. Who *was* he? And why did she feel so incredibly uneasy all of a sudden?

"Hey, check out the silver-handled cane," Greg whispered out of the side of his mouth. "Guy must think he's some bad dude."

"I'm more interested in finding out what he's doing in a highly restricted area without a badge," Juliet muttered, coming to herself with a jerk. She reached for the headphones hugging her neck and slipped them over her head. "Here," she said curtly, handing them to Greg. "I'll get rid of him before Poseidon totally loses his concentration."

"Go get him, boss," Greg muttered under his breath.

The stranger's eyes followed her without blinking as she hurried toward him. She strode purposely over the rough surface of the wooden planks, her wet rubber soles leaving small footprints behind her.

As she drew closer, Juliet's steps slowed. He was waiting, his expression one of lazy interest, and she could sense an air of suppressed excitement building within her as she approached.

"May I help you?" she demanded when she reached the end of the pier. She tilted her head upward to meet his gaze. His eyes were very blue—as blue as the superbly fitting blazer hugging his massive shoulders—and surrounded by thick russet lashes that curved upward and were tipped with gold.

No man should be allowed to have eyes like that, Juliet thought in sudden bemusement. They were simply too gorgeous—and far too potent. She blinked rapidly, and the man grinned in amusement.

"You sure have a way with those animals," he said in a husky baritone, his gaze flowing like flame-warmed brandy from the top of her head to her toes and back to her face.

Juliet was suddenly conscious of the skintight suit sheathing her body. She was completely covered, except for her hands and face, yet she felt frighteningly exposed, as though his piercing blue eyes could penetrate the insulating material all the way to her naked skin.

"Look," she said in a voice that sounded oddly breathless, "this is a restricted area. See?"

She pointed to a large white sign on a steel pole a few feet to his left. Bold red letters proclaimed the area off-limits to anyone but authorized personnel.

The man nodded in careless acknowledgment as his gaze followed her pointing finger. "I know that, ma'am," he said, tilting his head as though he were vastly entertained by her caution. "And I assure you that I am authorized. I'm not a man to deliberately break the rules."

I'll just bet, Juliet countered silently, watching the way his lashes brushed against his autocratic cheekbones. Power, that's it, she thought suddenly. That's what this guy projects. Power and confidence. And a subtle sense of danger.

Thunder rumbled in the distance, and Juliet shot a worried glance toward the black clouds overhead. The storm seemed to be coming closer, causing the air between them to crackle with static electricity, and she rushed into speech. "I need to see your badge before I can let you stay around the tank."

The man dipped his head in lazy assent. Even this small movement had a sinuous charm that served to underscore his rugged virility, and Juliet was suddenly very much aware that she was a woman.

"Whatever you say, ma'am," he said politely as he reached into the back pocket of his tailored twill slacks and pulled out a scuffed pigskin wallet. He flipped it open and extracted a yellow plastic badge, which he held out to her.

Juliet's fingers brushed against his as she took the laminated ID card from his hand, and the unexpected contact sent a shivery jolt of pleasure through her taut nervous system. His skin was warm, the texture slightly rougher than hers, and his fingers had felt hard when they'd slid past hers.

Anxious to regain her composure, she took her time, thoroughly studying the card in her hand. He was authorized, all right.

The picture was a decent likeness, better than most she'd seen. He wasn't handsome in the conventional way that her father had been handsome. His chin was too square, his nose too large and bent slightly to one side, as though displaced by another man's fist, and his brow, beneath his shallow widow's peak, was seamed with permanent lines.

No, she decided, there was nothing pretty about this man. Except his mouth. His lips were firm and well-shaped, and there was a tantalizing softness to his upper lip that seemed to suggest an underlying sweetness, perhaps even a vulnerability that he kept well hidden.

She sneaked a peak through the veil of her feathery lashes at that mouth. She could almost feel those lips sliding invitingly over hers, could almost sense the tender urgency behind that devastatingly white smile. He would be a good kisser, this big man with the seductive eyes and harshly sculptured face.

Juliet gave herself a mental shake. Why in the world was she wasting precious time on thoughts of kisses from a perfect stranger? It must be the storm throwing her off balance, she told herself firmly, returning her attention to the ID card.

The man's name was Roarke Randolph McKinley, and his date of birth made him forty-two.

"Roarke," she murmured aloud. The name flowed over her tongue like sweet molasses. "What a beautiful name."

To her surprise, he flushed a dusky red. "It's a family name. On my mother's side. People call me Mac," he said brusquely.

Juliet hid a smile. The man had the physique of a prize fighter and the face of a riverboat gambler, yet he blushed like an awkward adolescent. It was a devastating combination, raw male strength and poetic sensitivity, and much too sexy to contemplate.

Juliet flicked the alligator clip attached to the badge before handing the ID back to him. "Better wear it where it can be seen," she warned with a shaky smile. "Security is extremely tight around here."

Mac clipped the card to his lapel and cocked his head. "Since you know my name, how about telling me yours?"

"Juliet Prentice. I'm with the Dolphin Research Division."

"I'm very pleased to meet you, Ms. Prentice." His voice seemed to linger over her name with shivery slowness as he extended his hand and watched her expectantly. Juliet had no choice but to take the hand he offered so politely. He had a firm grip, but his touch was surprisingly gentle.

"Actually, I'm looking for Dr. Kurtz of Dolphin Research. I reckoned I must be fairly close when I saw the tank." For the first time Juliet noticed the provocative way his deep voice slurred vowels and slid over consonants. The soft drawl was in marked contrast to his rugged appearance, firing her curiosity.

Why in the world would a man like this be looking for Fred? she wondered uneasily. He didn't look like any scientist she'd ever known. For that matter, he didn't look like any man she'd ever known, and she'd known some of the most famous matinee idols of the last thirty years.

"Uh, look, I really have to get back to the tank," she said with a pointed glance over her shoulder. Her hand was still enveloped by his. "You'll find Fred in Building 3. Just follow this sidewalk up the hill and across the road." She tugged her hand from his grasp and pointed. "His office is on the second floor, last one on the right, and—oh, *rats!*" Two fat raindrops pelted her face as the wind began to gust in salty swirls around them. The storm had arrived.

Juliet groaned and spun around to yell at Greg. "Button it up, Greg. We've had it for today."

Her assistant waved cheerfully and began covering the instruments with specially designed shields as Juliet ran up the pier to retrieve the log.

Holding the clipboard against her body, she ran back to the spot where the visitor still watched. "C'mon," she said in a breathy rush. "Let's go."

"Yes, ma'am." He raised one brow mockingly and bowed slightly from the waist, and Juliet burst out laughing.

"Sorry, I didn't mean it to sound like an order. I'm just a little . . . frazzled this morning."

"No problem, Ms. Prentice. I'm working on a bad case of jet lag myself."

"Georgia, right?" she said impulsively. Her father, when he'd been preparing for one of his movie roles, had often practiced his regional dialects on her, and she'd gotten very good at distinguishing the various speech patterns.

Mac shook his head and fell into step beside her. "Close. Virginia, born and bred." He gave her a rueful look. "You've got a good ear, though. Most people think I'm from Texas." His voice had a steely quality that was only partially softened by the honeyed vowels, and she shivered involuntarily as she lowered her head against the gusting wind. He did have that tough cowboy look about him, especially with the weathered skin and the wrinkles around his eyes. But then, so did a lot of the senior naval officers she'd met in the six years she'd been working here on the base.

Was this man in the Navy? An officer? Was he to be the new Navy adviser to the project? Were they replacing the man to whom Fred reported? She hadn't heard of any new staff members, but the Navy rarely consulted its civilian employees when making a change.

She shot him a sideways look. His hair was short enough to be a military cut, and he had that air of unassuming confidence that most career officers had. But what about the cane? That certainly wasn't standard Navy issue. And he wasn't wearing a uniform, so perhaps he was a civilian employee, just as she was.

The temperature was dropping rapidly as the squall settled over the city, and she shivered in spite of the wet suit, automatically quickening her stride.

From the corner of her eye she noticed a tightening of the bronzed skin around Mac's lips, and she immediately slowed her steps.

The cane should have warned her, but his long legs looked strong and muscular beneath the tightly woven material of his trousers. When he walked, however, there was a perceptible hesitation in his gait, and his left leg dragged slightly.

Juliet's curiosity heightened as side by side they traveled up the hill toward the road. War wound? she wondered. Or an accident? Or maybe polio? No, definitely a wound or an accident. On a racecourse somewhere, or maybe on the side of a mountain. This was the kind of man who courted adventure, no matter what the risk.

"I thought I left the lousy weather back east," Mac said with a tantalizing grin as he wiped the moisture from his cheeks with a snowy handkerchief. "I was looking forward to the famous California sunshine you all have out here."

Juliet snorted. "It's famous, all right. And our testing schedule is set up on that premise, too. That's why a day of rain can set us back two days, or sometimes three."

"No wonder you looked stormier than this sky when I interrupted you. Sorry."

"No problem," she said after a slight hesitation. "You couldn't have known."

Juliet found herself intrigued by the sexy way his mouth slanted upward on one side, the corner pushing a shallow crease into his tanned cheek. He should smile more often, she decided.

A large red motorcycle with chrome pipes suddenly sped past them, spewing exhaust fumes from its roaring engine.

"Damn it, Terry. *Slow down!*" Juliet yelled at the retreating rider, who raised a hand in salute as he made a skidding turn into the small parking lot adjacent to the road. He killed the motor and parked the bike by the heavy metal guardrail.

"Friend of yours?" Mac asked dryly.

Juliet stared down the hill, glowering at the muscular figure of the rider as he dismounted and removed his black helmet. A shock of long blond curls spilled over the collar of his blue work shirt before the wind whipped his flaxen hair into a tangle.

"That's Terry Burton, the janitor for our building," she said in a thin voice. "He's going to kill himself one of these days if he's not careful."

A vision of her brother's scarred body rose in her mind, and her face paled. Rex had been no match for the skidding driver who had hit his cycle and slammed him into the pavement, crushing his spine.

A sudden spatter of rain dotted the rutted road beneath her feet as though to punctuate her troubled thoughts, and Juliet shivered. She cupped her hand around her mouth. "I'm going to report you for reckless driving!" she shouted into the wind, knowing that the earphones of Terry's radio blocked her words.

"I don't think he heard you," Mac drawled as the young man boogied up the road to the beat of his private concert.

"He wouldn't listen to me anyway," she said with an expression of disgust. "I just hope I'm not visiting him in the hospital one of these days."

Juliet had a sudden vision of herself almost nine months ago, summoned by the police to a local trauma center. For three days she'd paced the corridors of the hospital, praying that Rex would live. When he'd finally opened his eyes and whispered her name, she'd thought the worst was over, but she'd been wrong.

Now, in silence, she and Mac came abreast of the building, and she glanced at the narrow wooden stairs leading to the second story. The staff routinely used those stairs as a shortcut to the offices above, but with his stiff leg, this man would never be able to manage the climb. Thank God for the elevator, she thought with a pang of sympathy.

As though reading her thoughts, Mac gave her a speculative look, and Juliet rushed into speech. "This is our building, and that's the infirmary down there beyond the parking lot. Next to it are the PX and the cafeteria." She pointed downhill to a small clutch of beige buildings nestled in a tidy grove of palm trees.

Mac followed her gaze across the sparse landscaping that did little to camouflage the dreary architecture. "All Navy bases look alike to me. Someone sometime must have gotten a great deal on tan paint."

Juliet laughed and led the way around the corner of the building to the main entrance. "I think you're right." Inside the lobby she punched the button for the elevator and inclined her head toward the nearby wall. "And sea-foam green for the interior."

The doors slid open, and they stepped into the stainless-steel car. She noticed the way he braced most of his weight on his right leg and, embarrassed, quickly glanced down at the clipboard in her hand. He appeared to be so strong, even potentially dangerous, that it didn't seem quite fair that he should be flawed in any way. She punched the Up button with particular vehemence.

"Hold still." Mac's voice vibrated close to her ear. "You've got something tangled in your hair."

"I do? What?" Juliet stood perfectly motionless, her body tensed as Mac's hand threaded through the thickness of her ponytail. She could sense his large body behind her, even though they weren't physically touching, and his fingers seemed to linger for an uncommonly long time against the nape of her neck.

"Did you get it?" she asked in a voice that reverberated unnaturally in the enclosed space.

"Just a second," he murmured, tugging slightly on the tangled strands. His knuckles brushed the skin of her scalp, and Juliet jumped at the jolting sensation his touch elicited. "Sorry. Did that hurt?"

She shook her head. She could feel the heat of his body through the fabric of her suit, and suddenly she wondered what it would be like to lean back against that strong torso, to rub her shoulder blades against his chest, to feel the hardness of his belly against her spine.

Heat rose to her cheeks as the elevator doors slid open.

"Here it is," Mac said with a rumble of triumph as he stepped back and held up a gnarled twig. "Some kind of woody thing."

Juliet laughed and took the tiny twig from his hand. "It's a piece of mesquite. When the wind blows, we get debris from the tip of Point Loma. It's a national monument, and the vegetation on the hillside is all native. This time of year the mesquite is fairly brittle." She could still feel the imprint of his fingers against the nape of her neck. Roarke McKinley was one very different man.

Mac's eyes were curious as she preceded him into the small lobby. "I thought mesquite grew in the desert."

"Without irrigation, that's exactly what we'd be here," Juliet explained, and he nodded.

The lobby was small and sparsely furnished, with room for one desk opposite the elevator and a small adjacent anteroom where a hard vinyl couch occupied the far wall beneath a faded portrait of George Washington.

Building 3 had been built as a barracks in 1942 and remodeled into office space in the early fifties, when comfort was considered secondary to efficiency.

Recent remodeling had added a computer room and a spacious rest room, with lockers and a shower for the convenience of the staff, but the offices themselves were still as dreary as they'd been during the austerity program of the Korean War era.

The project secretary, Maria Martinez, a dark-haired woman in her early twenties, had looked up in surprise as Juliet stepped out of the elevator. The surprise in her black eyes had quickly turned to open curiosity when Mac had followed Juliet into the lobby.

"Morning, Dr. Prentice." Maria directed her comment to Juliet, but her eyes were on Mac.

Juliet hid a smile as she introduced the pretty young woman. Dressed in bright yellow, Maria, with her wide smile and friendly air, was a cheery spot of color in the drab lobby.

"Welcome to California, Mr. McKinley." Maria gave Mac a bright grin of greeting as she half rose from her chair to shake his hand. "Dr. Kurtz is expecting you."

"Please call me Mac," he said in a courteous drawl, flashing her a crooked grin.

Maria brightened immediately and touched her hair in a strictly feminine gesture that had Juliet mentally shaking her head in amusement.

"I'm going in, Maria," she said evenly. "I'll show Mr. McKinley to Dr. Kurtz's office."

Maria's eyes flashed in disappointment, but Juliet ignored the signal. The last thing she wanted to do was encourage the young woman's fantasy. She had a strong feeling that Mac was not the type of man this sheltered young woman needed in her life.

A single hall bisected the second floor, with two offices on each side. Fred Kurtz, as the director, had the largest office, which included a separate conference room.

The portly director seemed as surprised by Mac as Maria had been. Short and squat, with thinning brown hair, Dr. Kurtz had always reminded Juliet of the perfect civil servant.

He wore conservative clothes, drove a three-year-old sedan, and lived in a tract house in the suburbs. In the winter his clothes smelled of mothballs, and in the summer of spray starch.

"Welcome to California, McKinley," Fred said heartily, pumping Mac's hand, and Juliet winced. Thank God she hadn't said the same thing, or the man would think everyone in California spoke in cliches. She glanced at Mac, only to have him wink at her, and she hid a grin.

"Thank you, sir," Mac remarked politely. "I understand you have a slight problem with your computer system."

Juliet listened with mild interest as Mac commiserated with the director over the protracted delay in the delivery of their new system. It had been promised three months ago and was still only a distant hope.

Several times she tried to catch Mac's eye in order to make her excuses and leave, but he continued to talk. Fred ignored her completely, making her fume inside. Her hair was drying in stiff waves, and the salt from the seawater was tightening her skin while the two men droned on and on.

Juliet tried to edge toward the door, but Mac stopped her with a friendly hand on her shoulder. His touch was light and not in the least provocative, but Juliet could feel the sensual shock waves spreading along the nerve network beneath her skin.

"...so if you don't mind," Mac drawled with a persuasive smile, "I'd like to borrow Ms. Prentice here as a sort of liaison, someone to help me hit the floor running, so to speak." He squeezed her shoulder firmly and then released her.

Juliet's head jerked up in surprise, and her gaze shifted to the right, only to find the knot of Mac's tie. She forced her gaze higher, past his strong chin to his eyes. Oh no, she thought in dismay as his eyes smiled down at her. This is definitely *not* a good idea.

"But I don't know anything about computers," she protested as calmly as she could. "I don't see how I could possibly be of any use to you." And besides, you're much too unsettling for my own good, so let's just forget this nonsense, she added silently and fervently.

Mac met her gaze squarely, accepting her tacit challenge with one raised eyebrow. "But you know project procedures, Ms. Prentice. That's what I need."

"Dr. Prentice," she corrected with a taut smile. Talk about arrogance, she thought ruefully. The man acts as though he's used to getting his own way—especially with women. Not this time, she told herself firmly.

His lips quirked. "I beg your pardon," he said with a gallant nod. "*Dr.* Prentice."

His eyes were smiling, but his jaw was set in a resolute line, and his shoulders were rolled back in determination. Juliet was beginning to feel trapped.

"I'm sure Juliet will be very happy to accommodate you," Dr. Kurtz said firmly, giving her a warning scowl. "Won't you, Juliet?"

"Ordinarily, I would, but really, I'm swamped right now," she responded quickly, giving both men a wide smile deliberately tinged with regret. "I have two reports due at the end of the month, and this morning, with the storm and all, I had to abort the procedure." She tried to sound as harried as she felt. "I'm sure you understand."

The director's expression darkened. "We're *all* busy, Juliet. You'll find a way to get everything done." His eyebrows screwed into a wavy line of disapproval. "I have every confidence in you."

Juliet could hear the warning in his voice. *Do it or else.* Damn you, Fred, she raged silently. This is not what I need right now.

"I guess I'm all yours, Mr. McKinley," she capitulated aloud, and then stiffened as she realized the double meaning in her words. "Professionally speaking," she added quickly, her cheeks reddening with embarrassment.

"Yes, ma'am," he drawled. His expression was perfectly sober. It was the wicked gleam in his eyes that worried her.

Chapter 2

Mac sat at a corner table in the crowded cafeteria, his blazer slung over the back of his chair, his shirtsleeves rolled to his elbows, his tie loosened. It was a few minutes past noon, and the large room, with its bright yellow walls and white plastic furniture, was nearly full.

He was waiting for Juliet Prentice to join him for lunch, and he was getting damned hungry. His stomach, still on eastern time, had been telling him for the past hour that it was time to eat.

His plane had arrived a few minutes past dawn at North Island Naval Air Station across the bay from Point Loma. There, in an empty room reserved for visiting brass at the bachelor office quarters, he'd slipped out of his uniform and into his role as a computer consultant.

By nine he'd checked into a room in a nearby motel, called Dr. Kurtz to confirm his eleven-thirty appointment and studied the city map provided by the car rental firm. On the way to the base he'd driven through the surrounding streets, memorizing the names and picking out landmarks, until he had a working familiarity with the area.

The moment he'd driven past the gate, his course had been set. Meet the people involved, stir up the waters and see what surfaced.

Mac glanced at his watch. "Give me twenty minutes," Juliet had said when she'd left Kurtz's office, and already he'd been waiting thirty.

His gaze flicked with studied nonchalance around the room, returning every few seconds to the door leading to the outside. A feeling of taut excitement hummed through his body as he waited for her to arrive.

He could still see her striding up and down the pier, the curves of her body molded by the stretchy fabric of her suit, a sea nymph as graceful on land as she was in the water. He hadn't been able to take his eyes off her.

It's the case that's so intriguing, not the woman, he reminded himself as he tried to make his long legs comfortable despite the thick pedestal of the small round table.

It was always this way at the beginning of the chase. Every cell in his body was tuned for battle, his senses heightened, his mind focused. His spine pressed against the back of the molded vinyl chair, each vertebra tensed with anticipation as adrenaline pumped through his veins in an exhilarating rush, preparing him to face the enemy.

The first time he'd felt this way was on the bridge of a destroyer sitting off the coast of North Vietnam. The sound of the five-inch guns sending shell after shell into the beach had pounded into his head until his thudding heart had begun to echo the deadly cadence.

He'd been a gung ho ensign, fresh from the academy, convinced that his country would prevail. He'd been eager to taste combat, determined to test his courage under fire, anxious for the thrill of victory. So anxious that as soon as he was qualified, he'd volunteered for Swift Boat duty in-country, an assignment that was considered suicidal by the old-timers.

Mac's lips quirked briefly in a self-mocking grimace. He'd been so naive, that shavetail ensign. He'd disappeared somewhere in the middle of a steamy river in the jungle, replaced by the cold-eyed cynic who greeted him every morning in the mirror, a man who'd seen too much pain, experienced too much deceit, a man who had few illusions. Everything—and everyone—was for sale. For the right price.

Mac shifted restlessly in his seat and sent another glance at the door. As though summoned by his thought, Juliet stood framed in the doorway, her clear brown eyes searching the room.

Mac started to stand, only to be shocked into immobility by the searing pain shooting through his hip. Slow and easy, his therapist had drummed into him. No sudden moves. Clenching his teeth, Mac eased himself to his feet and raised a hand to attract her attention.

A spontaneous smile crossed her face as she caught sight of him and began weaving her way toward him through the densely packed tables.

She'd changed into dark brown tailored slacks and an ivory-colored oversized cotton shirt that complemented her tan. Her freshly shampooed hair had been pulled away from her temples and tucked into tortoiseshell combs behind her ears, and the dark blond mass hung in asymmetrical ringlets against her fragile neck.

She moved like a prima ballerina, her legs gliding forward with a liquid grace, her hips swaying to an inner tempo, her head tilted slightly to one side, as though she were listening to an interior melody.

His body reacted immediately, reminding him in strictly masculine terms how long it had been since he'd had a woman. Mac gritted his teeth and tried to ignore the insistent signals from his loins. This case was definitely not starting out the way he'd planned.

He forced a casual smile to his face as she reached the table and pulled out a chair. "Sorry I'm late," she said in a rush. "The shower was occupied, and I had to wait my turn."

Mac winced inwardly as a vivid picture of Juliet's willowy body, wet and rosy from the steamy shower, took shape in his mind. She would be perfect, all firm curves and glowing golden skin. He forced his mind into safer channels.

"No problem," he said with easy charm. "I used the time to jot down some notes about that dinosaur of a system we're replacing." He indicated the yellow legal pad on the table in front of him.

Juliet glanced down at the illegible black scrawl that filled two-thirds of the page. The world of computers was a total mystery to her. She loved people and animals, not cryptic symbols without passion or warmth. What on earth would they talk about for an entire hour?

Juliet slung her shoulder bag over the arm of the chair and gestured toward the line that had snaked around the end of the salad bar. "Shall we? I'm starving."

Mac nodded and reached for his cane. He allowed Juliet to precede him, then fell into step beside her. He noticed that she was very subtly adjusting her pace to his.

Frustration knifed through him, and he forced himself to walk faster. He didn't need any favors, especially from her.

At the end of the line, they stopped behind two men in business suits. "Surely you don't fight this crowd every day, Juliet?" Mac said with a look of amazement at the packed room.

It was the first time he'd said her Christian name, and the fluid vowels sounded lyrical when uttered in his softly slurred baritone—and very sexy.

"Usually I brown bag it," she said, resisting the urge to inch away from his side. He was standing much too close for her peace of mind. "To save time. I'm incredibly busy these days." She turned her head, intending to give him a warning look, only to find herself looking directly at his mouth. Instantly she raised her gaze, encountering amused blue eyes watching her with an intimate look of interest.

"I really appreciate your help in easing me into the project like this," Mac drawled softly, bending closer so that she could hear him over the lunch hour din.

His breath was warm on her skin and scented with peppermint gum. His after-shave was a subtle blend of spices that reminded her of a fall morning in the mountains.

Juliet was finding it unusually difficult to breathe; for some reason all the air seemed to have been sucked out of the room, and the noise was beginning to give her a headache.

"No problem," she said with a faint smile. "We all pitch in when we can." She managed to keep her voice carefully non-committal in spite of her discomfort. Why was she so jittery, for heaven's sake? She'd had lunch with male colleagues before. Right here in this room, too. It must be the storm, she told herself staunchly. It's making me as high-strung as the dolphins.

They reached the head of the line, and Juliet took two trays. She handed one to Mac and began to make her selections.

As they made their way along the steam tables, she started to worry. Would he be able to manage both the tray and his cane? He didn't seem to be able to walk without it. Should she offer to help? Something about the proud set of his shoulders told her that her offer would be forcefully rebuffed.

Juliet chatted with the cashier as she paid for her meal and waited for Mac. He paid and returned his wallet to his back pocket. Propping his cane against the counter, he lifted the tray with both hands, then slid his right forearm under the entire width, gripping the edge with the tips of his fingers and balancing all the weight on one arm.

He glanced up to find her watching him, and his face tightened as he reached for his cane. She stiffened as a dark scowl pulled his thick chestnut brows together.

"Aren't you going to offer to help?" he asked with chilly sarcasm.

Juliet glanced down at her well-laden tray. "Not me. I have enough to carry as it is."

Some of the dark clouds left Mac's face as he looked first at her tray and then at his own. Hers contained nearly twice as many dishes. "Do you eat that much for lunch every day?" he asked in obvious amazement.

Juliet colored. "Usually. I have one of those metabolisms that burns hot. I'm always hungry." As she began threading her way toward their table, she could hear his deep-throated chuckle following her.

They ate in silence for several minutes. Mac finished his hamburger and pushed aside his plate. "Not bad for institutional food."

"You sound like you're an expert." Juliet spread jam on her roll and took a healthy bite.

Amusement flashed in Mac's eyes. "Come to think of it, I guess I am. I've been eating in places like this on a regular basis since I left home to attend prep school. My mother keeps trying to lure me down to the farm so she can fatten me up."

Juliet glanced at the hard midriff above his belt buckle. She could feel the tug of purely feminine curiosity, the urge to let her eyes drift lower, but the edge of the table was in the way. "Doesn't look like she's succeeding," she muttered, and then immediately regretted the offhand remark as he threw back his head and laughed. It was a warm infectious sound that brought the sting of heat to her cheeks.

"Mama truly believes that a man on his own has to be malnourished, at the very least."

"I take it you're not married?"

He shook his head. His distantly remembered marriage to his childhood sweetheart had lasted barely eighteen months, thirteen of which he'd spent driving his Swift Boat up and down the muddy brown rivers of Vietnam. The Officer and the Debutante, he thought with a twinge of nostalgia. Had he ever really been that young?

"I'm divorced," he amplified. "For many years. How about you?"

He leaned forward and rested his forearms on the table, and Juliet's eyes flickered across to him. His arms looked strong, and she had a feeling that the sun-bleached hair covering the thick muscles would be very soft to the touch.

She curled her fingers into her palms and gave him a steady look. "No, I'm happily single."

"Ah, a modern lady." The obvious approval in his deep blue eyes made her feel warm all over. And more than a little uneasy. This was beginning to feel more like a blind date than a business lunch.

Juliet decided to change the subject before her imagination took her into territory better left unexplored. "Is this your first visit to California?"

Mac took a sip of milk and licked the residue from his bottom lip with his tongue. "I came through here years ago—on my way to Vietnam. From the little I've seen, San Diego has really changed."

Juliet nodded. So she'd been right about one thing. Mac had served in the war. "Is that where you hurt your leg?" she asked in a quiet voice. "In the war?" Juliet noticed that the deep lines bracketing his mouth seemed to deepen as though in painful memory.

"Yes, in the war." The lie came automatically. No one, except his family and a select few of his fellow officers knew the real story behind his disability.

Juliet caught the gruff note in his voice and dropped her eyes to her plate. Hastily she cast around for a less painful subject. "You mentioned a farm. Is that where you grew up?"

"Yes. My father and my brother raise tobacco. The first crop was planted in 1728 by my great-great-great grandfather, Thomas Roarke."

"Sounds very homey." She wiped her mouth, then looked up in dawning surprise. "You're Roarke Industries!" The old-line company was one of the giants in the tobacco industry and had recently assumed the status of a conglomerate by buying out several other companies that dealt in food and beverage.

Mac chuckled. "Not really. That's my daddy and my brother. I just have a few shares of stock." He lifted one shoulder as though he were embarrassed at having shared the personal information.

Juliet smiled her understanding. A tiny piece of the puzzle that was Roarke McKinley slid into place. Mac came from money. Old money. Hence the polished manner and relaxed self-assurance.

"So how come you're not a tobacco farmer, too?"

Mac shrugged. "I was an idealist." His lips twisted. "I thought my country needed me."

"So you joined the Army?"

"The Navy, actually. My daddy wangled me an appointment to Annapolis." His eyes flashed with something that could be pride—or derision. Juliet couldn't quite decide.

"I'm impressed," she said quietly.

"Don't be," he shot back laconically. "My idealism lasted about six months, until I had my first Swift Boat shot out from under me." He leaned back to hook a muscular arm over the back of the chair. The starched cotton of his blue and white striped shirt tightened over his broad chest, instantly reminding Juliet of a large cat lounging in the sun. Relaxed, and yet filled with controlled energy, ready to spring at the first sign of danger.

"Now that I'm a civilian," he added with a lazy smile, "I just collect my pay and let the politicians deal with the heavy stuff."

Juliet looked down at her plate. "That's a pretty cynical attitude, don't you think? I mean, you work for the government."

"Maybe, but I've paid my dues."

Juliet didn't know what to say. It wasn't as though he were breaking any rules, written or unwritten. Whereas she, in her desperate need for money, had broken several. Hastily she forced her mind away from that painful thought.

This conversation was becoming far too personal. Where was the boring technical talk about bits and bytes and operating systems? That she could handle, even if she didn't like it.

Juliet could feel the tension snaking down her spine, and she longed to make her excuses and leave. She hadn't felt this dizzy since her first deep-water dive.

She would force him to talk about the tedious technical stuff, whether he wanted to or not. Anything was better than imagining those broad shoulders naked and exposed to the hot California sun. Or wondering how those long legs would feel pressed against hers on the sand.

Juliet turned her involuntary groan into a cough. "Uh, where'd you learn about computers?" she asked, sugaring her coffee.

Mac looked down at his own hand curved around his glass. They were treading on ground that he'd fenced off years ago, ground that he didn't want to retrace. "There was a fellow officer in the hospital with me who had a degree in computer programming. We used to talk, and, well, I guess he just got me hooked." It wasn't quite the truth, but close enough. The man had been a CIA specialist who'd been badly injured in an auto accident, and he and Mac had shared more than a room. They'd shared long pain-filled nights, as well.

Mac shifted in his chair, feeling the hard cuff of his brace tug at his trousers as his leg moved against the plastic seat. He forced a smile.

"Are you from this area?" he asked, knowing that she wasn't. His purpose in arranging this lunch had been to charm her into trusting him, to begin to insinuate himself into her life, but he was finding it hard to concentrate on his goal. Especially when she kept looking at him with those wide brown eyes that seemed to caress his face like velvet.

Juliet speared a bite of salad and shook her head. "I'm from L.A. Well, actually, Beverly Hills. My father was Justin Forsythe Prentice." There was a note of pride in her voice, and something more. Pain perhaps. Or even defensiveness. Mac couldn't tell.

"I saw your father on stage once when I was younger," he said casually, draining his glass. "In *King Lear*. My mama believed in exposing her children to culture as often as possible, even if she had to threaten us with a lickin' to do it. Your father was very good."

"Yes, Daddy *was* good," she said with a slight catch in her voice. "Great, in fact. Everyone said so."

She'd been so happy as a child, being the daughter of a famous and beloved man, and so sure her idyllic life would last forever. Justin Prentice had adored his golden-haired little girl. He'd taken her everywhere, introducing her to his fellow actors as his "angel sunshine."

Juliet's mother, born and bred in Back Bay Boston, had been more reserved in temperament, but equally loving, providing a stable environment while Justin Prentice provided the glamour.

And then, without warning, Juliet's world had splintered into a sordid public soap opera. She had been appalled. In addition, she'd been terrified to think what her father's desertion would do to her mother, who'd been bedridden for years with arthritis.

She'd pleaded with him to reconsider, but Justin had been adamant. He was still a young man. He deserved to enjoy life.

Everything had been different for Juliet from that moment. The social whirl that had seemed so important had suddenly seemed empty. She had thrown herself into her studies, making top grades and winning honors in marine science.

Justin had been generous about a settlement and continued to pay for Juliet's education. Child support for Rex and alimony for Althea had allowed them to relocate to a smaller but comfortable home in Beverly Hills.

Althea, however, had seemed to lose heart from the moment her husband left her, spending her days quietly paging through the scrapbooks she'd kept of their life together.

Justin had died of cancer in the fall of Juliet's senior year, leaving an estate that barely covered her mother's escalating medical bills.

"I suppose you want to know what it was like, being the daughter of a man like Justin Prentice," she said bluntly, lifting her chin higher as she regarded him across the width of the table. It was a question she'd heard her entire life, and she was vastly bored with her own answers.

Mac shrugged. "Not especially. I know what it's like to be in the spotlight, maybe not in the same way, but close enough." He glanced down at the gold signet ring on the third finger of his right hand.

"Once, when I was seven, I got caught swiping a soda from the local market, and my daddy nearly wore out my behind for disgracing one of the oldest names in Virginia." He chuckled. "For years, I was determined to change my name to Smith, just as soon as it was legal."

Juliet watched his lips curve slowly into a wry smile. There was too much firepower in one of those grins, she decided. She would have to be careful.

"So how come you didn't?" she asked, wrenching her gaze away from his mouth. "Change your name, I mean." The room was definitely becoming uncomfortably warm. The management really shouldn't let so many people in here, she thought peevishly.

"Because by then I'd gotten interested in girls, and they were mighty impressed by my so-called connections."

Juliet laughed at the self-deprecating humor. He was unpredictable, this big man with the hard-bitten lines in his face. And he had a fascinating combination of cynicism and charm that she found enormously appealing—and far too dangerous.

After years in her father's orbit, she understood the rules of flirting, and this man was a master. But there was also a disturbing undercurrent flowing between them that she couldn't identify. Nor did she want to try.

Juliet finished her coffee and glanced at her watch. "It's getting late, Mac," she said with what she hoped was the right amount of regret, "and I've got a pile of work waiting for me, so if you're finished..." She glanced toward the door and waited for him to take the hint.

He didn't move. Instead he seemed to deliberately ignore her suggestion. "Tell the truth now," he challenged. "You were mad at me out there on the pier this morning, weren't you? I could see little gold flecks darting around in your eyes like the very devil."

He shifted in his chair, and Juliet could see the muscles of his stomach ripple beneath the striped cotton. He would be as hard as seasoned oak beneath those civilized clothes. And his skin would have the sheen of sleek good health, she was sure of it.

She blinked, trying to banish the intimate image, then blushed as she realized he was waiting for her to speak. "You did distract Poseidon at a critical time," she admitted with a smile. "Otherwise, we might have managed to squeeze in the final test before the storm broke."

A sheepish grin of apology tugged at his mouth. "It would ease my conscience if you'd let me make up for my blunder by taking you to dinner some night while I'm here."

More than anything, Juliet wanted to say yes, but she didn't dare. Her life was too complicated already. Still the thought was tempting....

She rushed into speech before she could change her mind. "That's very nice of you—"

"If you say *but*, I'll be sorely disappointed, I promise," Mac interrupted smoothly. "Not to say insulted."

Juliet forced herself to ignore the beguiling way his deep-set eyes crinkled into sexy lines at the corners whenever he was amused. "It's just that I'm so busy working on reports in my spare time, I don't know when I'd find a free evening."

"No problem." Mac's voice dropped into a lower register. Lower and more intimate and containing an unspoken promise that had Juliet pressing her knees together under the table. "I'll bring dinner to you. Just tell me when and where." His eyebrows rose whimsically, as though his thoughts were even more intimate than his tone.

She cleared her throat and curled her fingers around the strap of her purse. "I . . . that's very generous of you, but I've made it a strict rule never to see anyone from work socially."

It was the truth. Not once in the five years at the NRC had she ever dated a fellow employee. She'd lost track of the number of invitations she'd turned down before the word spread that Dr. Juliet Prentice was not available.

She forced a smile as Mac regarded her with disbelieving eyes. "I'm sure you understand."

Mac's lips curved wryly. "I guess I'll have to, won't I?"

"I guess you will." Juliet heard the whisper of disappointment in her own voice and stiffened. What was the matter with her? She wanted Mac to keep his distance, so why was she feeling so . . . let down?

A silver glint surfaced in his deep blue eyes as he crumpled the paper napkin in his big fist and threw it onto the table. "But that doesn't mean I won't try to change your mind." His jaw set, and his chin lifted. "I warn you, I'm a pretty determined guy."

Juliet didn't doubt that for an instant. "Thanks for the warning," she said with a casual laugh. "But I warn *you*, you're wasting your time with me."

All expression fled from Mac's eyes. "I don't think so, Juliet."

He pushed himself to his feet. Then, with a grace that seemed at odds with his size, he rolled down his sleeves and slipped into his jacket, shrugging to settle the coat into place.

It was a commonplace gesture, one she'd seen hundreds of men make hundreds of times. Yet when Mac did it, her pulse seemed to leap into high gear, sending the blood rushing through her veins.

It's chemistry, she told herself with rising urgency. Plain old-fashioned sex appeal, that's all. The man has it by the bucketful and doesn't mind spreading it around. Just stay out of his way and you'll be safe.

As they made their way through the crowded cafeteria, Juliet was aware of the eyes following them, mostly feminine, and nearly all directed at Mac. In some of the faces she could see pity, in others, hunger. In all of them she saw the same fascination she was feeling.

Outside the cafeteria the cool air had a deliciously fresh smell that made Juliet want to slip off her shoes and run in the thick green grass.

The storm had blown over, and the sky was brighter, with a few patches of blue visible through the thinning cloud cover.

Across the bay a large helicopter painted deadly black was making touch-and-go landings at North Island Naval Air Station, filling the air with the throbbing noise of its huge rotors.

Below them, Poseidon and Dolphus were together in Alpha tank, swimming in slow circles around the perimeter, while the females across the pier were huddled at the lip of Beta tank, their snouts waving excitedly in the air.

Two figures in wet suits were standing in front of the monitor board. The shorter one, a round man in ill-fitting black, was shaking a finger in the face of a tall, thin woman sheathed in brown.

Arguing again, Juliet thought wryly. The Felicity and Fred Never-Agree-On-Anything Show.

"What's going on? More testing?" Mac asked as he pointed his cane toward the tanks.

"No. Bubbles, one of the females and the most temperamental of all the dolphins, has been refusing food lately, and Fred and Felicity have different opinions as to the cause."

"Felicity?"

"Dr. Feldman. You haven't met her yet. She was one of the original team members when dolphin studies began here twelve years ago."

Mac frowned. "Looks like a pretty heated discussion from here."

Juliet chuckled. "Take my advice, Mac, try to stay neutral. Otherwise, you might get wounded by a stray insult."

His nickname felt cold and hard on her tongue. She much preferred the more poetic name he'd been given at birth. Not that it mattered, she told herself hastily, sneaking a sideways glance at his bold profile. His eyes were narrowed in concentration, and he had an alert tilt to his head that Juliet found strangely disturbing.

"So those two don't get along," he said as though to himself, watching the tank intently.

"Not exactly, no."

A burst of laughter interrupted the question Juliet could see forming in his eyes, and Mac shifted his gaze toward the foot of the fire escape, where Greg and Terry stood chatting with the project secretary. Maria's olive face was wreathed with laughter as she responded to their banter.

"Is that usual?" Mac drawled. "I mean, the janitor and that skinny grad student of yours hanging around together. I wouldn't think they'd have much in common."

"I'm not sure they're friends, exactly. More like beach buddies. They're both surfers, even though Greg doesn't really look the type."

Mac nodded.

As they neared the stairs the young woman suddenly poked Terry in the ribs, then turned and sprinted up the wooden stairs, her sandals slapping loudly against the rough boards.

The two young men exchanged looks, then hurried after her, calling her name. They caught up with her at the landing, and all three were laughing as they went inside.

Juliet sensed rather than saw the stiffening of Mac's body beside her. His eyes slowly moved from the stairs to Juliet's face. Her stomach lurched as she saw anger tighten his bronzed features.

"The staff shortcut, I take it," he said with a controlled smile.

"Yes." She couldn't lie to him. That would only make things worse. She'd tried to spare his feelings earlier by leading him to the elevator, and now he'd figured it out. She could see the bitter realization in his eyes.

Mac jerked his gaze away from her face and began walking stiffly toward the main entrance. His hand was white where it gripped the cane, and his face was a frozen mask.

Juliet followed in an agony of silence, privately cursing the rotten coincidence that had placed Greg and the others at the foot of the stairs just as she and Mac were passing.

Inside the elevator Juliet paused and turned to face Mac. "I'm sorry," she said with a helpless smile. She knew it was the wrong thing to say the moment the words had left her mouth.

"Don't be," he said in a clipped tone that sent shivers cascading down her spine. She watched silently as he reached behind her to stab the Up button with a blunt forefinger.

Mac glanced down at the cane in his left hand. He was accustomed to it now, so accustomed that he sometimes forgot why he needed it. Until an incident like this reminded him.

His gut writhed in frustration. He hated to be pitied—by anyone. He looked up to see tears welling in the corners of her lustrous brown eyes.

"Don't do that," he muttered between clenched teeth. "I don't want your tears." He felt a primitive need to wipe the sympathy from her face, coupled with a desperate urge to erase those glistening drops. Too many times over the past few years

he'd been attracted to a woman, only to discover that she'd really wanted to mother him because of his disability.

The thought that Juliet felt only pity for him filled him with helpless rage, and he didn't dare analyze the reason why. He moved quickly, pinning Juliet against the back of the small cubicle while at the same time punching the red Stop button with the heel of his right hand.

Before she could react, Mac was kissing her, his lips hard and insistent against hers. His eyes were closed, and his brow was furrowed into deep lines, as though he were in pain.

His right hand was folded around her shoulder, and his fingers were digging into her skin, as though he were afraid she would slip away.

Fury exploded inside her. How dare he? she raged, trying to turn away from his warm and insistent mouth. No man had ever treated her this way. No man had ever kissed her like this.

Let me go! The words pounded in her head as she stiffened and tried to push him away. But his chest was as immovable as granite.

He moved back slightly, his mouth softening on hers, caressing her with a whisper of sweetness. His fingers eased the pressure on her shoulder, moving gently against the thin cotton, exciting a low voltage tingle beneath her skin—as though her body were actually purring.

Juliet felt an urgent, primitive warmth overwhelming her anger, absorbing, neutralizing, defusing the feminine outrage. This wasn't an assault, she realized with blinding insight. He wasn't trying to hurt her. She only had to move sideways a few inches and she would be free. He was allowing her the choice.

Juliet felt light-headed, adrift somewhere between fantasy and reality. She should move away and stop him now. She should; she would. Soon. But this felt so good, so very good. His lips were so warm, so inviting....

Desire swirled around her, wrapping her in a wonderful cloak of delicious pleasure. Her body felt alive, reborn, pulsating with life. She inched her hands up his chest to his strong neck, framing his jaw with her slim fingers. His skin felt slightly raspy and hot to the touch.

Suddenly, Mac shuddered and stepped back, cursing violently under his breath. He looked stunned, as though he'd just had a serious shock.

Juliet dropped her hands and blinked up at him in a daze of confusion. "Wipe your eyes," he said hoarsely, glaring at her with stormy eyes. "And while you're at it, save your pity for someone who appreciates that kind of stuff." He stabbed the Up button and turned his back on Juliet as the car jerked in response.

Juliet's jaw dropped, and she bristled at the blunt command, her sympathy turning to outrage, swamping the pleasurable feelings still heating her body. "Fine. I'll remember that, *Mr.* McKinley."

The elevator doors slid open and, without looking at Mac, Juliet bolted into the lobby.

Maria looked up in surprise as Juliet brushed past. "Anything wrong, Dr. Prentice?" she asked, her black eyes wide.

"Just everything, that's all," Juliet muttered in a low voice without stopping.

Greg was seated at a small table in a corner of her office, talking on the phone, when Juliet stalked through the door and threw her purse onto her desk.

He looked up when she entered, and she scowled, still seething.

With an unsteady hand she opened the venetian blinds covering the window by her desk and glared at the familiar vista beyond. Not even the brightening sky could lighten her mood.

Nothing she'd done had deserved that kind of ill-tempered response. She'd only tried to spare the man embarrassment, just as she would have done for anyone in his situation, and he'd acted as though she'd insulted his manhood. And as for that kiss, she simply wasn't going to think about it. It didn't deserve even the slightest mental energy on her part.

Juliet scowled again and turned to stare at her assistant. The lunch hour was over. Didn't he know that?

Greg's shoulders hunched as though in self-defense, and he grimaced. "Uh, look, hon, I've got to go now," he said hastily into the receiver before hanging up and jumping to his feet.

He winced and turned bright red as he bumped his hip on the table, upsetting a coffee mug containing an assortment of stray pens and pencils. Hastily he shoved his hands in the pockets of his jeans as he eyed Juliet warily.

"I know I'm not supposed to use the phone for personal business, Dr. Prentice, but I thought since you were still out to lunch it would be okay."

He seemed to run out of breath then, and Juliet felt some of her anger dissipate. It had been a long time since she'd been in love. Not since she'd fallen for her faculty adviser in graduate school.

The professor had wooed her, bedded her and then appropriated part of her research as his own, thereby putting her federal grant at risk and damaging her credibility.

She'd never forgiven the man for his tawdry behavior, nor had she forgiven herself for her stupidity in falling for his practiced line. After that she'd vowed that she would never again become involved with anyone with whom she worked.

"That's all right, Greg," she said with an indulgent sigh. "Just don't make a habit of it." She nodded toward the phone. "You know how sensitive security is about calls going out of here."

Regulations were very specific in any secure area. Outgoing calls unrelated to work were strongly discouraged, as were incoming calls of a personal nature.

There was only one phone per office, with the connection routed through a central switchboard, and no telephone or telephone line was allowed within six feet of a classified computer terminal. It had been explained to Juliet when she'd first arrived that computers gave off electrical signals that could be read over a phone line by unauthorized persons using the proper equipment. It was inconvenient, having to cross the room to use the phone, but the staff had come to accept the restriction as necessary.

Greg gave her a hesitant look. "Uh, Dr. Prentice, are you all right? I mean, you look kinda . . . hot about something."

Juliet opened her desk drawer and took out a peppermint. She avoided Greg's eyes as she removed the wrapper and popped the candy into her mouth. "I just had a . . . difference of opinion with someone," she explained tersely, crunching the hard candy between her teeth.

Mac's taut face rose in her mind. He'd looked more than angry when he turned away from her in the elevator.

Juliet sighed as she worked the combination to the small safe built into a large double drawer on the left side of her black metal desk. Most of her notes and all of her computer diskettes were contained in that safe.

The office was tiny, so space was at a premium. Even the books in shelves along one wall were stacked too deep.

"Greg, let's go over this morning's procedure so we can duplicate it tomorrow."

He looked disappointed at the change of subject, and Juliet hid a wry smile. Poor Greg. He loved to gossip.

"So how's it goin', doc?" Terry Burton stood in the open doorway, a wide grin on his face. Blond hair as dry as summer grass was swept behind his ears, and his skin was burnt a deep brown. His radio was clipped to the waistband of his khakis, and his earphones dangled around his short bull neck.

Juliet gave him a tight smile. "Terry, I wish you'd be more careful on that red monster you drive around here. You wouldn't be much of a match for a speeding car, or even that heavy metal guardrail in the parking lot."

The janitor looked unconcerned. "Hey, doc, I'm cool, really. You saw my helmet. I'm no fool." He shrugged off her worry, then looked upward. "Got a flickering bulb there, doc. Want me to replace it for you now, while your terminal is shut off?"

The rules at the research center were very strict. Personnel without proper clearance were never allowed in a room when a secure terminal was in operation.

Juliet glanced upward. One light was definitely dimmer than the other three. "While you're at it, replace the others, too. Greg and I have some work we can do down by the tank until you're finished."

The janitor nodded. "I'll just go down to the storeroom and get the bulbs. I'll be back in five."

Juliet removed her clipboard with the test sheets from her safe, locked her purse inside and grabbed a pen from her desk.

She glanced through the window at the tanks. The water had calmed, and the tide was going out, exposing several inches of sandy shoreline.

"Juliet? Do you have a minute?" Mac was standing in the doorway, a tight, almost self-conscious expression on his face.

Juliet felt her pulse begin to race. She clutched the clipboard in fingers that had suddenly begun to shake.

"Actually, I'm rather busy now, Mr. McKinley," she told him with distant courtesy. She indicated the papers in her hand. "Greg and I have some work to do."

Mac's eyes shifted to the clipboard and then to Greg, who was standing frozen by the table. In three long deliberate strides, Mac crossed the room, plucked the clipboard from Juliet's fingers and shoved it into Greg's stomach.

"Here," he said in a low, no-nonsense voice. "You can get started doing whatever it is you need to do, and Dr. Prentice will join you in a moment."

Juliet opened her mouth, but nothing came out. She was too mad for coherent speech.

Greg blinked nervously, then loped to the door. "I'll be at the tanks, Dr. Prentice," he said in an edgy tone, his eyes sliding away from hers.

Coward, she thought in rising anger, glaring at the disappearing form of her assistant. "Now listen here, McKinley," she began in a fury-choked voice. "Don't—"

"No, you listen," he interrupted, closing the door and locking it. "I came in here to explain, and it's hard enough for me to do without an audience."

Juliet's mouth shut with an audible snap. "Explain?" she asked suspiciously.

Mac raked his hand through his hair. "Yes, explain, damn it! I acted like a jerk in the elevator."

"You certainly did," Juliet retorted sharply, crossing her arms over her chest. "I didn't deserve that." She took a deep breath, then plunged ahead. "The last thing I wanted to do was embarrass you. I was just trying to be helpful."

She felt her heart pounding in her chest as he stared at her, his eyes roaming her face so intently that she could almost feel his gaze against her skin.

"I know that—now," he drawled slowly, as though that fact surprised him. He moved a step closer, then stopped abruptly, suggesting to Juliet that his step had been involuntary.

"Look, I know it's probably hard for you to understand, but I don't think of myself as a person who needs help. And when it's given, I . . . don't deal with it very well." He shrugged, and a grimace of mocking amusement tightened his lips. "But I guess you know that."

Juliet felt her anger evaporate. He was a proud man, and this was probably as close as he would ever come to an apology.

He moved closer, raising her head with a hard hand under her chin. "I've never been a particularly patient person, even before I was . . . injured. But I shouldn't have taken out my frustrations on you."

"Actually, I have an idea how you feel," she said in a matter-of-fact voice that stirred some of the troubled shadows in his deep-set eyes.

"I'm not sure you do, Juliet. I'm not sure anyone really understands until he—or she—finds himself . . . restricted in some way."

Restricted? Juliet resisted an urge to laugh. The man might have a few limitations, but she had a feeling nothing could keep Mac from doing something he really wanted to do.

She took a deep breath. "My brother is . . . a paraplegic," she said, nearly choking on the words. The clinical term seemed so cold, so distant from the real horrors of Rex's condition. "That's why you saw tears in my eyes, Mac. I was thinking about Rex and all the problems he's going to face." It wasn't strictly true; she'd been thinking of Mac, as well, but she could see no benefit in admitting that to him now.

His glance met hers, and Juliet felt as exposed as a butterfly fluttering in a net. His eyes changed, darkened, then began to glint with sapphire brilliance. He wanted her. She could see it. And this time it had nothing to do with his private frustrations.

His warm hand flattened against her jaw, sliding slowly along the side of her neck to tangle in the thick curls cascading down her back.

She was powerless to speak, to move, impaled by those eyes that pulled her to him with a force she couldn't begin to understand. Or resist.

"I don't want your kindness, Juliet," he murmured in a husky drawl. "Or your sympathy."

He gently massaged the tense muscles at the back of her neck. His fingertips were pleasantly rough, arousing a delectable chill in the sensitive nerve endings under her skin.

"I know," she said in a breathy voice that didn't sound anything like her usual brisk tones. She was rapidly losing control of her thoughts.

"Do you?" His voice was a lazy whisper of sound, deep and resonant, calling up visions of moonlit nights spent on white-columned verandas, with the scent of magnolia hanging sweet and enticing in the heavy air.

He was so big and strong, yet his touch was so soothing. Was he so gentle because of all that he'd suffered? Had his disability given him more sensitivity than most men possessed? Juliet felt a shaky sigh whisper from her lips, bringing a slow smile to his mouth.

"I didn't hurt you, did I, Juliet? I didn't mean to." There was a wealth of regret in his sexy drawl and shadows in his blue eyes. Juliet shook her head.

"You didn't hurt me," she said softly, watching his smile broaden, a sexy white slash against his bronzed skin.

Mac's fingers left her neck to trail along the fragile line of her jaw. Her skin warmed under his touch, and her breathing faltered. She liked the feeling of his hand against her face; she reveled in the strength she could feel there.

"Come here," he whispered, reaching down to lift her to her tiptoes with one strong movement.

Juliet felt herself cradled in his powerful grip against his massive body, and she stared up at him in confusion. He was going to kiss her again, and she was going to let him.

It was foolish; it was completely out of character; it went against her own rule. But more than anything else in the world at this moment, she wanted to feel Mac's sensuous lips on hers, wanted to feel his sinewy body pressed against her, wanted to be enfolded in those strong arms.

"Juliet," he whispered, bending closer. His eyes were so deep, his lashes the thickest she'd ever seen on a man, and there were three golden freckles above the bridge of his nose, whimsically softening the harsh lines of his face.

Juliet parted her lips, and Mac groaned softly. "This is a mistake," he whispered, "but I'll take the risk." The words made no sense, but Juliet didn't care. She was enmeshed in a web of vibrant awareness.

With each breath she swam in the spicy scent of his after-shave. With each blink of her eye she could see the need sizzling in his fathomless blue gaze. With each electrically charged second that passed, she could feel the invisible thread of desire between them pulling tighter.

Mac let her slide down his body until her feet touched the linoleum. The floor seemed to tilt, then steady beneath her. She swayed against him, her mind powerless to control her body. The attraction she felt for this man she barely knew was alive and irresistible.

Juliet found herself stretching upward, her arms curving around his neck, her lips searching for his. Was she really doing this? Kissing him as though they'd been lovers for years?

And then, as his lips slanted over hers, Juliet stopped debating with herself. His appeal was simply too powerful, her resistance simply too weak.

She heard him lean his cane against the desk, and then she felt his arms tighten around her, his hands moving down her spine in a slow caress, igniting the sensitive nerve endings to a feverish excitement.

His mouth began to move, investigating hers with delicious thoroughness, tasting, stroking, nibbling on the curving corner where the tiny dimple sometimes appeared.

He was so persuasive, his lips dominating hers even as they explored. His power was tantalizing and exciting, his bold advance thrilling and irresistible.

Juliet couldn't seem to think. She could only feel, could only ride the crest of the tidal wave Mac was generating. Nothing was more important than this overwhelming bliss. No one mattered more than this big man with the sexy eyes and soul-shattering smile.

"Dr. Prentice? Are you in there?" The janitor began tapping on the door.

Mac groaned and buried his face in the curve of her shoulder. Juliet tried to ignore the insistent signals of protest her body was sending to her brain. She felt suddenly disconnected, and very chilled. If Mac hadn't locked the door...

He sighed, raised his head and smoothed a few tendrils of honey-colored hair away from her face. "I guess you can say it now," he said with a droll smile that didn't entirely erase the smoldering heat in his eyes.

"Say what?" Juliet asked in a shaky voice. Her head was still buzzing.

Mac lifted her hand to his lips and kissed her palm before giving her a crooked smile. "Welcome to California."

Chapter 3

"Watch it, Greg! You nearly brained Poseidon with that grappling hook." Juliet closed her eyes in frustration as her assistant jerked the long pole straight up in the air and hung his head in apology.

Greg was standing on the man-made ledge inside the lip of the tank, retrieving the last of the packets from the water.

"Sorry," he said solemnly. "I guess I didn't see him."

Juliet bit back a sharp retort and answered Greg's apology with a weary wave of her hand. Poseidon was over five feet long and weighed nearly six hundred pounds. How could Greg miss seeing him?

Juliet sighed and finished recording the data in the log. She couldn't help it if Greg's feelings were hurt. Better his feelings than a valuable animal like Poseidon, she thought in rising irritation.

What was wrong with Greg? she wondered. For that matter, what was wrong with her?

Over the last day or so—since Mac had arrived, in fact—she'd become increasingly short-tempered. She was beginning to feel smothered by his constant presence.

He seemed to be everywhere, peering over her shoulder when she was working on the computer, asking questions in that deep drawl that could make her shopping list sound intriguing, boldly flirting with her when no one was looking.

Glancing at her diver's watch, Juliet made a note of the time and signed the log. By squeezing in an extra session after the females were finished with their test, she and Greg had managed to make up some lost time, relieving some of the pressure that had kept her tied in knots.

Absently she tucked a windblown curl behind her ear and glanced at the large American flag whipping back and forth against the tall pole in the center of the military complex. Already the edge of the tough nylon was beginning to fray under the constant pounding of the wind.

She was as vulnerable as that proud flag, Juliet realized glumly. Her carefully planned life was already beginning to unravel around the edges.

Sighing, she raised her arms over her head and stretched, flexing the tired muscles of her back and shoulders. She bent from the waist and touched her toes, wiggling from side to side. Arms dangling, she slowly raised her torso, letting each vertebra slide into place without strain.

Fully erect, she took a deep breath and held it. She slowly opened her eyes to find Mac standing a few feet away, watching her with those thickly fringed blue eyes that she couldn't seem to get out of her mind, no matter how hard she tried.

He was dressed in a thick white sweater with the sleeves pushed carelessly to his elbows and light brown cords that clung to the hard lines of his thighs.

His stance was relaxed, his legs apart, his left hand barely resting on his cane. His expression was bland, but there was a suspicious crinkling at the corner of his eyes.

"Do you always sneak up on people like that?" she groused, scowling up at him.

Mac cocked his head and pretended to ponder her question. "Actually, I didn't want you to skitter away from me before I got a chance to discuss something important with you. You're a hard lady to catch."

"I've been very busy," she hedged politely.

Mac's lips quirked. "Are you sure you're not avoiding me, Juliet?"

"Of course not," she denied staunchly, not quite meeting his eyes. "Why would I do that?"

His shoulders lifted in a nonchalant shrug. "Maybe you're afraid of me?"

Juliet's jaw dropped, and her eyes shifted a fraction of an inch to zero in on his. "That's ridiculous," she snapped in irritation. "I'm just busy, that's all. If you'd get that stupid computer system up and running, we'd all have more time." It was a thin excuse, but the only one that came to mind.

Mac chuckled. "I reckon you're right. That's what I want to talk with you about."

"As I've told you before, you have the wrong person," she protested forcefully. "I hate computers, and the more I know about them, the more confused I get."

Mac raised a skeptical eyebrow. "C'mon, a bright woman like you? I expected you to be a whiz."

"That's just it. I know I have a pretty decent brain, but that rotten computer makes me feel so stupid. Push the wrong button, and the thing keeps beeping and beeping at you—or just wipes out hours of work without even a shred of guilt. It's frustrating, believe me."

Mac laughed. "I see I have my work cut out with you, lady." His eyes flashed with some elusive message that Juliet couldn't catch.

"Just tell me what buttons to push to do what," she said tartly, "and what buttons not to push, and I'll be fine."

Mac shifted and glanced toward the tank. Greg and Dolphus appeared to be carrying on an animated conversation in the corner.

"Is he supposed to do that?" Mac asked curiously, watching as the dolphin pushed Greg against the side of the tank, trapping him there.

"Hey, cut it out," Greg yelled in irritation, trying to side-step the animal's hard snout.

Juliet stiffened and shouted in sharp command, "Dolphus!" She raised her hand, drawing the dolphin's immediate attention.

"Greg, you didn't give Dolphus vitamins this morning, did you?"

Greg looked startled. "Sure, that's my job," he answered, his shoulders hunched defensively. "I gave them all a tablet apiece."

"Damn," Juliet muttered, then raised her voice. "You forgot to note it on his card, and I thought you'd forgotten, so I gave him another dose."

Juliet grabbed several fish from the bucket and threw one to each male in the tank, effectively distracting the excited dolphin.

"That vitamin compound is extremely volatile, Greg. In heavy doses, it can create a temporary condition very much like insanity in the dolphin's brain." She gave Mac an impatient look. "There's your bureaucracy for you. The powers above tell us the supplement is safe, but we know it isn't. I don't know how many forms I've filled out, how many letters I've written, but they keep sending us the same stuff."

She sighed and tossed several more mackerels, holding the animals' attention while Greg gingerly climbed out of the water.

"Remind me to stay out of that tank," Mac said with a wary look at the males.

Juliet frowned. "Don't worry. I wouldn't let you that close to the dolphins unless I was sure it was safe. They aren't pets. They can be highly dangerous when provoked. And those teeth can bite off an arm—or a leg—so we don't take careless chances, no matter how friendly they might seem."

Mac nodded. "I'll leave them to you. My job is systems support. Speaking of which—"

"Don't tell me we're back to computers," Juliet grumbled, securing the covers over the instrument and pulling down the waterproof metal hood to seal the panel.

"Well, it's like this. I need a place to work, and Dr. Kurtz suggested your office, so—"

Juliet's cheeks flamed. "You're kidding, I hope."

"No, I'm not. Do you mind?"

"I most certainly do," she said, mimicking her father's most imperious manner. "Greg's already using the extra desk, and there's not enough room in my office for another person."

"Dr. Feldman has graciously offered to clear a spot for Greg in her office." He held up a large square palm. "No, hear me out," he ordered softly as she started to sputter in protest. "Your office has the only extra terminal. Surely you can see the logic of a systems person needing access to the computer."

Turning abruptly, she began walking down the pier, with Mac following closely behind. At the end she stopped. "Look, can we talk about this later? I need to get out of this suit and wash the bay out of my hair before it turns green."

Mac chuckled and reached over to lift a silky ringlet. "I admit I like you better when your hair smells like roses instead of kelp." He let the soft strands slip through his fingers, an intense look on his face as he studied the blond curls.

Juliet forced herself to stand perfectly still. As a coquette she felt out of her depth, especially with this man. She had a feeling that the games he played had different rules from those she knew—if they had any rules at all.

Mac's eyes returned to her face. "So, do we have a deal? You share your office with me, and I'll do my best to teach you to make friends with your terminal." He let her hair fall against her neck and shoved his hand into his pocket.

Juliet had been outmaneuvered again—by a master. For one reckless split second she was tempted to refuse, loudly and in no uncertain terms, but grim reality intruded. Nothing had changed. She still needed her job.

Control, she told herself firmly. That was the key. And congeniality. Her mother had told her many times that a kind word and a friendly smile would solve almost any problem. And this man was definitely a problem.

"You've got a deal," she said with as much civility as she could manage. "Just don't talk to me while I'm working, okay?"

Mac gave her a strange look, then held up his hand in surrender. "Okay. It's your office. You get to set the rules."

Oh, yeah? she thought silently as they resumed walking toward Building 3.

Juliet returned to her office from the shower room to find Mac seated at her desk, his fingers flashing over the keyboard of her terminal. At her entrance, he looked up and grinned. "Feel better?"

She inhaled sharply as his eyes examined her khaki jumpsuit with a maddening thoroughness.

"Yes, thank you," she said pleasantly, resolutely ignoring the way her pulse was hammering in her ears. She dropped the canvas tote containing her wet clothes behind the door, then stood waiting, uncertain what to do next. As long as he was sitting at her desk, she was stuck.

"I'll be done in a second," he said with an apologetic nod toward the screen.

Mac finished typing, then punched the Enter key, and the screen went blank. He pushed himself to his feet and reached for his cane.

"There were a couple of calls for you while you were in the shower," he told her as he limped past her to the other desk. "I put the messages under your diary."

Juliet smiled her thanks and sat down. The cushion beneath her thighs felt warmer than usual, touched by the heat from his body. Instantly an image of hard buttocks and taut thighs leaped into her mind, awakening the deep feminine yearnings she'd tried to bury, though without much luck, since the kiss they'd shared.

Pheromones, she told herself with stern logic as she restrained herself from squirming in her chair. Every species produces them in order to stimulate a response in a member of the opposite sex. Mac's pheromones must really be powerful, she thought with dark humor. Triple strength, at least.

She resisted an urge to giggle. It was all very natural. He was a man who exuded sex appeal and masculine self-assurance, and she was a woman who had a healthy appreciation for male mystique. No wonder he had her emotions wobbling near overload.

Stifling a sigh, Juliet retrieved the pink slips from beneath her office calendar, glancing at the spiked backhand curiously. Left-handed, she thought idly, then froze as the content of the message sank in.

"Peter called. Can you come early tonight? Wants you to call immediately!" Several heavy slashes underlined the last word. She could almost hear the command in the bold handwriting.

Juliet shot a quick glance across her desk. Mac was seated in front of the other terminal, his palms flattened against the edge of the desk, his head bent over a thick manual open in front of him.

His dark red hair caught the light, revealing a sprinkling of wiry gray mixed with the chestnut. The short curls were thick, too thick to comb easily, and Juliet could almost feel the coarse texture against her fingers. But the tanned skin of his neck below the dark thatch would be smooth to the touch and enticingly warm. She had only to lean over and reach out her hand...

Juliet tossed her head in private rebuttal and pushed the unsettling image away. She had more serious thoughts to occupy her mind. Like the message from Peter.

Juliet crumpled the pink square in her fist and tossed it into the metal basket by her desk. Adrenaline pumped through her system as she realized what a close call she'd just had. She had told Peter not to call her at work, but apparently he'd felt that his reason was important enough for him to ignore her warning. Well, she would have a word with him about that!

The other message was from Dr. Green, her brother's doctor at Mar Vista. Juliet slid her chair backward and reached for the phone. As she punched out the number she saw Mac turn toward her in open curiosity.

The doctor was in his office and took her call immediately. "Dr. Prentice," he said in a harried voice, "I'm sorry to interrupt you at work, but I felt it was warranted."

"Of course." Juliet could feel flutters of dread in her stomach. What now? she wondered with weary resignation.

"Rex is refusing to cooperate with his therapist. He threw a barbell at her this morning, as a matter of fact."

Juliet felt her spirits plummet. "Did he give any reason? For the barbell, I mean?"

"None that made any sense. He just told her to get the hell out of his sight and stop torturing him."

"You think he means the pain of the therapy?"

"Maybe. He refused to answer my questions when I saw him about an hour ago. I was hoping he would tell you."

Juliet closed her eyes. "I'll do my best."

"Then you'll stop by this evening?"

"Yes—*no*! I can't tonight. I—I have an unbreakable appointment, but I'll come tomorrow—right after work." She closed her eyes in frustration.

"Please let me know if you find out anything."

Juliet could hear the disappointment in the doctor's voice, but there was nothing she could do. Peter was her lifeline. Whatever he wanted, she would try to give him. Until Rex was home and safe. Her hand was shaking as she hung up the phone.

"Trouble?" Mac asked.

"Nothing I can't handle," she replied with more sharpness than she intended. "But thank you for asking."

He nodded briefly and returned his attention to the manual.

Juliet took a shaky breath and signed on to the terminal. Her personal problems would have to wait. She had work to do.

"Quitting time, Juliet. Greg and I are stopping off for a drink. Want to come?"

Juliet looked up to find Felicity Feldman standing in the open doorway, her purse under her arm. She was a tall woman in her late thirties, stylishly slim in her designer sportswear and meticulously groomed. Juliet had never seen her without nail polish or eye shadow, even in the tank.

"Thanks, Felicity, but I can't. Maybe next time." Juliet was surprised to see relief flicker in the woman's amber eyes at the refusal. Her surprise turned to understanding as Felicity's gaze swung to Mac, who'd risen at the woman's entrance and was regarding her with frank interest.

"How about you, Mac? Care to join us for a drink?"

Juliet nearly broke out laughing at the unfamiliar purr in her co-worker's normally brisk voice.

Mac hesitated, then grinned. "Why don't you tell me where you'll be? If I finish here in the next fifteen minutes or so, I'll join you." His voice had a lazy purr of its own.

Felicity's face lit up. "Great. I'll save you a seat." She started to leave, then turned back to add in a congenial tone, "Just ask Juliet how to get to Grogan's. She's better at directions than I am." With a jaunty wave of her well-manicured hand, Felicity spun on her heel and left.

Juliet stared at the amber letters marching across her screen. The sentence she'd just typed made no sense. Scowling in irritation, she deleted the gibberish.

"Nice lady," Mac said with a wry grin. "Very friendly. She's been more than helpful since we met."

Juliet looked up sharply, searching his face. Did he mean that *she* hadn't been? His bland expression gave no clue.

Juliet managed a polite smile. "Felicity is our resident sunshine." She smiled. "I've never known her to be depressed."

"What about the day I arrived? Down by the tanks? She looked pretty upset to me."

Juliet frowned. "Upset? Oh, you mean the Felicity and Fred Show?"

At his look of confusion, Juliet recounted the full name. "*They* even call it that. I think they enjoy baiting each other."

His resonant chuckle filled the room. "It's not serious, then?"

Juliet shook her head. "No, not really. Oh, I think Felicity was disappointed when Fred was brought in from the outside as director, but even she admitted that his credentials were as good as hers."

"She was in line for the job?" He leaned back against the edge of the desk and crossed his arms over his wide chest. His thigh muscles flattened against the hard surface, and Juliet could see the latent power beneath the nubby fabric of his cords. She inhaled deeply, then released the air in a steady rush.

"Yes. Officially, she's assistant director."

"And what about you? Are you angling for the top spot?"

Juliet heard a warning bell. Watch the personal stuff, she told herself sternly. The less he knows, the better.

"Not me," she said with a light laugh. "I'm happy being number three—and trying harder."

Mac nodded. "Less stress that way, I imagine."

"Absolutely."

Juliet returned her attention to the screen, but she'd lost her train of thought. Glancing toward the window, she could see the line of cars snaking up the hill toward the main gate. Traffic along Rosecrans Street would be a mess if she didn't leave soon. She riffled through her notes, gnawing her lip in concentration. There was at least another hour's work to be done.

"Sure you can't join us for a drink?"

She looked up to find Mac watching her. His pose was casual, even indolent, but there was something incongruous about the sharply interested light in his eyes. Always look at the eyes, her father had told her repeatedly. You can see a man's soul in his eyes. Remember that.

She tried, but as soon as she met Mac's gaze, he looked down at his feet. His loafers looked new and very expensive, but they couldn't be all that interesting, she thought wryly.

"I'm sure," she said as pleasantly as she could. "I'm busy tonight."

"With Peter?" His grin was roguishly challenging, and Juliet tried to answer in kind.

"Yes, with Peter." She hoped her curt tone would discourage further questions, but Mac refused to take the hint.

"Is he your—what does my baby sister call it?" He snapped his fingers. "Your significant other, that's it."

Juliet blinked. "I—you could call him that, yes." Actually it wasn't really a lie, she rationalized, averting her gaze. Next to Rex, Peter *was* the most important person in her life right now. Without him, she would never be able to cover the bills that fell through the cracks of her insurance coverage.

Mac levered himself erect. "Lucky guy," he said with what sounded like regret. Still standing, he returned his attention to the screen, and Juliet did the same.

Ten minutes later, Mac signed off and reached for his cane. "Well, good night, Juliet. I hope you and Peter have a great evening."

Juliet looked up in confusion. "What? Oh, right. Thank you. I'm sure we shall." Oh, great, Juliet. Right out of Jane Austen.

But to her relief, Mac didn't seem to have noticed her stiff response. He simply nodded and said pleasantly, "If you don't mind giving me those directions . . ."

Juliet hastily complied, and Mac limped out of the room. She could hear his uneven steps on the linoleum floor, fading gradually as he moved toward the lobby.

It would be fun to join the others for a glass of wine and light conversation. She hadn't been able to do that in a long time, and she missed the camaraderie. But Rex needed her, and she didn't begrudge the time she spent with him at the hospital.

Juliet listened for the whir of the elevator, but her office was too far from the lobby for the sound to carry. Where she sat, the only sounds in the building seemed to be the sibilant hum of her computer and the discordant whine of Terry's floor polisher in the conference room at the end of the hall.

She and the janitor were alone on the second floor, two islands of life in a deserted after-hours sea.

Juliet groaned and buried her head in her hands. She was tired. Bone tired. When Rex was home again and everything had returned to normal, she would take a nice long vacation. Somewhere warm and peaceful and private, where she could take stock of her life.

Her eyes closed in desperation. So much was riding on her ability to juggle all her responsibilities without dropping any. Her concentration had to be absolute. And that meant she had to put her personal life on hold.

Somehow she had to keep Roarke McKinley out of her mind. She had no choice. Her future and Rex's depended on it.

* * *

The moon, nearly full and silvery bright, was peeping over the edge of downtown San Diego when Juliet pulled up to the curb in front of a Moorish two-story home in the affluent Loma Portal district of the city.

As she climbed out, an airplane roared over her head, its lights flashing against the low-lying clouds. Lindbergh Field was directly between her downtown, and its one runway pointed toward the sea.

Juliet slowly walked up the curving brick walk, mentally preparing herself for another exhausting session with Peter.

The man was a perfectionist, a nitpicker who was never satisfied. No matter how hard she tried to give him exactly what he wanted, he always wanted more.

Tonight she simply wasn't in the mood. The temptation to skip this meeting had been strong, but Peter was paying her another installment this evening, and the hospital expected payment on the first. She had to keep her appointment with Peter or risk his anger.

Juliet sighed deeply as she climbed the tall steps leading to the large stucco residence. All during her hasty dinner, she'd thought of Rex. He had to get better. He had to learn to live a full and productive life in spite of his paralyzed legs. He just had to. She would never be able to stand it if he didn't.

She was fumbling for the bell when suddenly the door opened and a small woman with heavy features and a matronly form smiled up at her. Her voice when she spoke was thick with the ponderous consonants of her native language. "I told Peter I heard your car, but you know him. He never believes anything until he sees it with his own eyes—or hears it with his own ears."

Juliet forced a smile and leaned down to give Natasha a hug. She respected Peter for his brilliance and his dedication to his country, but she loved Tasha. In many ways she'd become the nurturing mother Juliet had never had.

"How is the old bear tonight, anyway?" Juliet whispered as she followed Peter's wife into the luxurious home.

"Grumpy," the woman said with a fond smile. "As usual, no?"

Juliet nodded and glanced up and down the street without noticing what she was doing before closing the door behind her. When she left tonight, Peter would have his precious pages, and she would have two thousand dollars.

Mac sat in front of the window in his motel room, a bottle of brandy on the small table by his elbow, his left leg resting on an empty chair across from him. From where he sat he could see the lights of the city sparkling like rhinestones under the stark winter moon.

The night was still, and the bay was a shimmering mirror, reflecting the moonbeams in a wavering silver line that stretched from shore to shore.

Below his window, gentle waves lapped against the moored sailboats, rocking the white hulls in a chorus line of motion and tipping the tall masts in jagged unison.

Mac had just hung up the phone after reporting to Carter Hendricks. The admiral had been pleased that he had managed to settle in without exciting any suspicion. The fact that the computer operating system was overdue for an update had been a stroke of luck for Naval Intelligence, which for once found itself the beneficiary of the customary bureaucratic delays.

Mac had succinctly summarized the days since his arrival. "No new leads, Carter. Nothing." He'd gone on to detail what he'd discovered about the staff.

Kurtz was dull, predictable and eager to please. His prime interest seemed to be the installation of the new system.

Greg Handleman was a possibility, but his access to classified material was limited. He was behaving erratically, however, from what Mac had been able to pick up from the random remarks of the others. The rumor had to do with his girlfriend, a bit of a kook from what Maria had told him, and a political radical. Handleman's political leanings, however, were unknown.

Feldman, too, was a possibility. She had access, but what about motive? As far as Mac could see, she was bright, ambitious and shrewd. She was extremely attractive, perhaps even promiscuous. But where was the motive? Her financial records revealed no vast amounts of unexplained funds, no enormous debts, nothing incriminating. As far as Mac could tell, she was also apolitical. No affiliations, no campus protests in her youth. Nothing.

Both Mac and Hendricks had agreed that Juliet Prentice was still the most likely suspect. According to the files, the next payment for her brother's care was due on the first of March, in two days' time.

Commander Cahill, at Mac's direction, had made arrangements to contact the accounting clerk at the hospital on that date to see if the payment had been made. Then they would wait to find out if Hydra received another call from Alexey with further information to be passed along in Vienna.

They discussed the possibility of surveillance, but Mac was opposed. "Too risky until we have more reason. If Prentice is meeting Alexey, one of them would be sure to spot a tail sooner or later. Alexey probably knows half our people by sight, as it is. Let's wait."

The admiral had agreed. "Stay on her, though, Mac," Hendricks had ordered before they'd hung up. "Get inside her head. Beat her at her own game."

Now Mac tipped his chin back and looked at the ceiling, as though to see Juliet's face reflected there. How could he get inside her head when, every time he tried, she somehow managed to turn things around so she was inside his? He dropped his chin to his chest for a moment, then lifted it again.

"Damn it, Juliet. Who are you?" Mac stared at the photo propped against the brandy bottle and tried to find the treachery in those big brown eyes.

Her features seemed to take on a new life now that he'd met her. Her natural expression was somber, even troubled, as though she carried the weight of the world on her slim shoulders. And yet, when she smiled, her eyes sparkled, her skin glowed, and everything seemed brighter somehow.

Like vintage champagne, her smile was deliciously intoxicating and just as potent in its aftereffects. Her laughter could draw a man toward her like an especially strong magnet, and Mac could still hear it.

Ever since his arrival, he'd tried to find the key to her personality, doing his best to charm her into lowering that prickly guard of hers.

Using every nuance of the aristocratic Southern courtesy his mother had drummed into him as a gawky adolescent, he'd teased her, flirted with her, even tried to flatter her, but nothing seemed to work.

Every time he appeared to make progress, she danced away from him again, leaving him holding nothing but his suspicions.

There had to be a weak spot in her armor somewhere.

Mac took a sip of brandy and leaned back. The wrinkled chair cushion rubbed against his shoulder blades as he tried to find a comfortable position. Nothing felt right these days, not even his suspicions of Juliet Prentice.

She had him confused. Who was this woman he was stalking? His eyes darkened in reflection as he studied the amber liquid in his glass.

Most traitors did it for one of two reasons—ideology or profit, that much he knew to be true. Of the two, the zealots, the dedicated anti-Americans, were the most unpredictable.

Mac's gut churned as he remembered the look of fanatic zeal on Misrani's face when she'd spat on his battered body as he lay chained to the floor in a rat-infested hovel. Before he'd learned of her treachery, he would have died for her, while she would have died only for her beliefs—which she probably had by now. Mac twisted in his seat and took a deep breath.

It still hurt, even after the time that had passed. It hurt to admit that he'd been so badly fooled, to accept the cruel fact that the woman he'd loved so desperately had felt nothing but contempt and hatred for him, even as she was offering her body to him with vows of passionate love.

"I'm going to have your child, McKinley," she'd whispered to him as they worked him over. "And I'm going to teach him to kill Americans."

Mac had told himself over and over that she'd been lying, that it had been a subtle form of psychological torture to weaken his resistance, but deep inside he was afraid she'd been telling the truth. And sometimes, late at night in the hospital, he'd prayed that the child would simply cease to exist. His mind had never been able to take him past that thought.

When he'd left the hospital, for the first time since he'd taken his first steps under the protection of his nanny, Mac had felt alone. And in spite of his family's unflagging support and love, he had gone on feeling alone—until that moment in Juliet's office, when she had lifted her lips to his.

Damn! Mac breathed silently. She'd made him feel again, this vibrant woman with the loving eyes. Holding her strong and eager body in his arms had made him yearn for things he'd rejected a long time ago. Things like love and warmth and tenderness. And that wasn't all she'd excited in him.

Mac's teeth clenched in frustration as his body stirred. From that moment she'd come charging down the pier to confront him, her cheeks flushed, her eyes glittering with the light of battle, he'd wanted her.

All through their shared lunch, he'd been fighting an urge to lean across the table and kiss those soft coral lips into smiling just for him.

While he'd been trying to pump her for information, his attention had been focused on her face, on the way her full mouth curved into a seductive bow whenever she smiled. Instead of listening for incriminating statements, he'd been watching the quick flash of humor in her luminous brown eyes as he'd baited her.

Mac's skin began to burn as the memory of her tears took shape in his mind. Maybe she'd been crying for her brother, but she'd been crying for him, too.

He'd meant to punish her with a kiss, to drive the pity from her eyes, to make her so angry that she couldn't cry for him, but he hadn't been able to summon the rage he'd needed. Instead he'd found himself responding to her, found himself longing to make the kiss real. He'd found himself wanting her with a helpless intensity that had shaken him badly. He hadn't felt that way about a woman since Misrani. He hadn't even thought that he could.

He clenched his fist on his thigh and struggled against the frustration that buffeted him. Once, before his injury, he would have run off his more turbulent feelings. Or played a furious game of tennis with his older brother. Now, however, he was forced to wait them out. To simply endure, until the emotions exhausted themselves.

But what about the driving desire he felt for Juliet Prentice? How was he going to wait that out? Every time he saw her, he had to remind himself that she was a suspect, a possible spy. A potential enemy. And the most desirable woman he'd ever met.

The bay smelled of salt, seaweed and creosote from the heavy pilings supporting the B Street Pier. Scavenging gulls swooped overhead as the tourists strolled along the brightly lighted embarcadero, their muted voices blending with the lapping of the waves against the cement breakwater edging the bay.

It was nearly midnight, and the fog was slowly rolling in through the entrance to the channel inside Point Loma. The sound of shrill laughter drifted over the water as the sailing ship *Invader* neared her pier, her deck crammed with partying passengers, a necklace of white lights strung over her two masts from bow to stern.

A man in a well-fitting conservative gray suit sat on a bench near the pier, watching the approach of the blue-hulled schooner with hard eyes. He was handsome, with dark curly hair and a lean face that was filled with cunning.

His eyes slid toward the left as a nondescript man in equally nondescript clothes approached the bench and sat down, his hands wrapped around a container of black coffee.

"Medusa is frightened," the newcomer said tersely, sipping his coffee without looking at the other man. "Someone new has been assigned to the project, a computer expert. Been asking a lot of questions."

The tall man in the suit stared straight ahead. "FBI?"

"Hardly. He's a cripple. Has a bad leg, walks with a cane. Big guy with a Southern accent." His voice took on a harsh edge. "Medusa's been distracted since he arrived."

"Why?"

"He's bound to have access to the files—all of them—and when they've been accessed and by whom."

The man with dark hair muttered a vicious curse in his native language. "Maybe he won't understand what he sees."

"Medusa doesn't want to take that chance. She thinks he's pretty sharp."

"How much longer before you'll have the documents you need?"

The casually dressed man waited until no one was near before he answered in a low voice. "Two weeks, three at the most."

"Good. Get what you can and get out."

"And Medusa? What if she becomes a liability?"

The tall man stood up and waved at a strikingly beautiful woman in black who was coming up the ramp from the berthed *Invader*. "Simple. You will terminate her."

Chapter 4

W hat's this all about, Felicity?" Juliet slid into a seat next to the assistant director and flipped to a clean page in her notebook. "I don't have time right now for unscheduled meetings."

Greg, who'd followed Juliet into the conference room, walked around the circular table to take a seat as far away from the director's empty chair as possible.

"Beats me," Felicity replied with a shrug. Her hair was swept up into a casual twist of auburn ringlets, and she was wearing a tailored wool dress of bright apricot that Juliet had never seen before.

Juliet frowned as she glanced around the sparsely furnished conference room. She felt a chill, but the windows were closed, and dust motes waltzed in placid circles through the shafts of bright afternoon sun streaming through the panes.

Felicity looked at Juliet and grinned. "I hope this isn't another one of Fred's pep rallies. You know, come early, stay late, write brilliant reports. Rah, rah, team."

Juliet shook her head. "Naughty, naughty, Felicity. Fred's going to overhear you one of these days, and he'll have your head."

Felicity waved an immaculately manicured hand in casual unconcern. "No way, José. I'm a civil servant, remember? The government says I can't be fired."

"Right. But what if he finds some reason to get your clearance revoked? You might end up the only Ph.D. clerk on the federal payroll."

"Oh, piffle," Felicity retorted airily. "My life's dull as dishwater. Work, eat, sleep. Now and then I chase men."

Juliet laughed. "Why do I think you're leaving out the X-rated parts?"

Felicity directed her amber eyes toward the closed door leading to the director's office, then leaned over to whisper in dulcet tones, "Not X-rated, sweetie. Just plain old R." Her eyes shifted toward the other door. "And speaking of which," her voice rose to a welcoming purr, "come right on in, Mac. Have you been sentenced to this meeting, too?"

Mac walked over to the table and pulled out the chair next to Greg's. He was dressed in faded jeans and a worn maroon sweatshirt with cutoff sleeves and a ragged neck, reminding Juliet of the stevedores she'd once seen unloading cargo on the B Street Pier.

"Uh-oh," he drawled with a slow grin. "Do I detect rebellion in the ranks?"

"Don't mind Felicity," Juliet said with a smile. "Happy hour's already started at Grogan's, and those dollar margaritas are calling to her."

Felicity assumed a haughty air. "Don't listen to her, Mac. She's just trying to cover up for our esteemed director's poor timing." She pulled a comical face. "I mean, who can concentrate on work at four-thirty on a Friday afternoon?"

Mac grinned, and his eyes slid over Felicity's apricot brightness to rest on Juliet's more subdued lavender. His grin widened, and his lashes dipped in a sexy salute as his gaze lingered for a heart-racing second on the tailored V between her breasts.

Juliet felt impaled, branded by his intimate gaze, and she groaned inwardly as her nipples tingled beneath the thin silk.

She'd chosen to wear the silk blouse especially for Rex. It had been his gift to her on her thirtieth birthday last year, and it was one of his favorites.

The heated look in Mac's eyes, however, told her that the sentimental gesture had been a mistake. More than that, it had been a foolish risk to take. After all, she berated herself, a woman who'd sworn to avoid entanglements at work shouldn't deliberately wear a provocative outfit to the office. Not unless she wanted that assertion challenged.

Feeling distinctly uneasy, Juliet sat back in her chair and avoided Mac's gaze. She wouldn't make the same mistake again, not while he was around.

"I guess you managed to find your way home all right last night," Felicity said in a friendly tone as Mac levered himself into his chair.

"No problem at all," he said amiably. "Your directions were as good as Juliet's." His eyes smiled at both women as he laid his cane on the floor and stretched out his legs.

Home from where? The question popped into Juliet's mind and refused to be dislodged. Had Felicity and Mac shared more than a drink? Had they been at her designer-decorated condo in Mission Hills? An unwelcome tension invaded Juliet's body at the thought, and she forced her muscles to relax.

Why should she care if Mac and Felicity got something going? They would be perfect together, two gorgeous people looking for a good time. It certainly didn't matter to her.

She glanced up at the clock on the wall. It was almost four-forty, and Rex would be expecting her soon. She sighed and twisted in her seat. Hurry up, Fred, she urged silently.

Her impatient gaze drifted toward the door to the director's office, only to be intercepted by Mac, who was regarding her with keen interest. She grimaced involuntarily, and one thick male brow slid upward in question. It was surprisingly boyish, his look of puzzlement, and decidedly incongruous on his rugged face.

"How was your evening?" he drawled softly, tilting his head to one side and watching her closely.

"Fine," she said curtly, wishing fervently that she hadn't left her blazer hanging on the back of her office door. Not that Mac was staring at her. He wasn't. But he was aware of her. Very aware. She could feel it.

Juliet smoothed her palms against the wool of her gray slacks and slid her thighs together. Fully three feet of shiny walnut separated her from Mac, yet she felt as though he was touching her, as though his hand was actually tracing the modest cleavage of her blouse.

Shivering, she instinctively glanced across the table at those hands. They were very big, bigger than Greg's, bigger than most men's. Powerful, too, with long fingers and a broad palm edged with thick muscle. On his right hand there was a thin white scar slanting from the knuckle of his little finger to his wrist. It looked like the slice of a sharp knife, or perhaps a razor blade.

"Where did you go? To dinner at Peter's?" His tone was perfectly polite, but Juliet heard a distant note of purely masculine interest, the kind that led to more than the kisses they'd shared. Or was it because of the kisses that she was imagining that subtle vibration beneath the words?

"We had a lovely evening," she said primly, flushing as his eyes glinted.

"In other words, mind my own business." His grin cut a beguiling crease in his cheek.

Juliet laughed. "Exactly." She ignored the curious looks that Felicity and Greg were shooting at Mac and then at her. Let them think whatever they want, she thought grumpily. It's really none of their business.

Felicity touched her lightly on the arm. "Remember that new seafood place I told you about last week, Juliet? The Blue Fin?"

Juliet nodded. "The one with the chef who knows how to fix blowfish without killing off his customers?"

"Yes, that's the one. I was telling Mac about it last night. You'd never believe a fish that could be so deadly in the water could be so scrumptious on the plate."

Juliet gave Felicity an indulgent look. "I'll pass, thank you. I have enough trouble worrying about whether or not my pork chops are cooked all the way through."

Mac threw his head back and laughed. It was a rich sound, like dark chocolate melting on the tongue, and Juliet found herself laughing along with him.

Felicity tossed her head in gay dismissal. "How about it, Mac? I can't get any of these cowards to go with me. Want to meet me there at seven? It's delicious, I promise."

Mac's bronzed face assumed a regretful frown. "I'd love to, Felicity, but I'll have to ask for a rain check. Juliet and I have plans for dinner." His deep blue gaze slid toward Juliet, a veiled plea evident beneath the thick screen of his rusty brown lashes. Help me out, his expression plainly telegraphed.

Juliet felt an instant urge to giggle. So he wasn't quite as fearless as he seemed.

Felicity was undaunted. "Why don't I join you, and we'll all three go to the Blue Fin." She glanced expectantly at Juliet.

Juliet felt trapped. She didn't want to hurt Felicity's feelings, yet she didn't dare antagonize Mac by branding him a liar in front of Felicity and Greg.

Before Juliet could formulate an answer, Mac interjected smoothly, "Actually it's more of a business dinner, Felicity. I've asked Juliet to show me around the area before we eat. I want to rent a place of my own while I'm in San Diego."

Felicity's mouth curved upward in a regretful smile. "I'll hold you to that rain check," she promised, as unruffled as usual, and Mac nodded.

"Sure. Maybe next weekend, if you're free." His grin flashed with roguish charm. "I'll need a little time to prepare myself."

Greg gave Mac a speculative look before mumbling, "I don't think I'd ever be ready to eat somethin' that's meaner'n me."

Everyone laughed, and Greg flushed a bright pink as he ducked his head in embarrassment.

"You've got a point there, son," Mac drawled, leaning back in his chair. "I'll give it some thought."

At that moment the door to Dr. Kurtz's office opened, and the portly director entered in a rush. The smell of the aromatic pipe tobacco he favored clung to his tweed jacket, and Juliet wrinkled her nose.

Dr. Kurtz nodded to Mac, then glanced around the table. "Sorry to keep you waiting, ladies and gentlemen," the director said briskly as he settled into his chair. He cleared his throat and pulled his pipe and a pouch of tobacco from his pocket. "I'll be brief."

Thank God, Juliet breathed silently, sneaking a look at her watch. As soon as the meeting was over, she would call Rex to let him know that she was on her way.

Dr. Kurtz inclined his head toward Mac and smiled. It was the oily politician's grin he reserved for visiting brass. "You've all met Mr. McKinley—and welcomed him warmly, I'm sure." His eyes swept around the table in open challenge, and the staff nodded in polite unison.

"As you know," the director continued, "he's been sent here by the Navy department to do the interface for the new database so that the transfer to the new system will go off without a hitch."

He began filling his pipe with tobacco, and the staff exchanged long-suffering glances. Oblivious to the others at the table, Kurtz finished packing the pipe and meticulously tamped the bowl before flicking his lighter.

He puffed furiously, and a cloud of gray smoke encircled his head, obscuring his balding pate for a moment. Juliet stifled a sneeze as the scent of cherry reached her nostrils.

A folded linen handkerchief came sliding across the table, and she looked up to find Mac's eyes narrowed in sympathy. She smiled her thanks and pressed the handkerchief to her nose as another sneeze shook her. His handkerchief smelled like him, spicy and with a hint of some elusive male scent that defied description, but which made her throat tighten in response.

The director gave Juliet an apologetic look before he went on to explain the procedure for the next few weeks, during which Mac would be working out a new file management system.

"But why don't I let him explain all that to you himself?" Kurtz said with a tactful nod in his direction. "Mac?"

Mac leaned forward and folded his hands in front of him. A crooked grin gleamed against his sun-darkened skin as he acknowledged the director. "I know you all have better things to do on a Friday afternoon than listen to me drone on about the intricacies of setting up new directories, so I'll be as brief as possible. As Dr. Kurtz mentioned, I'm really just an advance man for the hardware people who'll install the new network. My job is to have everything converted and ready to plug in when the equipment arrives."

Quickly and concisely, he outlined his intentions, and Juliet found herself listening with interest in spite of her innate dislike of the subject. There was something about the man that compelled attention, something charismatic that had her hanging on every word in spite of her impatience.

"Any questions?" Mac asked in conclusion, his eyes sweeping the table.

Felicity raised her hand. "About the backup, are we still going to use the disks?"

Mac nodded. "Yes. Very little will change in the way of procedure. I'm not here to complicate your life, believe me. If I do my job right, I'll simplify things for everyone."

"That's what we need, isn't it people?" Fred commented quickly, directing another toothy smile toward Mac.

"Oh, one more thing," Mac added, leaning forward slightly as though for emphasis. "I'll need to go through your files individually, to see if I can uncover any duplications or wasted storage space. Part of the appeal of this system is its versatility, so we want to make sure we take advantage of it."

The three scientists looked at each other with question marks in their eyes. Felicity was the first to respond. "Are you authorized?"

Mac acknowledged the question with a faint smile. "Absolutely. Fred has seen my clearance." He glanced at the director, who hastily nodded.

Juliet felt her face grow cold and then hot as panic shot through her. An accounting of Peter's payments to her and another of her payments to the hospital were hidden away in her personal files, the only record she dared keep. Somehow she would have to expunge that record before Mac began his survey.

Her heart began to pound. Before this moment, each scientist had kept his own records, contributing test results to a shared database, but keeping the raw data in individual files. It had seemed more convenient that way.

Mac made a steeple of his fingers against his lips and watched Juliet through the screen of his lashes. She was frightened; he could see it. But why? Was there something in the files that shouldn't be there? Or something that should be there that wasn't? His chest filled with some emotion that he preferred not to identify.

Maybe tonight, if he could keep her from breaking the date he'd forced her into, he might be able to probe further. After all, he thought sardonically, he was a good listener. Everyone said so. Listening, however, wasn't the only thing he wanted to do whenever he was around Juliet Prentice. No, he wanted to take her to his bed and spend an eternity exploring that deliciously ripe body of hers. He felt an ominous quickening in his loins and shifted impatiently in the hard chair. Wouldn't this meeting ever be over? he grumbled silently.

"I guess that's it, people," Dr. Kurtz said with a brief nod. "Have a nice weekend."

The others responded politely and pushed back their chairs. There was a flurry of good-byes, and then Juliet and Mac were alone.

"Thanks for the hanky," she murmured, handing the folded cloth back to him.

"Thanks for helping me out of a tight spot," he countered as he returned the handkerchief to his back pocket and reached for his cane. "Experimenting with exotic food is not really my idea of a good time."

Juliet chuckled. "It's not mine, either." She closed her notebook and stood up. "Felicity's sweet, but she can be pretty overpowering if you're not used to her."

Mac grinned and got slowly to his feet. "Actually she reminds me of Suzanne, my sister," he drawled. "Suzanne's had two husbands and is working on the third."

As they walked toward the hall, Juliet noticed that her high-heeled pumps had raised her mouth to the level of his chin. Perfect for kissing, came the unbidden thought, but she hastily pushed the idea away. She had other things to worry about.

"Look, I know I put you in an awkward spot, Juliet," Mac said, stepping back to let her precede him out the door. "But I really would like your advice about where to find a decent apartment. I hate living in a motel."

Juliet turned into her office, and Mac stopped in the doorway, leaned his shoulder against the wooden frame and waited.

He looked so hopeful, she thought with an uneasy feeling of guilt. As though it really mattered whether or not she helped him out. But that's nonsense, she told herself firmly. The man seems more than capable of taking care of himself. She opened her mouth to make an excuse, then closed it with a snap as a sudden thought occurred to her. Maybe they could trade favors.

"Mac, I'm late for an appointment right now, but . . . well, maybe we could help each other out."

As matter-of-factly as she could, she told him about her brother's motorcycle accident and his lengthy recovery. "He's in some kind of funk right now, and he won't cooperate with the people who are trying to help him." She paused to take a deep breath. "I thought you might be able to talk to him, maybe give him some...encouragement." She held her breath, but Mac's face remained impassive.

"Maybe he just needs more time," Mac said evenly, watching her intently.

"Tell that to the insurance company," she said in a bitter tone. "They have this stupid rule that says they won't pay for a patient who refuses to cooperate in his treatment."

Mac's expression didn't change. "Can they do that? Legally, I mean."

Juliet snorted in derision. "You bet your life they can," she said. "They have all the power. Rex is just a number to them." She took a deep breath in an effort to calm down. She'd been through all this before, with the patient representative at Mar Vista who'd called to warn her that the insurance carrier was requesting additional information on Rex.

"You sound angry about that," he said in a neutral tone. "Do you think that's unreasonable?"

Juliet jerked her hand toward the bay. "Day after day I watch big old Navy ships steaming out of the harbor, carrying billions of dollars' worth of killing firepower, and I ask myself how come it's only the rich who can afford superior care in this country?" Her shoulders drooped. "It's not fair."

"You make your living working for this country," he said softly. "As you once reminded me. Someone's got to defend it."

Juliet stiffened, her eyes flashing angrily as she glared across the small office. Mac had sounded almost . . . disappointed in her.

"You're right. I . . . forget what I said." She forced a laugh as the anger drained away. "It's been a long week."

Mac pushed himself away from the doorjamb. "You need a drink," he said firmly. "C'mon. I'll buy."

Juliet shook her head. The idea was surprisingly tempting, in spite of her resolve to avoid any further entanglement with this man. "My brother is waiting. I promised to bring him a take-out burger."

"Fair enough. You buy the dinner, and I'll buy the drinks after we've seen . . . Rex, is it?"

Juliet nodded. She suddenly felt as though a great weight had been lifted from her shoulders, at least temporarily. "Yes, Rex Richard. Justin was playing Richard the Third on Broadway when Rex was born."

Mac's face became pensive. "Your father died a few years back, didn't he?"

"Yes," she said in a strained tone. "In November it'll be nine years."

Mac nodded in sympathy. "You must miss him very much."

Juliet nodded. Especially now, when she was feeling so alone and scared. She averted her gaze.

"Ready to go?" Mac glanced toward the vista beyond the window. "Looks like the traffic's thinning some."

Juliet folded her blazer over her arm and reached for the large canvas tote that contained her wet suit and towels. Before the meeting she'd locked her notes in the safe and secured her terminal.

The elevator was on the way up when they reached the lobby. Mac smiled warmly at her as they waited. "This is a rare treat, Juliet. I haven't been out with a lady as lovely as you in a long time."

The door opened then, sparing her from replying, and she hurried inside. Mac followed and punched the button. With a violent lurch, the elevator started downward, tossing Juliet against Mac's side. Automatically his arm came out to steady her.

"This thing bucks like an old tractor we had once on the farm," he drawled, and Juliet felt a tiny shiver of pleasure as his breath warmed her skin.

Subtly she tried to edge away, only to have Mac tuck her more firmly against his side, her shoulder squeezed against his chest, her hip against his. He had only to rotate his body a few inches and they would be face to face, chest to chest, thigh to thigh. Mouth to mouth.

Juliet stopped breathing. Would he move those few inches? Did she want him to? A powerful urgency shook her to the marrow. God help her, she did.

The door opened on the ground floor, and Mac gave her shoulders a strong hug. "Darn, I was hoping it would get stuck," he said in a husky voice as he released her.

Juliet pretended to be offended. "What is it with you, Mac? Do you have some kind of thing for elevators?"

He frowned, then burst out laughing. "Not really. At least, not before I met you. Maybe you just have a way of inspiring me." His grin took on a rueful slant, and Juliet laughed.

"Remind me to take the stairs from now on," she said playfully, then froze. Had she said the wrong thing again?

But Mac seemed more amused than angry. "No fair, lady," he teased as he held the outer door for her. "You wouldn't do that to a war veteran, would you?"

"Try me," she answered in a bantering lilt, giving him a warning look that had his brows rising in an expression of mock fear. Excitement and something that felt strangely like happiness began filling her, lightening her step and making her eyes twinkle.

"I'll drive," she said as they entered the lot. "It's easier than directing you." She indicated a yellow sports car sitting alone in the first row. It was old, but the paint gleamed from careful waxing, and the interior was immaculate.

"Nice car," Mac commented as she unlocked the passenger door before rounding the car to unlock her own. "You've really kept it up."

Juliet slung her satchel into the narrow back seat and slid beneath the wheel.

Mac folded his body awkwardly and backed into the low bucket seat. She averted her eyes as he circled his left knee with both hands and pulled his leg inside the car. He held his cane between his knees and closed the door.

"Actually, Rex was the one who did most of the restoration work," she said with a fond smile as she buckled her seat belt. "He made it a summer project the year he graduated from high school. I'd had this car since college, and it was getting pretty beat up."

Her father had given it to her for her eighteenth birthday. It was the last gift he'd ever given her, and in spite of its unreliable performance in recent years, she hadn't been able to part with it.

She inserted the key and glanced at Mac inquiringly.

"What?" he asked with a puzzled half smile.

"Seat belt."

His lips twitched. "Why? Are you a bad driver?"

She grinned. "No, but there's no sense taking chances."

Mac gave her a long-suffering look that was more flirtatious than complaining and buckled the strap across his wide chest.

Juliet nodded in satisfaction and turned the key. Nothing happened.

She tried again, praying that the old car wouldn't let her down now. But her prayer went unanswered. The only sound was the metallic click of the ignition switch as she turned the key again and again.

"I think your battery's dead," Mac said in a wry voice.

She nodded dispiritedly. "I know. It's the generator. I've had this trouble before." In rising frustration, she hit the steering wheel with the heel of her hand. Wasn't anything ever going to go right in her life again?

Mac reached over to cover her hand with his. "Hey, don't sweat the small stuff," he said in a forceful tone. "We'll take my car and call the auto club from the hospital. Okay?" His long fingers closed over her slim hand in a gesture of comfort, and Juliet felt some of the tension drain from her.

"Okay," she said with a wan smile. "But I'll drive. I know it sounds silly, but I'm a very nervous passenger."

Mac gave her a curious look. Juliet thought he was going to object, but he simply shrugged and removed his hand. "Okay with me," he said with easy acceptance as he opened the door and awkwardly swung his legs out.

As Juliet locked her door, she glanced across the top of the low-slung car. Mac was using the top of the door to pull himself to his feet, and his huge body seemed to reduce her compact vehicle to the proportions of a kiddie car she'd once had.

She glanced toward the rental sedan he'd indicated several rows away. It was midsize, dark blue in color, an ordinary American car. No real power, no glamour, no danger. Definitely not the kind of car she would have expected Mac to drive.

As she fell into step beside him, she wondered what he drove when he was home in Virginia. Something large and lethal, with rakish lines and a real leather interior, she guessed, sneaking a look at his bold profile. A lean mean machine, she thought, echoing one of her brother's favorite phrases. It was an over-worked cliché among Rex's generation, but in this case it was true. She just wasn't sure whether she was describing the car or the man.

Mar Vista Rehabilitation Center was housed in a rambling one-story building adjacent to the large medical complex known as San Diego General Hospital.

It had been built the same year that Rex was born, a coincidence that Juliet found somewhat macabre, especially since the memorial celebration marking that milestone had been held on Rex's birthday.

Not that she believed in fate, but the longer she lived, the more she did believe in her father's favorite axiom: "God must have had a sense of the dramatic. Why else would he have invented earthquakes and opening nights?"

"Classy place," Mac commented as they crossed the large, bright lobby. The walls were painted a restful pink, with accents of pale blue and lavender provided by several contemporary prints framed in chrome. Clay pots filled with greenery provided walls of privacy around the free-form but comfortable-looking chairs.

"I'd give up some of the original art and glitzy magazines for lower fees," Juliet retorted in a whisper. She took a tighter grip on the three white bags bearing their dinner and tried to ignore the tantalizing smell of hamburgers and French fries wafting toward her nostrils. She's skipped lunch in order to leave on time, and she was ravenously hungry.

Mac gave her an odd look. "Maybe it doesn't seem important when you're not the patient," he said in an even voice, "but staring at blank walls and ugly plastic furniture can get awfully tedious after a while."

Juliet tactfully remained silent. Mac was right, of course. She was being petty, but the strain was beginning to wear on her. Sometimes she thought she would shatter into billions of individual cells if she had to cope with one more pressure.

* * *

Juliet paced the corridor with long nervous strides. Up and down, twelve steps from Rex's room to the nurses' station and back again. Her narrow heels clicked out a staccato rhythm on the linoleum, jarring her concentration with each sharp tap.

Her thoughts were with Rex and Mac behind the closed door. What was Mac telling her brother? Would it help or hurt the confused young man?

Juliet sighed and clasped her hands tightly in front of her. It had started so badly.

Rex had been startled to see his sister with a stranger, a man with hard features and intimidating shoulders who walked with a cane. She'd seen the wariness creep into her brother's green eyes, although Rex was too well bred to be deliberately rude.

She'd tried to cover the awkwardness with congenial chatter, the kind her mother had done so well. She'd served the food, teased Rex about his ghastly choice in cuisine, then blushed when Mac pointed out just how much of that awful food she'd consumed.

Mac. Juliet felt her confusion deepen. He was an enigma, a man she couldn't read in spite of her finely honed ability to detect subtle signals—in people as well as dolphins.

Juliet bit the inside of her lip in pensive deliberation as she paced. Whenever she was around Mac, she felt disoriented and confused. It was as though she'd accidentally entered a dark underwater cave that was filled with tantalizing exotic creatures who were drawing her deeper and deeper into the unfamiliar cavern until she was hopelessly lost.

Being with Mac would be just like that, she knew without doubt. He would pull her into his powerful male orbit, tantalizing her, seducing her, absorbing her, until she was powerless to resist him. And eventually she would be lost, her control gone. And then what? Mac would go back to Washington, and she would be here by herself, feeling more lonely than ever.

Juliet reached the nurses' station and turned to retrace her steps. Her heart was fluttering with nervousness. She shouldn't have left them alone, but Mac had practically ordered her to fetch coffee for the three of them.

"From the cafeteria," he'd told her firmly. And Juliet had taken the hint. The coffee was there on the floor by the door. The Styrofoam containers would keep it warm.

But for how long? It had been over thirty minutes since she'd left. Should she barge right in, or would Mac come looking for her? It wasn't like her to be so indecisive, but somehow, without her really knowing when or how, Mac had taken over.

He was in charge now and, oddly enough, in spite of her personal confusion, on some deeper level she was relieved. She'd been the parent for so long—since her mother had died eight years ago.

She was making the turn at the end of the hall when she heard the door open. Mac stuck his head around the frame and looked up and down the corridor.

Catching sight of Juliet, he motioned for her to come inside. "Hey, lady, you've got two thirsty men in here just waiting for coffee," he said in that slow intimate drawl that made her stomach quiver. "What kept you so long?"

Juliet hurried toward the door and reached down to pick up the three cups. "I'm coming, I'm coming," she said lightly, but her eyes were filled with worry as they met Mac's.

His blue eyes shone steadily into hers, reassuring her, bolstering her. It's going to be all right, they signaled, and Juliet nearly sagged in relief.

"You have to have a little patience with my sister, Mac," Rex called from his bed. "She's gotten a little weird from being in salt water so much."

Juliet swept by Mac with a haughty swish. "Listen, if you two guys were in such a hurry, why didn't you go get the coffee yourselves?" She held her breath. Rex's sense of humor had been noticeably unpredictable since the accident.

She nearly wept with relief as a jaunty grin spread over her brother's milk-white face. "Next time we will," he said with a grin at Mac. "You can sit here and make pictures on the walls."

Juliet looked from one to the other in confusion. Both men wore that smug look of primitive male superiority that she abhorred. What had Mac been doing all this time? Telling her brother dirty jokes instead of giving him a pep talk?

Mac caught the suspicious look on her face and winked. "Drink your coffee, Juliet, and stop glaring at us. I promise we didn't drag two nurses in here while you were gone, although we did consider it."

Juliet's mouth popped open in outrage. She took a deep breath and prepared to blast him, only to freeze as she heard the sound of her brother's laugh. It sounded strange, rusty and thin, and more wonderful than she could ever have imagined.

He'd laughed like that often before the accident, usually when he'd teased her into a temper. It had been a cherished game between them in those days—Rex saying outrageous things to get a rise from his proper sister, Juliet exaggerating her response to bring a triumphant glow to her brother's eyes. She'd missed their banter more than she had realized.

"Listen, I'd better not catch either one of you fooling around in here. I value my reputation, even if you two jokers don't."

Hands on hips, she glared from one set of smug masculine eyes to the other. Rex struggled to keep a straight face, and Mac hung his head. She wanted to hug both of them.

"Aw, c'mon, Juliet. You know we're only teasing—although Mac did want to invite that cute little blond nurse in here to give us both a back rub. But I told him she had cold hands, so he decided to wait until later—when you could do it."

Mac looked pleased, and Juliet felt herself blushing furiously. "Sounds like a terrific idea to me," Mac said with a wry grin. "I can't remember the last time I had a good massage."

"Sorry, I'm fresh out of rubbing alcohol," she shot back flippantly. Her stomach was tumbling erratically, and her head felt odd, as though it were floating several inches above her shoulders.

She couldn't seem to get the image of Mac's muscular torso, stripped and gleaming with oil, out of her mind. Would his skin feel silky beneath her palms, or would the tiny strawberry blond hairs matting his arms give his body an enticing roughness? Juliet gave herself a mental shake. Her libido was certainly behaving strangely lately.

Rex pushed a button of the side rail of his bed, and his shoulders rose higher. He took the white cup from the bedside table and began to sip the coffee. His brows furrowed, then cleared as he took another sip. "Hey, this is good. As soon as I get the hang of that chair, I'll hot rod down to the cafeteria at night and get my coffee there. The stuff the nurses brew on the ward is awful."

Juliet was afraid to breathe. She could feel hope begin to take root inside her. Had Rex really made a joke about his hated wheelchair? She was afraid to trust her hearing. Not when it meant so much to her.

After one glance at her, Mac began to tell Rex about the bootleg hootch one of the sailors had fermented in an unused storage room at the hospital in Bethesda.

Juliet listened absently, her eyes fixed on her brother as he watched Mac attentively. Physically, he looked the same as he had two days ago. Silky auburn hair, dramatic green eyes, a pug nose dotted with freckles. But instead of dropping in defeat, his colorless lips were curved upward in a smile. Instead of hunching in dejection, his bony shoulders were thrown back confidently.

He was almost back to normal. Almost. Except for the thin legs lying limply under the covers, unmoving, without feeling. He would never be considered normal by society's standards again.

A burst of laughter greeted the end of Mac's story, and Juliet smiled with real happiness.

Rex gave her a sly look. "Mac said you're going to help him find a place to live," he remarked in a tone of open curiosity.

"Well, I'm going to show him around," Juliet hedged.

"I told him he should look in Ocean Beach," Rex continued in an eager tone. "There are always vacancies in your area."

Juliet lived in a small frame cottage on a cliff overlooking the Pacific. She'd taken the small one bedroom bungalow when Rex had moved into his fraternity house on campus at the beginning of his sophomore year.

"Yes, that's a good idea," she said. "We'll be sure to look there first." Juliet could have strangled her brother then and there. The last person she wanted for a neighbor was Mac.

Rex grinned as though pleased, then drained his cup and tossed the empty container toward the small plastic trash basket near the head of the bed.

The crumpled Styrofoam hit the rim of the basket, then bounced onto the floor. Rex started to reach over the side to retrieve it, only to topple forward as he lost his balance.

Moving more swiftly than Juliet would have thought possible, Mac lurched forward to catch Rex, pushing him back with a thrust of his powerful forearm.

Rex muttered a vicious curse. "See what I mean," he said to Mac in a strangled voice. "I can't even pick up after myself."

Mac took a step backward. "Try it again, and this time hang on to the side rail." His voice was firm and without pity.

Rex gave him a measuring look. Juliet could tell that he wanted to do as Mac said, but a part of him had already given up. He'd fallen out of bed once getting into his wheelchair and had steadfastly refused to try again, so every day the orderly helped him into the chair in the morning and back to bed in the evening.

Mac stood silently, his expression blank. Juliet wondered what he was feeling behind those deep-set sapphire eyes.

Rex glanced down at the crumpled cup. His chest heaved once, and he squared his shoulders. His hands were shaking as he placed one on the rail and began reaching toward the floor with the other. There was only a foot or so between the tips of his fingers and the cup, an easy reach for someone as tall as Rex—if he could brace himself with his legs.

Juliet held her breath as Rex leaned lower. Sweat dotted his forehead, and his labored breathing seemed unnaturally loud in the quiet room.

And then he had it. With a triumphant cry he tossed the cup into the basket and flopped back against his pillows. The neck of his gown was wet, and he was shaking, but his grin was steady, and his eyes seemed to glow with triumph.

"Way to go!" Juliet cheered, and Rex beamed. They both knew he'd just taken a giant step along the path to recovery.

"It's easy, once you know how," Rex said with a smug laugh. His eyes swung to Mac. "Right?"

"Right." Mac grinned, but there was a preoccupied look in his eyes.

Juliet moved closer to the bed. Rex was beginning to look tired, and she was emotionally exhausted. "Well, kiddo, I think we'd better be going. Mac promised me a drink, and you need to get your rest. Dr. Green said you have things to do down in the gym."

Rex looked distinctly uncomfortable at the mention of the gym, but Juliet didn't press. He'd had enough for one evening.

"'Night, sweetie." She kissed him on the cheek, then hugged him fiercely. She was so proud of him.

She stepped back, and Mac moved forward. The two men exchanged handshakes.

"Give 'em hell," Mac said in a brusque tone.

"I'll try," Rex returned in a strong voice. "And I'll remember what you told me. Slow and easy."

Mac grinned and lifted a thumb in salute. "You got it."

Juliet tossed a kiss over her shoulder as they went out the door.

The corridor was beginning to fill with visitors. After eight months Juliet knew many of them by sight, if not by name.

A man in a garish Hawaiian shirt stopped her and, giving Mac an apologetic look, Juliet exchanged pleasantries, listening attentively as the man talked about his son's progress.

Mac edged closer to the wall, his eyes fixed on the end of the corridor. His breathing quickened, and his stomach churned as stifling tension tightened the muscles of his gut. He wanted to run, but he couldn't. The best he could do was put one foot in front of the other in the careful measured way he'd been taught.

Coming here, seeing Rex struggling with the horrors of his crippled legs, listening to him describe his frustrations, had brought it all back, every gut wrenching minute of it.

Juliet finished her conversation and returned to Mac's side. "Sorry," she muttered as they began walking toward the lobby. Mac could feel her eyes on him, but he ignored the silent question.

How could she possibly understand what it had been like? How could she imagine the mind games he'd played with himself just to stand the pain one more second, one more minute, without screaming?

In the middle of the night, lying endlessly in the same uncomfortable position, he'd heard the same kind of sibilant footsteps trudging up and down the hall outside his door.

In the first few weeks he'd listened in rigid longing for that sound, praying for the presence of a nurse with a needle that would send him off into a few coveted hours of oblivion before the murderous pain racking his battered body would jerk him awake again.

But that hadn't been the worst of it. Each day for two weeks he'd waited for the doctor to appear, waited to hear that he could keep his splintered left leg one more day.

He'd prayed then, prayed as he never had as a child. But mostly he'd waited, learning to endure the pain and the uncertainty one more minute, one more hour, one more day.

He'd learned a lot about himself during those times. That he was stronger than he'd ever imagined. That he could hate with a fierce heat that drove away the hurt of betrayal. That he would never let a woman get that close to him again.

"This place is beginning to feel like a second home," Juliet murmured with a cheery wave at another acquaintance. "I can even tell what's on the menu for dinner by the smell."

"All hospitals smell alike," Mac muttered, forcing a light note into his voice.

Juliet nodded, her smile freezing on her face as she noticed his pale cheeks. She felt as though a large hand had reached out to slam her against the wall. How could I be so stupid? she thought in dismay.

She'd asked Mac to do what no one should have to do—relive a nightmare. And she'd done it in all innocence. In her total concern for her brother, she hadn't considered what it might do to Mac.

This was pain she was seeing. Well masked, but real nonetheless. Juliet felt her cheeks grow warm in mortification. Mac had told her nothing of the incident that had injured his leg, but she'd learned enough from Rex's ordeal in the last few months to know that his recovery must have been rough.

Coming here, seeing the white uniforms, hearing the soft voice of the paging operator, must have felt like the worst kind of déjà vu to Mac.

He was handling it well, but she could see the way his big fist whitened around the handle of his cane, and a helpless feeling of guilt buffeted her.

"Mac?" She placed a tentative hand on his arm, forcing him to stop.

His throat tightened as he saw the growing look of dismay in her expressive eyes. Sympathy, pain, self-reproach—he saw them all. And something else, something sweet and enticing that made his breath catch in his throat.

"Thank you," she said with quiet sincerity, her hand tightening on his bare forearm. "You've really helped Rex. I could see it."

"You're welcome," he said, forcing a smile. Don't look at me like that, he thought. Don't make me want things I can't have. He fought down the urge to run his fingertip along the swelling curve of her bottom lip, to kiss her frown of concern into a sultry, passionate smile just for him.

Juliet nodded her understanding, dropping her hand, and they resumed walking.

Mac glanced down at his feet. He'd managed to get out of Bethesda on his own two legs, and every day since he'd walked alone. He'd reconciled himself to solitariness, even convinced himself that he preferred the life of a swinging bachelor. Until now.

Mac slid his eyes to the side. Juliet was clearly upset, upset because she'd caused him pain. He could see it in the heightened color of her dewy cheeks and in the quick rise and fall of her breasts beneath the lavender silk.

Mac's body stirred, even as he dropped his eyes. She had a dynamite body, the kind that moved with natural grace no matter what kind of clothes she was wearing. And her skin would be smooth and tight and tantalizing to the touch.

Sure, he wanted her. What man wouldn't? But it was more than that. He'd had enough women to know that her appeal was more than sexual, more than physical. Something about this woman had him tied in knots, and he hated it, even as he yearned to take her to his bed.

He'd thought about her all during the meeting, which had made it extremely difficult to concentrate. And even now his body was responding to her nearness.

Damn! he thought in simmering frustration. What the hell was he supposed to do about her?

Chapter 5

"Are you sleeping with this guy Peter?" Mac stirred the ice in his double bourbon with a blunt forefinger and watched Juliet with hooded eyes.

Juliet nearly choked. "That's none of your business," she said in a firm voice, feeling her temper begin to simmer.

Going out with Mac had been a mistake. For some reason he'd been verbally sparring with her from the moment they'd entered the tiny neighborhood bar.

Juliet stared at the garish neon sign in the window, telling herself that she was going to get up and leave as soon as she finished her drink.

Mac had barely said a word as she'd driven them to Ocean Beach. He seemed locked somewhere inside his own thoughts, his face closed to her.

She'd suggested that they forgo the drink, but Mac had insisted. "I promised," he'd said with a grim smile, and Juliet had decided not to argue.

Besides, she told herself that it might help him to be with someone after his experience at the hospital. After all, he'd been there for her. Now it was her turn.

Juliet sighed and let her eyes drift around the room. She'd chosen this bar because it was close to the beach and because she thought Mac might enjoy some local color.

The interior was dimly lit from above, and the rough redwood paneling on the walls absorbed most of the light from the flickering candles in the middle of each round table.

The decor was haphazard, a mélange of beach life, with an ancient fiberglass surfboard hanging on the wall next to a frayed fishing net festooned with colored glass bottles that had once been used as marker buoys.

"If you're not sleeping with him, how come he acted like he owned you on the phone yesterday." Mac seemed to be baiting her.

"I told you, Mac. Peter's a . . . friend of mine. A good friend." Juliet concentrated on her breathing. Mac had become a different person, sarcastic and arrogant, yet strangely withdrawn.

He drained his glass and signaled the waitress for another. It was his third. "You remind me of a woman I once knew," he said in a silky drawl. "Only you're more beautiful."

Juliet sipped her drink and tried to decipher the unfamiliar expression in his eyes. Mac caught her gaze on him and lowered his eyes to the sputtering candle in the middle of the table. "Have you ever been in love, Juliet?" he asked suddenly, keeping his eyes fixed on the flame.

"Yes, once," she said. "Or at least I thought I was."

"What happened?"

"He wanted my research more than he wanted me."

A muscle jerked along Mac's jaw, and his hand tightened around his glass. "Hurt like hell, didn't it?" His voice had a savage intensity that sent prickles of uneasiness skating across her shoulder blades.

"Yes," she said bluntly. "It hurt like hell." She took another sip, grimacing as the whiskey burned all the way to her stomach. Her father had taught her to take her liquor straight and to stop at two drinks, and it was a rule she'd never broken. But tonight she was tempted.

The mini-skirted waitress brought Mac's drink, her perky smile faltering as she caught sight of his taut face. He grunted his thanks and tossed a large bill onto the tray, indicating with a wave of his hand that the woman should keep it. She left without a word.

"I was in love once, too." Mac leaned back and studied his bourbon with opaque eyes. "I wanted the whole package. Marriage, kids, a nice place in Virginia, a few horses, maybe a rose garden. Even bought the ring." He tossed down half his drink in one swallow.

"What happened?" Juliet asked softly. Her growing anger was forgotten in her concern for Mac. She had a feeling he was undergoing some kind of catharsis, dredging through his past in order to find peace. She'd done that once, a long time ago. Right after she'd discovered what a gullible fool she'd been.

"She . . . changed her mind," Mac drawled, his lips thinning at some inner irony. "After she'd gotten all she could get out of me." He downed the second half of his drink and signaled the waitress. This time he ordered another whiskey for Juliet along with his bourbon, quirking an eyebrow in her direction as though daring her to protest.

Juliet dropped her eyes, tacitly accepting his challenge. For some reason he seemed eager to pick a fight with her, perhaps to unload some of the rage she could feel simmering behind his civilized facade.

"I'll drink with you, Mac," she said after the waitress had brought the drinks and departed, "but I won't let you punish me for something another woman did to you. It's not fair, and I don't deserve it."

His eyes flashed before his lashes dropped. "Is that what I'm doing?" he asked in a dangerously quiet voice.

"I think so, yes."

"Maybe I am at that." Mac toyed with the handle of his cane. "You'd never do that. Betray a guy, I mean. No, of course you wouldn't. I can tell you're the loyal type. Just look at the way you take care of your brother."

His voice roughened suddenly, and Juliet was caught off balance. Was he being sarcastic, or did he really mean what he said?

"You make that sound like some kind of a crime," she probed. "Like loyalty is a dirty word."

Mac's gaze lingered on her face, his brows knotted in puzzlement, as though she were an alien creature he'd just met. "On the contrary," he countered in a silky drawl, "I believe in loyalty. It's love I don't believe in." He nodded to the candle that had burned almost to its end. "See that flame? Love's like that. From a distance it's great, but get too close and you'll get burned every time."

Juliet's gaze automatically fell to the flickering candle. "I'm not sure I agree," she said slowly. "At least, I don't think I *want* to agree."

"So you've forgiven this guy who romanced you for your research? Is that what you're telling me?"

Juliet looked up to find a cynical half smile playing around his lips. She answered with a shrug. "I can't say that I don't have some pretty negative feelings still, but life goes on. I wouldn't say that I've been scarred forever by one mistake."

"No? So how come you have this rule about never dating a co-worker?"

"Because I'm not stupid," Juliet shot back with a defiant look, causing Mac to blink in surprise.

"Stubborn, though," he drawled in a wry undertone, and Juliet burst out laughing.

"I prefer determined," she answered pertly, relieved to see that the sexy slash was back in his cheek and that the sleepy-eyed look of masculine sensuality was in his eyes again. Whatever had been tormenting him earlier seemed to have disappeared.

Mac leaned forward suddenly, reaching across the table to smooth an errant lock of hair away from her temple. "Stubborn," he repeated in softly slurred tones. "And beautiful." His fingertips lingered on her skin, making her instantly aware of a new and heightened awareness between them.

"Who are you, really?" he murmured, watching her intently with midnight eyes that seemed to reflect the shimmering glow of the candle. "I wish you'd let me see behind that beautiful face of yours."

Juliet felt desire shiver through her. "What do you want to know?" she asked softly, fascinated with the masculine curve of his mouth. There was a triangular indentation above his upper lip that was just the right size to accomodate the tip of her tongue.

Mac's fingers slid into her hair, and he pulled her toward him. "Will you have dinner with me tomorrow night?" His drawl was laced with mischief, and Juliet blinked in surprise.

"You're impossible," she sputtered, taking hold of his wrist and pulling his hand away. Instantly he twisted in her grasp until his fingers were holding hers.

"True enough," he murmured, lifting the back of her hand to his lips. His tongue slowly traced the intricate lines of her veins beneath the sensitive skin until she couldn't stand it any longer.

"Mac, people are staring," she whispered, trying to pull away.

Mac lifted his eyes and glanced around the room. "No, they're not." He pressed her hand between his palms. "And from the looks of this place, we could strip naked on the floor and nobody'd much care."

Juliet tried to look stern, but the twinkle in his eye defeated her, and she giggled. "I guess you're right at that."

She smiled up at him, her eyes brimming with laughter, her delicate features bathed in the soft glimmer of the flame.

God, she's beautiful! Mac thought in a blinding surge of desire. So beautiful. And completely out of bounds.

Silently, his heart racing with emotions he didn't dare analyze, he released her hand and picked up his drink, downing the bourbon in one swallow. Not this time, he vowed. This time he wasn't going to be blinded by a woman's beauty. This time he was going to make the rules. He searched the room for the waitress. He needed another drink.

* * *

"That's it there. The one with the green trim." Juliet pointed toward a row of four tidy wood-frame bungalows perched on a cliff overlooking the Pacific.

Each cottage was painted a snowy white and trimmed in dark green. A tiny square of thick Bermuda grass separated each house from its neighbor, and a short white picket fence enclosed the small community on three sides, leaving the fourth open to the sea.

A large black sign with For Rent spelled out in orange letters had been tacked to the fence, and Mac's eyes sharpened with interest. For once his luck seemed to be holding.

He pulled into the nearest parking space and turned off the ignition. "Which one's yours?" he asked with the barest suggestion of a smile.

Juliet frowned. "That one," she repeated impatiently. "With the pink geraniums in the window box." She sighed. "The mildew almost got 'em, but I saved 'em." Her lips parted in a triumphant smile. "Aren't you proud of me?" She was beginning to feel light-headed.

Mac looked down into her shadowed face. Light from the street lamp seemed trapped in her honeyed curls, turning the soft tangle to shimmering platinum. Beneath her long lashes, her brown eyes looked velvety black and were filled with golden light.

Slowly he reached out to smooth back a stray curl. His fingertips rested against the satin curve of her cheek, savoring the warmth he could feel blooming beneath his callused skin.

The feathery tips of her lashes brushed against the heel of his hand, reminding him of the delicate wings of a monarch butterfly he'd once captured as a child.

His breath caught in his throat as he remembered the horror he'd felt when he'd opened his hand to discover that, in his excited pleasure, he'd crushed the beautiful creature to death.

"You're shaking," he said in a low voice. He hesitated, then slid his other hand across her cheek to frame her face. Her skin was as fragile as fine porcelain, and just as smooth.

"I should have worn my blazer," she murmured, wondering if he would kiss her, even as she tried to pull away.

Mac slid his hand behind her slender neck and pulled her toward him. "I like your blouse," he answered in a husky voice that sent shivers along her skin beneath the silk. "It's very...elegant."

His lips brushed hers before he buried his face in her neck. Juliet rubbed her cheek against his temple, and Mac sighed. His lips nibbled at the thin skin above her open collar, and she held her breath. She wanted those soft lips to move lower, to spread the delectable warmth over her breasts. But suddenly he stiffened, sighed again and released her.

"It's late," he drawled hoarsely. "I'd better get you inside."

Juliet straightened her hair and took a deep breath. She felt just a bit tipsy all of a sudden, and very depressed. Of course, she hadn't really wanted Mac to kiss her. Not really. But he could at least have tried.

Mac came around to open the door for her, and she took the arm he offered with a polite smile. His fingers closed over hers, warmly intimate and oddly possessive, as they walked along the low fence.

At the gate, which was standing ajar, Mac paused and pointed to the sign with his cane. "How'd you like a crusty old bachelor like me for a neighbor?" he asked in a bantering tone.

"No!" Juliet's hand flew to her mouth in mortification. "I— that is, uh..." She didn't know what to say. How could she tell him that she was afraid? Afraid that he'd batter down her defenses. Afraid that in a moment of desperate longing she would give in to the scorching attraction she felt for him and invite him into her bed.

"I didn't mean that," she said in a small voice, gazing up at him helplessly. The last thing she wanted to do was hurt him.

His hand was gentle as he traced the line of her cheek. "Yes, you did," he drawled softly, watching her with brooding eyes.

Juliet blinked up into his shadowed face with a confused frown. Her mind seemed to be whirling, and she was so tired.

She'd had three drinks, and Mac had had six, but he seemed completely sober.

"C'mon, Cinderella," he muttered huskily. "I'll walk you to your door." He pushed open the gate with his cane and reached out to encircle her stiff shoulders.

Juliet sighed and leaned against him as they slowly walked up the path to her shiny green front door. His body felt hard and solid, and his distinctive walk seemed strangely comforting, as though he were somehow more real, more genuine, because of his uniqueness.

On the small porch, Mac waited patiently while Juliet fumbled in her bag. She grinned triumphantly as she found her key ring and held it up for his inspection.

His fingers brushed against her wrist as he took the keys from her and bent to open the door. Absently, her eyes fixed on the back of his head, Juliet rubbed the thin skin of her wrist with the fingers of her other hand.

With a sharp metallic click the latch gave, and Mac shoved the door open with the heel of his hand. Straightening, he deposited the keys in her palm. His touch was warmly reassuring as he folded her fingers over the brass ring and lifted her hand to his lips. Juliet felt a fluttering begin in her stomach.

Below the cliff, the waves pounded the rocky shoreline in a steady undulating rhythm. The scent of the sea lay heavy on the still night air, filling Juliet's nostrils with its familiar bouquet.

It was a lovely evening, crisp and clear, with the light of the rising moon casting a silvery reverse shadow on the dark sea.

She had a sudden longing to kick off her shoes and run on the beach. She could almost feel the salt spray on her cheeks and the sand between her toes.

"You know what I'd love to do?" she said impulsively, grabbing Mac's arm. "Right this minute?" Suddenly she didn't want this evening to end.

"What?" he answered with an indulgent smile. He shifted position, and Juliet caught a flash of moonlight from the handle of his cane. Oh no! she thought in frantic realization. He can't run on the beach.

"I'd like to...to take Rex on a picnic," she improvised swiftly as a dull wave of chagrin thudded into her stomach. "Now that the weather's getting nicer. Maybe to Balboa Park or...or on the hospital grounds, even." She forced a brilliant smile. "What do you think of that?"

Mac looked slightly taken aback. "I think you're a little tipsy," he said with a wry grin. "Rex is probably fast asleep by now, and that's where you should be, too."

He took her by the arm and turned her toward the open doorway. She could feel the strength in his hand through the thinness of the silk.

"Yes, sir," she said flippantly, hiding her embarrassment at the near disaster her muddled thinking had almost caused. She took a step, then halted and turned around.

"I'll always be grateful for what you did for my brother," she said softly, blinking up at him. On sudden impulse, she reached up to kiss him on the cheek. Her breasts brushed against his broad chest, and Mac's right arm came around to hold her as she tried to withdraw. "Not so fast, baby," he breathed in a husky whisper.

Juliet was crushed against him, her toes barely touching the stoop. She couldn't move, couldn't even seem to think. A hazy confusion blanketed her thoughts, and a strange lethargy soothed her first impulse of fear.

He gradually lessened the pressure on her spine, allowing her to slide down his body so that she was standing again.

"Mmm," she murmured, snuggling her cheek against his hard chest. The soft fabric of his sweatshirt felt comforting against her skin, and his body heat kept her from feeling the chill in the air. She would rest here a minute, just long enough to gather her wits together.

Mac caressed her back, stroking the curve of her spine in a hypnotic rhythm that was sending insistent messages to the pleasure centers in her brain.

Up and down his hand moved, leaving a trail of heat behind. Deep inside, Juliet felt a jolt of instant reaction, an awakening, a powerful surging to life of feelings that had long been dormant, and desire flooded her veins. She felt hot all over, as though every inch of her skin were covered by fire.

Mac bent his head to kiss her forehead. His lips felt cool against her heated skin, and Juliet sighed against his throat.

"Juliet? Look at me," he commanded softly, leaning back slightly in order to see her face.

Juliet, her eyes half closed, slowly looked up, her mouth open in silent question.

"This is me. Mac."

Of course it was Mac. She knew that. She blinked in confusion, nodding so that he wouldn't think she was completely crazy.

He frowned, then shook his head as though to clear it. "I just wanted you to know who was kissing you," he said in a gruff voice as he raised her face to his.

Juliet had no chance to reply. His lips came down on hers, hard and possessive. His hand cupped the back of her head, allowing her no retreat. His kiss was an assault on her senses. Dominant, encompassing, provoking a response in kind.

Juliet felt a hot rush of adrenaline flood her system, breaking through the fog of weariness to leave her clearheaded and exhilarated.

Mac was kissing her, his lips demanding and eager, and she was kissing him back—willingly, eagerly, retreating, advancing. Hard lips against soft ones, force against resilience, strength against strength.

She could feel the joy singing through the cells of her body, bringing her to life. It was as though she'd been in a deadening sleep for months, her senses numbed, her pleasure centers disconnected.

Her fingers dug into his shoulders, bunching the soft fleece of his sweatshirt. She strained against him, struggling to get closer. Electrical energy tightened her muscles, exciting her nerve endings.

It was as though her physical desires, once released, had come back stronger than ever, pushing the limits of her control. She wanted him. Totally, violently, without reason.

Joyously she opened her mouth to him, receiving the plundering tip of his tongue with heated eagerness. He shifted position, his right leg pushing between her thighs, and his hands cupped her buttocks, pulling her into the trim angle of his hips. His arousal was startling, evoking an answering swelling in her breasts.

She was out of control, her senses filled with him, her body craving his. Now. She whimpered deep in her throat, her muscles tightening in involuntary spasms of need.

Mac pulled away immediately, his face stricken. His eyes glittered in the artificial light, two vivid blue stars in the dark sky of his face.

"Did I hurt you?" he asked in a harsh whisper, trailing his thumb over the swollen fullness of her lower lip. He glanced around the darkened street, his brows pulled into a frown. "I must be drunker than I thought," he muttered in a strained voice.

Juliet was too shaken to speak. She stared up at him, the tidal wave of her emotions beginning to ebb. Was he telling her that the only reason he wanted her was because he'd had too much to drink?

Mac closed his eyes and tried to ignore the warm pressure of her thighs against his. But nothing about this woman was easy to ignore. Not her smile, not her feisty personality, and certainly not her lush curves. When she'd slid down his body, his loins had caught fire, punishing him with throbbing insistence.

She felt so good, snuggled into his arms. Her breasts were so soft crushed against his chest, and her nipples felt like tiny pebbles, erotically rubbing against his shirt until he wanted to strip the silk away and taste each perfect bud. But he'd vowed to exercise restraint, and he meant to keep that vow, no matter what it cost him in physical punishment.

His chest heaved in a deep sigh as he pushed her away. His hand caressed her cheek gently, then fell to his side. "You'd better go in now," he said in a flat tone. "Before we do something we'll both regret."

Juliet looked up at him in helpless confusion. Something they'd regret? Did he regret kissing her? Or was he worried that she would expect more from him than he was prepared to give? He'd sounded almost . . . accusing.

With a cry of distress she spun on her heel and fled inside, closing the door behind her. She felt like a fool.

"Does she know you've rented the place next to hers?" Admiral Hendricks' voice was distorted by the hum of the long-distance line.

"I doubt it. Not unless she called the landlord after I left her at the door." Mac plumped the pillow behind him and leaned back against the headboard bolted to the motel wall.

"She's not suspicious, is she?" came the gravelly question.

"No, she believes my cover. I'm sure of it. So do the others," Mac said slowly, rubbing his hand against the bristly stubble at the back of his neck. He could still feel Juliet's silken curls crushed against his palms, could still smell the flowery fragrance of her shampoo on his hands.

"Anything new to report?"

Mac glanced at the stack of folders in the open briefcase on the floor by the bed. "Nothing definite. I had a drink with Dr. Feldman last night, and the woman acted as if she'd been at sea for two months without shore leave."

Hendricks' chuckle rumbled through the phone. "Came on to you, did she?"

"Like a damned octopus." Mac closed his eyes and flexed his knee. He needed a long soak in a hot bath before turning in for the night. "I dropped the bomb on them today about the files." He hesitated. "Prentice was the only one who seemed upset."

There was a lengthy pause, and Mac opened his eyes to stare at the stars twinkling in the inky sky beyond the windowpane. Was Juliet already in bed, he wondered, or was she looking out at those same stars? Was she remembering the kiss they'd shared? Or had she already pushed him out of her mind?

"Sounds like we were right to suspect her," the admiral said at last.

"Perhaps, although she might just have been thinking about her brother. She's been…worried." Mac wasn't sure why he'd said that. Maybe it was because Carter seemed so certain that Juliet was guilty.

The admiral's sigh was audible. "So what are your plans now?"

Mac frowned. "I'm going to spend as much time with her as I can, see where she goes, who she knows, what she thinks. I intend to push her hard until she makes that first mistake." His lips tightened. "Or until someone else does."

"You sound strange, Mac. Anything wrong?"

Mac glared at his reflection in the mirror above the imitation walnut dresser. He could see the tension in the taut planes of his cheeks, and his hair was disheveled from the absentminded combing of his fingers. "I think I just need a good night's sleep."

"So why not take that Feldman woman up on what she's offering?"

He could tell from the tone of his superior's voice that their business had been concluded and Carter was ragging him as one old friend to another.

"I said sleep, Carter," Mac growled into the receiver, a cynical grin spreading over his face. "Besides, she's not my type."

He grimaced as he thought of Juliet's colleague. She was the kind of woman he'd been dating for years—attractive, intelligent, sexy as all get out. So why wasn't he turned on by her?

"What about Dr. Prentice? Is she your type?"

Mac's fist tightened around the receiver. "I'm not looking for a quick roll in the hay here," he said tersely, tempted to tell his friend exactly what he thought of his suggestion, but a Navy captain did not blast an admiral, no matter how tight the friendship.

"Couldn't hurt, though," Hendricks said blandly. "Besides, you might learn something."

"No way, Carter. I've been on the receiving end of that kind of deceit," he said with a savage edge to his voice. Mac felt his stomach twist with revulsion. He was overreacting, and he knew it, but Hendricks' words had touched a sensitive cord.

"Mac?" The admiral's voice was thick with irony. "I was only kidding." He paused, then added in a brisk tone, "Get some sleep, and call me as soon as you get something concrete."

"Aye, aye, sir," Mac said formally, and waited for his superior to hang up.

Hendricks broke the connection, and Mac dropped the receiver into the cradle. He tipped his head back against the wall and looked up at the ceiling. The pebbly surface was painted a stark white that reminded him of the room in the hospital where he'd spent sixteen endless months.

His body had seemed alien to him then, his skin puckered with purple suture lines, his powerful physique altered irreparably. He'd gotten used to the way he looked—eventually.

Mac sighed. Tonight had been a mistake. He'd let his runaway desire for Juliet's body get in the way. But maybe he'd learned something, too. She couldn't be getting what she needed from Peter. Not if she could kiss him the way she'd done tonight. So maybe Peter wasn't her lover. Maybe Peter was another name for Alexey.

His intuition told him that Peter was a key player in this drama, but what was his role? He'd have to find out.

Mac sat up quickly, wincing as his knee flared into pain. He'd had plenty of women, most of them beautiful and sophisticated, and all of them willing, but he'd never been as shaken by a kiss as he'd been tonight.

Juliet had wanted him as badly as he'd wanted her; he would swear to it. He'd felt the shuddering response of her soft body against his, heard the sweet little moans she'd made deep in her throat. Her eyes had smoldered with the same need he'd felt flaming in his own. If she hadn't shivered suddenly, if she hadn't cried out, he would have been beyond the point of stopping.

Mac groaned and flexed his shoulders, trying to work out some of the tension. He ran his hand over the heavy steel shaft of his brace. He needed to remember the mistake that had put him in that brace for the rest of his life. He needed to keep a clear head.

He grimaced as he swung his leg over the side of the bed and reached for his cane. Carter's words had struck a cord he hadn't dared acknowledge. In the deepest recesses of his soul, he was beginning to feel more than he should for Juliet Prentice. His objectivity was threatened, and so was his equilibrium. He felt as though he were walking through a battlefield. One false step and he'd be blown to bits.

Juliet wandered through her tiny living room, plumping the chintz-covered pillows of the rattan sofa, straightening the row of colorful floral prints on the wall, smoothing the fringe of an antique beaded evening bag lying on the coffee table.

The cheerful greens and yellows of the room failed to lift her sagging spirits, and the cozy ivory walls that had always seemed warm and soothing suddenly seemed flat and lacking in imagination.

Her bare feet padded silently on the sea grass mat covering the terra-cotta tile as she toured the room, searching for something else to pacify her nervous fingers and occupy her overactive mind.

She was dressed for bed in a nightshirt and faded pink bathrobe. Her hair, squeaky clean and blow-dried into a satiny fall of loose curls, hugged her neck, reminding her of the touch of Mac's hand against her skin.

Her face, scrubbed clean of makeup, still felt warm with the blush of passion, and her lips were still tender from his kiss.

It was after eleven, her normal bedtime, and she was wide awake. A projector was running continuously in her mind, playing back the scene beyond her front door minute by minute, second by second.

Mac hadn't intended to kiss her. She could still see the doubt in his eyes as he'd looked down at her—doubt that had slowly mingled with desire as she'd met his questioning gaze.

She'd been the aggressor, something that shocked her as much as it surprised her. Not that she wasn't confident of her own appeal when it came to men—she knew very well that she was attractive.

But years in her father's larger-than-life world, where relationships had been built more on expediency and impulse than on caring and commitment, had taught her to be careful with her trust. And her disastrous experience in graduate school had reinforced that reticence.

She'd done fine until Mac had opened up to her. In her mind he'd been a stranger until then—an attractive stranger, to be sure, but still a stranger. But once he'd shared his emotional pain with her, he'd somehow hooked her into caring about him, something she'd sworn not to do.

Juliet sighed and switched off the lamp. She padded down the short hall to her bedroom and pulled back the covers, then took off her robe and draped it over the foot of the old walnut sleigh bed she'd found in a secondhand store downtown.

Sighing, she reached for the switch at the base of the lamp. Her hand froze in midair as the phone rang. The bell seemed unnaturally loud in the silence, and her heart began to thump against her ribs.

"Hello?" she said curtly.

"Juliet? It's Mac."

She squeezed her eyes shut and bit her lip.

"Juliet? Are you there?" His deep voice enveloped her with remembered warmth.

"I . . . yes, I'm here. I was . . . sleeping."

There was a brief silence. "I'm sorry I woke you," he drawled in a more impersonal tone. "I just wanted to—to remind you about your car. We never did get around to calling the auto club."

Disappointment crushed her, stiffening her knees. What had she expected? Words of caring? Promises? Love? Grow up, Juliet, she told herself resolutely. Obviously the fireworks that had had her pacing the floor had fizzled for Mac.

"Thanks for reminding me," she said lightly. "I'll call first thing tomorrow."

There was another pause. "Good. Well, good night . . . Juliet."

She felt her lips tremble as his husky baritone lingered over her name, caressing each syllable with its sexy lilt.

"Good night," she replied softly. She couldn't bring herself to use his curt nickname when his real name had so much music in it.

As she hung up, her eyes fell on the ornate Shakespeare folio lying on the nightstand. With stiff fingers, she opened the cover and stared down at the currency tucked against the spine. Her lips tightened. Two thousand dollars.

Tomorrow, when she visited Rex, she would stop by the business office and pay her share of this month's charges. Juliet closed the book and climbed into bed, snapping off the light.

It's better this way, she told herself, staring at the gray shadows splotching the ivory ceiling. Outside, the waves pounded the cliffs, reminding her of the danger she was courting. Mac would never understand the desperation that drove her to take such a risk.

"I promised my mother," she whispered into the darkness. "When she was dying. I promised her I'd take care of Rex." Juliet sighed and closed her eyes. The room was beginning to spin in slow circles, and her brain felt overloaded.

She twisted onto her side and pressed her face into the pillow. Her body was wide awake and eager to finish what Mac had started.

But no matter how much she wanted to be with him, no matter how tempting the thought, she didn't dare. Once, before she'd learned a very painful lesson, she might have taken the risk, but not now. She didn't intend to repeat past mistakes.

Juliet groaned and hugged her pillow against her heated skin. She had a feeling it was going to be a very restless night.

Chapter 6

Juliet awakened the next morning with a dull ache behind her eyelids. She groaned and pulled the pillow over her head in a groggy effort to drown out the sound of a drum pounding through her bedroom.

A drum? She opened her eyes and tried to force a measure of alertness into her numbed brain.

"Someone's at my door," she muttered indistinctly into the foam rubber of her pillow as the pounding continued, jolting painfully through her head.

She threw off the covers and looked around for her robe. It was there on the floor beside the bed, next to her open briefcase.

The pounding stopped, then began again, reverberating loudly through her small cottage like an imperial summons. Juliet glanced at the digital clock by the bed and winced at the red numbers. It was almost ten. She'd overslept.

Struggling into her worn terry robe, she hurried down the hall to the living room.

The wooden blinds covering the seaside windows were open, revealing the usual hazy morning mist rolling in from the horizon. Below the cliff, the surf pummeled the rocks in the surging rhythm that signaled high tide.

Clutching her robe together at the throat, Juliet drew the bolt on the door and opened it a crack. "Mac? What are you doing here?" She blinked against the glare, stunned at the sight of the large male body taking up most of her tiny porch.

He was leaning against the wrought-iron railing, hands bracketing his lean hips, his cane leaning on the railing beside him, an easy smile softening the deep lines of his face.

"Rise and shine, sleepyhead," he drawled in husky, teasing tones as he reached down to pick up a white bakery sack that was resting on the cement beside his loafers.

Juliet gaped at him in silence as he held up the sack and shook it. "I brought breakfast."

Her sleepy eyes snapped to full alert. Just stay calm and everything will be fine, she told herself in fervent prayer, tossing her tousled head in unconscious defiance.

"Am I expecting you?" she asked in a deliberately distant tone. She tried not to notice the way the soft suede of his gray jacket and his blue flannel shirt emphasized the powerful angle of his shoulders, or the way his faded gray jeans stretched over the thick muscles of his upper thighs as he lounged negligently against the iron rail.

Mac shifted his weight as he prepared to stand, and Juliet found her gaze following the long line of his body as he moved away from the railing and pushed himself erect.

He looked hurt. "That's a modern woman for you. Invites a guy on a picnic and then forgets all about it." He grinned, his even white teeth a mocking slash against his bronzed skin.

Juliet frowned. "Picnic? What picnic?" She squinted in confusion as she took a firmer grip on the door handle.

"The picnic with Rex you were so excited about last night." One thick chestnut brow rose in disbelief. "Don't tell me you've forgotten already?"

"No, I haven't forgotten," she said warily, trying valiantly to bring the events of last night into sharper mental focus.

She had mentioned something about a picnic. What was it? Her mind felt sluggish, as though her head were filled with wet cement.

She nearly groaned aloud as the conversation on the porch drifted through the fog of memory to reach her brain. It had been an innocent mistake. She'd started to suggest a run on the beach, then remembered just in time that Mac would be incapable of that simple pleasure and covered her gaffe with the first thing that had come to mind—a picnic for Rex.

The irony was so overwhelming that she felt like crying. In trying to spare Mac's feelings, she'd apparently maneuvered herself into spending a day in his company.

She narrowed her eyes in concentration. "Are you sure I said to come by at ten o'clock—in the morning?"

There was something about his stance that was so still and watchful that it made her terribly uneasy. What had she said to him last night? Or done, to make him look at her with those fathomless eyes that seemed to be probing her soul as well as her face?

"Actually, you forgot to set a time. That's why I came so early. I wanted to get all moved in before we left for the hospital. I figured that since your car was out of commission you'd want me to drive." He took a step forward as though to enter, but Juliet refused to move, and he was forced to stop, his broad chest inches from her slender body.

"Juliet? I can't come in if you're standing in the doorway." His deep drawl carried a hint of indulgent amusement.

"Come on in," she muttered, standing aside. Maybe after she'd had her coffee she would be able to think more clearly.

He stepped over the threshold and waited for her to close the door. He followed her through the handkerchief-size living room as she led the way to the kitchen.

"What do you mean, 'before you move in'?" She stopped suddenly and whirled to confront him. Mac, only one step behind her, smacked into her head-on, and the white sack went flying across the room as he fought to keep his balance.

"Oomph," she gasped as the air whooshed out of her lungs. Mac's right arm encircled her in quick reaction, holding her against him to keep her from flying backward. His hand was splayed against her back, warm and hard.

Juliet stood with her face pressed against his solid shoulder, her hands gripping his hard biceps for support. His jacket smelled of leather and musk, and the muscles under her palms bulged as he righted himself with sheer brute power.

"Are you okay?" There was a rough edge of concern in his voice that surprised her. Juliet nodded against his shoulder, and Mac chuckled. "You shouldn't make those sudden moves, you know. I'm not real great with fancy footwork these days."

Juliet managed a smile. "I'm not real great with *anything* in the morning." She raised her head and tried to pull away, but he held on. Even with one hand balanced on his cane, he was too strong for her to escape him.

As they stood locked together, she could feel a strange lassitude enveloping her body, a blend of anticipation and surrender. It was as if by touching, they'd bonded in some primitive, deeply intimate way that was both mysterious and irresistible.

As though Mac could hear her thoughts, he groaned and pulled her tighter against him, wrapping his body around her in a protective curve, his shoulders bent, his thighs hard against hers. Bending his head, he rubbed his cheek against the thick tangle of curls at her temple.

Juliet could feel his muscles relax slightly, as if he were consciously trying to keep from frightening her. But fear wasn't one of the emotions warring within her tingling body. It was pure undiluted desire that was heating her blood and shortening her breath.

Her cheeks felt hot and then cold. Her skin seemed filled with electricity, as though touched by benign lighting. She wanted to sink into him, to lose herself in his potent male aura.

Juliet felt a rush of excitement as Mac's free hand came up to caress her cheek. His brows were drawn, and his jaw was taut as his intense gaze swept over her face. A tiny flame of emotion flared in his pupils, growing brighter as Juliet stared helplessly into his eyes.

His lashes dipped as his eyes fixed on her slightly parted mouth. His lips curved up at the corners, and Juliet stopped breathing as his head moved slowly downward. Her own lips tingled with anticipation, and her breathing resumed a shallow cadence as she closed her eyes.

His breath was warm on her face, minty fresh and moistly provocative. She smiled in welcome, her lips parting eagerly.

Mac felt her sigh against his mouth, the sound soft and hesitant and enticing. She needed to be kissed, and kissed hard, this sweetly smiling woman who, even in the harsh morning light, was so hauntingly lovely.

He hesitated, then allowed his lashes to drift down in surrender. He hadn't intended to touch her again. Not like this. But he couldn't seem to help himself.

He felt his face flush as his lips slanted over hers. He wanted her desperately, wanted her more than he'd ever wanted a woman and, God help him, he was going to have her.

Juliet felt excitement tingle through her as his lips took possession of hers. His mouth was firm and possessive, and his hand slid down her side to rest warmly on the curve of her hip. His long torso pressed against hers, hard and sinewy and demanding. His breathing became more ragged as she opened her mouth under the relentless onslaught of his tongue.

He shifted his weight slightly, and Juliet pressed closer, loving the slide of his thigh against hers. The slow friction was almost unbearably arousing, sending signals of building urgency through her legs and into her soft core.

His hand tugged on the knot of her belt, pulling insistently until the soft material gave way, allowing the robe to fall open. "So warm," he murmured, cupping her breast with his palm. "So sweet." His fingertips trailed along the swelling fullness to the nipple, which stiffened instantly at his touch.

Juliet burrowed her hands under the ribbed hem of his jacket, her fingers yanking impatiently at his shirttails until she found the warm flesh beneath the blue flannel. His back was hard, his skin smooth over sinewy muscles that stretched with latent strength along the bony ridge of his spine.

Eagerly she pressed her fingertips against his skin, sliding her hands under the low-riding waistband of his jeans to the spot under the nylon briefs where his lean hips flared into the hardness of his buttocks.

She loved the feel of his body under her hands, adored the swift intake of his breath as she explored lower, eagerly seeking the most intimate part of him. He was all man, hard and hot, and ready for love.

"Where's your bedroom?" Mac whispered in a thick voice, nuzzling her neck. His big hand was pressed against the small of her back, pushing her hard against him.

Juliet heard his husky question through a haze of desire, and it took several seconds for the meaning to register. Mac intended to take her to bed. Now, in the middle of the morning, without preamble and without even a pretense of love.

A shrill army of contradictory emotions rampaged through her head, blurring into a white noise of confusion. More than anything she wanted to give in, to lead him down the hall to her rumpled bed, to revel in the heated pleasure he offered, but a faint, insistent voice somewhere in her head shouted a strident warning. Was the risk of repeating her previous mistake really worth a few moments of pleasure? Especially since that was all Mac intended to offer?

No! came the resounding answer. She'd been burned once. It would be foolish to take the same chance again, no matter how strong the temptation.

She withdrew her hands to push frantically against his chest. His body was as hard as the oak of her front door, and just as unyielding.

"Please," she said in a faint voice that was scratchy from the conflicting emotions tugging at her. "I . . . need coffee."

Mac blinked in confusion as she continued to push at his chest. The blood pounded in his temples, and his skin felt seared where her fingers had been exploring. Surely she didn't expect him to stop now. Not now. Not when she had him so aroused he could scarcely stand.

"Coffee?" he grated in a husky voice. "You want coffee? Now?"

"Yes. Right now." Tormented by unslaked desire, Juliet failed to notice the deadly flash of anger in Mac's eyes as she closed the lapels of her robe and frantically cinched the belt.

Leaving him standing there, she hurried into the kitchen and plugged in the coffee maker she'd filled the night before.

Mac jerked his hand through his hair, his brow pulled down in a thunderous frown. He hadn't had a woman stop him short like this since he was an awkward teenager fumbling in the bucket seats of his older brother's sports car.

Muttering an obscenity under his breath, he limped stiffly across the room and retrieved the white sack from its resting place under the couch before following Juliet into the sunny yellow kitchen.

"What's in the bag?" she asked with a bright smile, her eyes sliding away from the noticeable bulge behind the fly of his jeans. Instant craving shivered through her, heating her bones, and she ground her teeth in frustration. She could feel the flush on her cheeks, and her hands were still shaking. She wanted him desperately.

"Croissants," Mac replied without inflection, tossing the sack onto the table. "Just out of the oven." He took off his jacket and hung it over the back of a kitchen chair. "I got 'em at an all-night coffee shop next to the motel where I was staying." His expression was carefully neutral, with all traces of their passion wiped from his face.

Juliet's eyes narrowed. "Was staying? Is that past tense?"

"I've rented the place next door for three months—starting today. Last night, when I called, the manager said he'd leave the key in the mailbox for me so I could move my things in this morning."

The mug she'd been reaching for slipped through her fingers and crashed onto the tile next to her feet. Resolutely avoiding Mac's eye, she stooped down to collect the shards of broken pottery. The mug had been her favorite, one of only a few remaining from her mother's handmade set.

"I'm sure you'll like it here," she said with a false smile as she tossed the pieces into the trash basket under the sink. *Why is he looking at me like I just snatched the last cookie out of the* jar? she thought in rising irritation. I just dropped a cup, for heaven's sake.

"If it's like this, I'm sure I will," Mac said mildly. "I like what you've done to it. It's very homey."

"Thanks. Most of these things were my mother's."

The custom-designed rattan furniture that had once occupied the solarium of their Beverly Hills colonial was all that had been left after the liquidation sale forced by her mother's creditors after Althea's death. Even Althea's wedding ring had been sold to help cover the enormous medical bills that had resulted from her last lengthy stay in the hospital before her fatal stroke.

Excusing herself, Juliet slipped past Mac to get butter and jam from the refrigerator that stood on the cluttered service porch, and then she began preparing breakfast.

"Can I help?" he asked as he unbuttoned the cuffs of his blue flannel shirt and rolled the sleeves back over his wide forearms. Juliet shivered slightly as she remembered the feel of his strong arms cradling her tightly. The power of those muscles had been held tautly in check, but she'd felt his enormous strength nevertheless.

Absently biting her lip, she slid her eyes away from his lean body and nodded toward the overhead cupboard. "Plates and napkins are in there. The silverware's in the drawer to the right."

Mac set the table, and Juliet poured the coffee. Then they sat down and began to eat.

"Are you the surfer?" Mac asked, inclining his head toward the orange and white board propped against the wall on the small porch.

Juliet shook her head as a wave of sadness replaced her angry frustration. The battered board belonged to Rex, left there during his last visit just before the accident, and Juliet kept it where he'd left it as a private act of faith.

"Whose board is it? Peter's?" Mac's voice was tinged with sharp male curiosity.

Juliet's heart lurched in immediate fear. Why did he keep mentioning Peter, for God's sake? She could feel her palms grow clammy as she forced a smile. "No, it's Rex's," she explained in a calm voice as she spread jam on her second croissant.

"Your brother's a gutsy guy," Mac said with a slow nod. "I think he'll make it."

She leaned over her cup and let the steam warm her face. A sudden thought occurred to her, and she sat up straighter. "Did you find out why he threw a barbell at his therapist?" She'd forgotten all about the incident that had precipitated their visit yesterday.

"Because she turns him on."

Juliet's jaw dropped, and her thickly fringed eyes widened in amazement. "What?"

Mac's lips twitched. "According to Rex, she's the most beautiful woman in the world. And the sexiest." His voice tightened. "That's the real problem. His body didn't respond to the sight of a beautiful woman the way he thought it should." He flexed his shoulders as though to ease a sudden stiffness. "It scared him."

Juliet felt like a fool. That Rex would be worried about his sexuality had never occurred to her. But why should it? That was one subject the two of them had never discussed in any detail. Rex had his private life, and she had hers. Which, she suspected, was far less exciting than her charming brother's.

"Don't look so stricken," Mac said in a gruff tone that was laced with humor. "He admitted that the doctors are optimistic, that they say his body simply needs time to heal. We talked it out, and I think I managed to reassure him—for the time being, anyway."

The rest he has to do himself, Mac thought in grim memory. It had taken him months after his release to test his manhood with a woman. And that was one encounter he wanted to forget.

"But why didn't he confide in me?" Juliet tried to mask the hurt she was feeling with a pose of sisterly irritation.

Mac threw her a mocking look. "C'mon, Juliet. You're his big sister, not his buddy. A guy doesn't like to parade his insecurities in front of a woman."

Juliet sighed. "More stupid machismo," she muttered under her breath, but Mac's keen ears picked up the indistinct mumble.

"Is it?" he questioned tautly. "I don't think so. I haven't met a woman yet who admires a wimp." His eyes narrowed in disgust. "I suppose Peter's your idea of a perfect man."

She clutched her mug tightly and forced herself to remain calm. "What is this obsession you have with Peter? I've told you before—he's just a friend."

"So how come Rex has never heard of him?"

"What?"

"If he's such a good friend, how come you've never mentioned him to your brother?"

Juliet felt as though he'd just dropped a bucket of ice down her back. "I, um, didn't realize I hadn't mentioned him," she countered, knowing that she had to say something. "I'm sure I did."

Mac relaxed in his chair and hooked an elbow over the back. The neck of his shirt gaped open, revealing the steady pulse at the base of his throat.

"You don't sound very sure."

Juliet studied the tiny beat, trying furiously to formulate an answer. As she hesitated, she could feel the tension building in the room, snaking between them as though it were alive. Think, Juliet, she ordered herself feverishly. But her mind went blank.

"Look, can we please change the subject?" she said curtly. "It's too early to argue."

"What do you want to talk about? Making love?"

Juliet's chin came up with a jerk. "What?"

"You heard me. Why did you suddenly change your mind?"

"I...don't know what you mean," she muttered, crumbling the half-eaten croissant between her nervous fingers.

Mac's cheek creased with a sardonic smile. "Like hell you don't. You were as ready as I was, Juliet." His voice thinned. "Why did you suddenly push me away? Is it because you're involved with this guy Peter?"

She carefully folded her hands together in her lap and took a deep breath. "I'm not involved with anyone. I just don't want to sleep with you. For a lot of reasons, but mostly because I promised myself a long time ago to keep my career and my private life separate.''

"Juliet, I'm not a member of your team. I'm not even a biologist. We're not co-workers. Not really.'' One brow lifted combatively. "I have a feeling there's something more, something you're not telling me.'' He leaned forward. "Am I right?''

Juliet inhaled sharply, and the air entering her lungs was charged with electrical tension. The room seemed filled with a force beyond her understanding, and she burrowed her folded hands between her tensed thighs.

"You're wasting your time with me,'' she said flatly, her heart pounding thunderously. "Why don't you concentrate on Felicity instead? She doesn't have the same kind of hang-ups I do.'' As soon as the words were out of her mouth, Juliet groaned inwardly. She had sounded catty—no, *bitchy*—when she'd only meant to sound firm.

Mac seemed frozen in the chair, and there was something about his expression that made her cringe inside.

"What kind of hang-ups are those, Juliet?'' he asked in a voice that was quietly menacing. "Do you demand perfection in your men? Is that it?'' His face twisted. "We can always do it in the dark.''

Juliet jerked, feeling as though he'd reached across the table and slapped her. "I don't deserve that, Mac,'' she said in a voice that vibrated with hurt. "And you know it.'' She felt as though the room were spinning violently around her, and her entire body was shaking. "Please lock the door when you leave,'' she said with prickly courtesy as she stood. "I have to get dressed.''

She left the kitchen quickly and went to her bedroom, closing the door firmly behind her.

Mac doubled his hand into a fist and beat it softly against the arm of the chair. Way to go, McKinley, he jeered silently. Nothing like losing your temper with the lady. That's really gonna make her trust you, all right.

Mac ground his teeth together in frustration. From the instant Juliet had opened the door looking like a sleepy, tousled angel with bare feet, he'd been off balance. In her soft furry robe, her face dewy and vulnerable from sleep, she'd been nearly irresistible.

In the living room, holding her in his arms, he'd wanted her so badly that his blood had seemed to burn in his veins. She fit against him perfectly, her slender body enticingly pliant against his. Her hair smelled of some exotic spice that reminded him of autumn leaves and pumpkin pie, and her skin had the freshness of a newly opened rosebud, the pale pink kind his mother raised in the formal garden behind the big white house.

What had started out as deliberate sexual banter in order to pry more information about Peter from her had somehow gotten completely out of hand. And it had been his fault. He'd been the one to lose control, lashing out at her like a horny teenager rebuffed by a haughty high school belle.

Mac's brows knotted in a dark frown as he viciously muttered a long string of richly imaginative curses that he'd learned as a boy in the tobacco sheds. He flexed his shoulders and glanced at the closed door that mocked him from the end of the hall.

For the first time in years he felt helpless to control his own emotions. It was as though he'd been cast adrift in a treacherous sea, buffeted on all sides by feelings and desires that could swamp him if he wasn't constantly on guard. And it was driving him crazy.

Worse still, he admitted with a savage groan of frustration, he knew very well that Juliet was getting to him, and the more he fought it, the more enmeshed in her spell he seemed to be.

"It stops now," he vowed in a gritty voice, reaching for his cane. He'd been in situations where one wrong word, one careless expression, one indiscriminate move, would have meant instant death, and he'd survived. He'd matched wits with some of the most brilliant and devious minds in the arena of international intrigue and won. Against all odds, he'd battled pain and discouragement to walk again, and he could damn well keep his desire for Juliet Prentice in check.

He heaved a decisive sigh and pushed himself to his feet. His body felt heavy and sluggish, and his head was beginning to ache. When this was over, he was going to find a willing woman, a woman who wanted only the pleasure he could give her, and he was going to purge his body of the feel of Juliet Prentice. There was no way he would ever let himself be vulnerable to this woman, to *any* woman, no matter how much he wanted her.

He glanced around the tidy kitchen, a look of pain on his face. If only Juliet fit the profile, if only he could make himself hate her the way he hated Misrani, if only...

He kicked the leg of his chair with his good leg, wincing as his battered knee took his weight. He wished he'd never heard of Project Ping Pong.

Juliet was slipping into her jeans when the knock came at the door. She tugged the bleached denim over her hips and closed the zipper.

"Go away," she yelled in shaky tones as she pulled a dark red sweater over her head. A warm shower had smoothed away most of her anger, but she was still feeling bruised by Mac's unexpected verbal assault.

The knock came again, this time with more force. "I said *go away.*"

She sat down on the side of her bed to tie her sneakers. She had one shoe done and was reaching for the other when the door opened and Mac walked in, a mug of steaming coffee balanced carefully in his hand.

Juliet glowered at him, her heart thudding. His big frame seemed to fill the cozy bedroom with raw male essence, making her feel as though she herself were being invaded.

"You didn't finish your coffee," he said gruffly. "Where do you want it?"

She met his question with stony silence, her eyes black with renewed anger.

"You're angry," he said bluntly, meeting her accusing gaze squarely.

FREE-GIFT COMPUTER CARD

TEAR OFF HERE AND MAIL THIS CARD TODAY!

SILHOUETTE FREE GIFT DEPT.

MAIL THIS FREE-GIFT COMPUTER CARD

to receive 4 FREE Silhouette Intimate Moments® ... *PLUS* a FREE Surprise Bonus!

Yes! Send me 4 Free Silhouette Intimate Moments plus A Free Surprise Bonus. Then send me four new Silhouette Intimate Moments each month and bill me just $2.49 per book (26¢ less than retail). No postage and handling charges. If I am not fully satisfied, I may return a shipment and cancel at any time. The 4 Free Books and Surprise Bonus remain mine to keep.

240 CIL YACX

FREE! AFFIX THIS STICKER IN SPACE AT RIGHT

Use this heart to get a FREE SURPRISE BONUS!

PRINT YOUR NAME HERE FOR DATA PROCESSING (Please PRINT in ink)

☐ MR.
☐ MRS.
☐ MISS

FIRST NAME | INITIAL | LAST NAME

ADDRESS

CITY | STATE | ZIP | APT.

FREE GIFT DEADLINE:

| S | E | P | T | 3 | 0 | 1 | 9 | 8 | 8 |

Offer limited to one per household and not valid for present Intimate Moments subscribers. Prices subject to change.

TEAR OFF HERE AND MAIL THIS CARD TODAY!

DATA PROCESSING #1348

00000000000000000000000
45 46 47 48 49 50 51 52 53 54 55 56
22222222222222222222222
1111111111111111111111

PLACE GOLD HEART HERE

to receive your **FREE** Surprise Bonus

Printed in U.S.A.

NO POSTAGE
NECESSARY
IF MAILED
IN THE
UNITED STATES

APPROVED
FREE-GIFT OFFER

BUSINESS REPLY CARD

FIRST CLASS   PERMIT NO. 717   BUFFALO, NY

POSTAGE WILL BE PAID BY ADDRESSEE

Silhouette Books ®

901 Fuhrmann Blvd.,
P.O. Box 1867
Buffalo, NY 14240-9952

"How did you ever guess?" she retorted, refusing to respond to the hurt look on his face. She finished tying her shoe and folded her arms over her chest.

Forcing a conciliatory smile, Mac crossed the room to set the steaming mug next to the folio. He hesitated, then sat down beside her. Somehow he would have to charm her out of her bad mood, or he might as well pack it in.

"I lost my temper," he said bluntly, looking down at the floor. "I got the feeling you were shoving me onto Felicity because the thought of sleeping with a cripple turned you off, and it . . . hurt." His gut twisted as he realized that he wasn't lying. It *had* hurt. Too much.

Juliet gave him a disbelieving look. "I can't believe you could think that of me."

Mac's lips quirked into a wry line. "Yeah, well, I suppose I just . . . reacted without thinking it through. This isn't the first time my temper has gotten me into hot water."

Juliet gave him a grudging smile. "Maybe it goes with the red hair."

Mac inhaled slowly. Her eyes had lost their hard sheen, and her lips had relaxed into a sultry pout that gave her the look of an adorable coquette.

"I was out of line, Juliet. I...apologize." He took her hand, half expecting her to jerk away. But she allowed her fingers to remain in his.

"Suppose we did become lovers, Mac?" she asked in a breathy little voice that sent shivers down his spine. "What happens when your work here is done?" She gestured impatiently, answering her own question before he had a chance to speak. "You'll leave, that's what. Oh, maybe we'll talk on the phone a few times. You might even fly out here for an odd weekend or two, but . . ." She shrugged. "It just won't work."

A slow sexy grin began forming on Mac's hard lips. "Why don't we try it and see?" His tongue slid over the softly spoken question as though savoring a fine wine, and Juliet felt a tug of longing. Instinctively, without really thinking about it, she curled her fingers around his broad palm.

"I want to, Mac, but I just…can't. Please don't make it any harder on me than it already is."

He squeezed her hand gently, a warmly intimate gesture that Juliet treasured. "Why don't we work on being friends? See what happens?" he asked in a cajoling tone.

Deliberately she curved her lips into a teasing grin. "You promise you won't try to charm me into bed?" Her heart rate accelerated to a gallop as she realized that her bed was exactly where they were seated. Mac had only to bend her backward a few feet onto the mattress, and she would be totally helpless to resist. The thought brought prickles of primitive feminine excitement to her skin.

"Let's say I'll be as good a friend as you want me to be," he answered with slow deliberation, a look of supreme male confidence stealing over his face.

"I'll remember that," she promised, pulling her hand free and standing up. She needed to put some distance between them before she forgot her resolve.

Watching her with amused eyes, Mac leaned back, his foot accidentally kicking the briefcase under the bed. "Oops, sorry. What did I kick?" He sat up and looked down at the corner of the briefcase that was protruding from beneath the box springs.

Juliet's throat tightened as she saw his eyes flicker toward the papers just a few inches from his toes.

"Moonlighting?" he asked casually, shifting his gaze to her face.

"Of course not," she said with a light laugh while praying that he wouldn't notice the color flooding into her cheeks. "You know regulations don't allow that. I was just going over some tax papers for my…my accountant, that's all." Swiftly she knelt, shut the lid and secured the lock.

Abruptly, Mac stood up and limped over to the window. He pushed aside the woven curtains and stared out at the brightening day. "Why don't you phone Rex and tell him we're bringing lunch while I put my things in my new place and check with the manager about my rent?" he asked, turning back to face her. His smile was as charming as ever, but there was a distant look in his eyes that hadn't been there before, a look that Juliet couldn't read.

"Sounds okay to me. Shall we plan for noon?"

He nodded, and she gave him a radiant smile. She was suddenly filled with energy and anxious to get on with the day. As she preceded Mac from the room she glanced over her shoulder at the patchwork sky. "I think it's going to be a perfect day for a picnic," she said with an eager lilt in her voice.

Mac risked one last look at her closed briefcase before he left the room. He felt sick.

At the suggestion of Rex's nurse, they had their picnic behind the hospital in an enclosed patio area outside the cafeteria.

It was a cheery place, with large molded concrete planters containing copper-colored winter chrysanthemums placed at intervals around the floor.

Metal tables and chairs painted bright red were dotted around the area, and a colorful mural featuring children and their pets decorated the four-foot fence separating the dining area from the sloping green lawn leading to the parking lot.

The three of them were seated at a small round table at the edge of the patio near a large mock orange tree. They were listening to Rex's portable radio and eating the chocolate chip cookies Juliet had brought for dessert.

"...and now here's another oldie but goodie from the Beatles. *Revolution*."

"Hey, Julie, does this song remind you of your radical past?" Rex cocked his head, looking from Juliet to Mac, a teasing smile on his lips.

Juliet flushed. "One peace march is hardly radical," she said with a grimace. "And I only marched in that one because I had a crush on Tommy Raye, and he was there."

Rex chuckled and shifted in his wheelchair. "You should have seen her, Mac. I was only six, but I remember how embarrassed I was that my sister was wearing a moldy old leather jacket and army boots in public. Boy, was she *ug-lee*."

Juliet gasped and threw a wadded napkin at her brother's head. Rex caught it and aimed it back at her.

Mac laughed as she missed the ball and cursed under her breath. "Temper, temper, Juliet. I promise not to tell the FBI your deep dark secret."

Her face flamed with heat. "I'm sure they already know about it. They comb through every tiny detail of your life." Absently she toyed with the apple that was all that was left of her lunch, twisting the stem around and around until it broke off in her hand.

"Hey, don't get her started on that," Rex pleaded with an exaggerated groan. "Juliet has a thing about background checks."

Mac raised his gaze on Juliet's strained face. "Oh, yeah? How come?"

"Because security people can make a person's life miserable without good reason." At his look of disbelief she added with more force, "Just last year a physicist I know at NRC lost his job because his wife's brother was an active member of some obscure left-wing activist group."

"Surely there must be more to it than that."

Juliet shook her head vehemently. "True story. He appealed, but it was no use. The government revoked his security clearance." Weary indignation crept into her voice. "The government doesn't have to give you a reason to pull your clearance. They can just do it."

"You think that's wrong?"

She sighed. "I think it shouldn't be so subjective. There's no way of telling what might trigger an investigation. Even a casual comment at a cocktail party could be reported, and the next thing you know, there's the FBI breathing down your neck. And God forbid you should fail to report extra income, even a legacy from a relative."

Juliet glanced up to see an arrested look on Mac's face. "Have you had a windfall like that?" he asked with lazy interest, leaning forward slightly. His thick crescent lashes lowered under her glare of indignation, obscuring his expression.

She fussed with her napkin and pretended nonchalance. "Don't I wish." She started to change the subject when the door from the cafeteria opened, and a group of four adults and two little girls spilled out onto the patio.

The adults, two well-dressed couples in their late twenties, carried cups and packaged sandwiches from the vending machines that serviced the hungry when the cafeteria line was closed.

The little girls were dressed in identical pinafores of pink and white gingham with white tights and shiny black patent leather shoes. One of them carried a bright red ball that was almost as big as she was.

"Cute kids," Rex said with an open-faced grin, and Juliet gave him a fond look. He'd always been good with children, far better than she was.

"The one with the blond hair looks like you, Julie," Rex said with a teasing grin. "See the bandage on her chin? Probably got it in a fist fight, just like you used to get into."

Juliet gave him a haughty look. "How would you know? You weren't even born when I was their age."

Rex smirked. "Mom used to tell me all about her wildcat daughter. She used to say that there wasn't an ounce of Boston blood in your veins."

Juliet laughed. "That's true enough. I never did learn to curtsy."

She glanced at Mac, only to find him staring at the giggling little girls with an odd look on his face.

Did he have a child from his marriage? Juliet wondered with sharp curiosity. He'd never mentioned one, but that didn't necessarily mean he didn't have one.

From behind the veil of her lashes, she studied his brooding expression. He was lost in thought, as though he were far away. Wherever he was, she had a feeling it wasn't a pleasant place.

Rex didn't seem to notice Mac's preoccupation. He was watching the girls. They were chattering happily as they tossed the large ball back and forth between them.

A squeal of protest interrupted their soft giggles as the taller of the two threw the ball over her sister's head. "No fair,

Tammy," the smaller girl shouted, her chubby face screwed into a frown.

The ball rolled across the smooth cement to stop next to Rex's chair. With a jerky movement, he reached over to scoop it up, then held it out to the little girl who approached with hesitant steps.

"That's a great ball you've got there," Rex said kindly, giving her a friendly smile.

"It's a present for my new cousin, but Mommy says we can play with it 'cuz he was just borned." The girl's voice was high-pitched and earnest.

Rex nodded soberly. "Mommy's right. Your cousin probably won't be needing it for a while yet."

He tossed the ball gently into the air, and the little girl caught it between her palms.

"Good catch." Rex applauded, and she took a step closer. Her small brow furrowed as she inspected the shiny wheelchair. Tentatively she reached out to touch one of the gray rubber tires.

"Is this yours?" she asked curiously, gazing wide-eyed into Rex's freckled face.

A muscle twitched along his jaw. "Yes, it's mine," he said with a twisted grin. "All mine."

"Do you have to sit in it all the time?"

He took a deep breath. "Yes, all the time."

The little girl frowned. "Does it hurt to be crippled?"

Rex's face twisted, and two bright spots of color appeared on his pale cheeks. "Yes, it hurts," he said in a strained voice.

The child took a step backward. "Mommy said me'n' Tammy shouldn't stare, 'cuz it isn't nice to stare at cripples." She gave Rex a wide smile that revealed two missing teeth, then ran back to resume her game.

Rex sat motionless, his face frozen into a bitter mask. He stared straight ahead, his eyes fixed.

Juliet jumped up to comfort him, only to have Mac stop her with a hard grip on her arm.

"It's just a word, Rex," Mac said evenly, his voice deep and sure. "Not a label—unless you let it be one."

Rex's face flushed. "I can't do it, Mac," he said in a voice that shook. "I can't shake it off. I don't want to be crippled." His face contorted into a grimace of agony. *"I hate it!"*

Mac's shoulders jerked. "So do I, but that doesn't change the way the cards were dealt. You and me, we've got two choices. Play the hand or fold." Mac met Rex's eyes squarely, and Juliet gnawed the inside of her lip as her brother sat silently, his expression stony, his shoulders hunched.

"Please don't give up, Rex," she said softly, her voice breaking. "Not now. Not after we've come this far."

Rex shifted his gaze to his sister. *"We,* Julie? Are you sitting in this chair, too?"

Juliet nearly gasped aloud at the anger she saw in his green eyes as he said in a dead voice, "I wish I'd died in that damned crash."

She stiffened, and the color drained from her face as he turned his chair and began wheeling himself toward the glass door.

It took him two tries and a lot of maneuvering, but he finally managed to swing the door wide enough to roll his chair through. He paused just inside as though to catch his breath and then, with a violent movement of his shoulders, set the chair in motion again.

As soon as Rex had disappeared from view, Juliet collapsed into her chair. Her knees felt shaky, and her stomach was queasy.

"Did you hear what he said?" She gave Mac a wan look and fought to keep from giving in to the tears that hovered behind her eyes.

He looked up and nodded, his intense blue gaze fixed on her strained face. "I heard."

"Did you feel that way? After you were hurt, I mean?"

Mac hesitated. "No. But I was pretty hard to live with for a long time. It's a wonder my folks still came to see me."

Juliet gave him a helpless look. "What should I do? I don't know what to do for him anymore."

"Maybe you've already done too much."

Juliet's brow furrowed. "Just what do you mean by that?"

He looked down at his hands. He wondered how she would react if he told her that he knew all about the payments to the hospital, payments made in cash that had no known origin. He gave himself a mental shake. This wasn't a parlor game he was playing here. This was a life and death situation. He forced a calmness into his voice that belied the frustration seething inside him.

"You have to let Rex fight his own battles, take his own blows, or he'll never develop the calluses he needs to deal with the problems he's going to face."

"What do you expect me to do?" she cried heatedly. "Let him just give up and waste away?"

"If that's what he has to do for a while, yes. It's his life, and you have to let him live it."

Juliet closed her eyes against the rising tide of truth, and a dry sob escaped her throat. "Ever since my... my father left, I've been the one to take care of things. I took care of my mother until she died, and then I started taking care of Rex. I guess I thought I could make up for Daddy's desertion that way."

She gave Mac a speaking look. "It hurt so much when he left. I'm not sure I ever really got over it. That's why I've always tried to be there for Rex. I've never wanted him to feel that kind of pain." She looked deeply into Mac's face. "Can that really be so wrong? To put the brother I love before everything else in my life?"

Mac dropped his eyes. His chest hurt, as though a giant boulder had been dropped on him from a great height. He looked up to find Juliet watching him with pleading eyes. His heart thudded against the painful constriction.

"Each one of us has to make his own choices," he told her quietly. He paused, then added in a heavy voice, "And answer for them."

Chapter 7

Mac drove them home. Juliet sat stiffly in the passenger seat, her mind numb, as though a switch in the back of her head had suddenly been turned to "off." She was tired, and deeply discouraged.

For the first time since Rex's accident she'd come face to face with the truth. Rex might simply choose to give up, to live out his life waiting to die, and if he did, there was nothing she could do about it.

"Juliet?" Mac's deep voice cut through her isolation. "We're home."

She glanced around, surprised to see that he had pulled into his space in front of their small enclave of cottages.

He walked her to the door and waited while she searched for her keys. Once they were inside, he carried the wicker picnic hamper to the kitchen, while she stood in the middle of her living room, staring out the picture window at the sea.

She gave him a vague smile of thanks when he returned to the living room and came to stand by her side. "I've seen a lot of oceans, but I've always loved the Pacific best," he said in a low tone, gazing past the breakers to the horizon.

The sea was a winter gray, laced with white patches of foam. A lone boat bobbed atop the gentle swells, its sails two distant white triangles against the pale blue sky.

Juliet turned her head to look at Mac's shuttered face. She could almost see him on the bridge of the ship, squinting into the sun, his blue eyes darker than the sea he searched.

He could have been a pirate, or maybe the captain of a Spanish galleon sailing along the jagged California coast, searching for new worlds to claim.

She felt a surge of longing. How wonderful it would be, discovering new worlds with this man at her side.

"Hey, look at that!" he exclaimed in throaty surprise. "Is that a whale?"

Juliet narrowed her gaze against the lemony glare of the sun on the water. Beyond the breakers the sea stretched smooth and unbroken to the horizon. She started to shake her head when a stream of water rose above the surface, barely visible to the naked eye, followed almost immediately by a rising gray mound that was the back of a California gray whale.

"They're migrating," she said softly, watching the animal glide smoothly through the sea. "I see one now and then in the bay."

The whale seemed to hesitate, then slipped headfirst beneath the waves, its huge tail flukes rising straight up toward the sky before disappearing beneath the spray in one smooth motion.

Juliet closed her eyes, visualizing the silent, watery world beneath the surface. It was peaceful there, and sheltering, with no pressures, no terrors, no pain.

"Hey, I didn't mean to make you sad, Juliet." His voice penetrated her rambling thoughts, and she jerked her head up to meet his gaze.

"I'm scared, Mac," she said in a thin voice. "What if Rex just . . . gives up? What if he doesn't fight?"

"He will—when he's ready. You can't give him the strength he needs, Juliet. He has to find it inside himself." He ran his hand up and down her arm, comforting her even as he excited shivers of sensation beneath the skin.

"He's always been a gentle person—like my mother," she said with a sigh. Juliet had been the one to inherit the fiery ambition and gritty determination of their flamboyant father.

Mac's hand cupped her shoulder, shaking her gently. "That doesn't mean he's not a fighter. You have to have faith."

She frowned. "I'm not sure I have faith in anything anymore, Mac. Not in the doctors, or in Rex…or in myself." Her voice trailed into silence, and her shoulders hunched.

"Tell me," Mac urged in a steady voice, his hand tightening on her shoulder. "Maybe I can help."

She lifted her eyes to find that his were filled with a troubled expression she couldn't understand. There was pain in those deep blue depths, and anger, and something more that frightened her with its intensity.

"I—thanks for offering, but I'll work it out. I guess I'm just feeling a little sorry for myself, that's all. Don't pay any attention to my ramblings."

"I think you have every right to feel sorry for yourself now and then. It can't be easy, watching someone you love in pain." His eyes darkened with some private thought. "I'd like to help."

Juliet shook her head. "I'll work it out." She could still hear a faint echo of her mother's cultured voice. *Ladies never whine, Juliet. It's most unbecoming, and men find it too boring for words.*

Mac looked disappointed, and his hand fell from her shoulder.

She forced a bright smile. "I'm sorry. You've been so nice to us—Rex and me, and I don't mean to repay you by being a Gloomy Gus." She gestured toward the kitchen. "How about a cup of coffee before you go? I'm afraid I don't have anything stronger."

Something powerful but indecipherable flickered in his eyes for an instant before he inclined his head in a nod of acceptance. "Coffee would be nice," he said in a voice that was surprisingly husky. "I don't need anything stronger when I'm around you, Juliet."

Juliet searched his face, but there were no clues to be read, no new lines to reveal his feelings, no heightened color in his hard cheeks. And yet she'd heard a note of longing in his voice.

Her heart began to pound, and her breathing changed as she looked into his face. It wasn't possible that she could love this man, so why did she feel like flinging herself into his strong arms and begging him to hold her?

She dropped her eyes, and her gaze fell to the tip of his shiny black cane. In the short time she'd known him, he'd done more for her brother than she'd been able to do in months, done more than even some of the professionals at the center.

He'd done it freely, without strings. And he'd been there for her, too. Teasing her when she was sad, listening to her when she was scared, soothing her when she was lonely.

Juliet felt herself freeze with the impact of her thoughts. Mac was a man who gave generously, without demanding more than she wanted to give. A man who could be trusted with her thoughts and her pain. And with her very soul. A man who could be trusted with her heart.

She held her breath. It's true. I love him, she thought in a shimmering daze. I really do. She exhaled a soft tumultuous sigh of exultation mingled with dismay, and his expression darkened with renewed concern.

"Juliet, he's going to be okay," he said in a deep rumble next to her ear. "Really."

She felt an involuntary shiver of response travel through her body as he slipped his right arm around her shoulder and pulled her snugly against his body.

Desire rippled through her, gathering strength with each heartbeat. She wanted to wrap herself in the warming glow that reached out to envelop her. She longed to lose herself in that crooked white grin that gentled the harsh lines of his face, to bask in the aura of supremely masculine charm that seemed to draw her like a powerful electromagnetic field.

"You smell so...so pretty," Mac murmured against her temple, his lips brushing lightly against her skin.

Juliet felt her stomach flutter with indecision. She had to think calmly and rationally. She had to catch her breath.

She tried to move, but he held her close. "Don't go," he whispered in a husky drawl that sent ripples of anticipation cascading down her spine. "You feel so good."

He moved, pulling her hard against his chest. He'd left his jacket in the car, and she could feel his heart pounding beneath the soft flannel of his shirt. Slowly, tentatively, she slid her hands over his shoulders and linked them behind the erect column of his neck. He was so tall that she had to stretch on tiptoe to place her mouth within reach of his.

Her breasts slid over his chest, softness flattening against hardness, and Mac inhaled sharply, tightening his arm around her.

His legs pressed against hers, hard and rigid, and Juliet could feel the cuff of his brace pressing against the top of her thigh.

She sighed and tipped her head backward, waiting. She wanted to kiss him again, wanted to feel his lips moving against hers. She could feel the hunger tugging at her and the flush of desire burning in her cheeks. Every muscle of her was straining with the urge to absorb his. With each moment the craving seemed to grow until she could scarcely breathe.

Mac watched her feathery lashes slowly close over the troubled fire of her vibrant brown eyes. Her face was soft, her mouth sweetly vulnerable. Her body, so lush even in its athletic slimness, was exciting him beyond his ability to resist.

He felt drugged, his rational mind clouded. Nothing seemed to make any sense. He wanted her, but why? Because she was a beautiful woman, and he was only taking what she offered? Or because he had a job to do, and making love to Juliet was a part of that job? Or because she was sweet and kind and dear, and he was beginning to crave being with her in ways that were threatening his objectivity?

Juliet opened her eyes, gazing up at him with a searching, hesitant expression.

Mac groaned and lowered his head. The hell with logic, he told himself angrily. And the hell with Project Ping Pong. At this moment, the only thing he wanted was Juliet.

"Sweet Juliet," he murmured in a rusty whisper, brushing his lips over hers.

She closed her eyes and met his seeking mouth with a sigh of eagerness. He tasted like soda pop, and his breath was hot and urgent against her mouth as he probed her lips gently with his tongue.

She opened her mouth to him, welcoming him with a drugged lassitude. This time his kiss was tender and coaxing, his lips softening into gentleness as they explored hers with deliberate slowness.

She could feel the muscles of his torso contract violently as she pressed her breasts against him, rubbing the nipples against the hardness of his chest to ease the tingling ache he was arousing in her.

Mac groaned, ending the kiss. His face was flushed, and his eyes were midnight dark as he raised his head. "Stop me now, Juliet," he said in a strained tone, his voice sliding possessively over her name, "or I won't be able to stop myself. I want you too much to hold back."

Tumbling feelings cascaded through Juliet's body, brushing her cheeks with pink and widening her eyes, which glowed with the inner fire of her desire.

"I...oh, Mac, I want you, too," she whispered in a shaky voice, clutching his neck with trembling fingers.

Time hung suspended as she clung to him, her senses exploding in a chorus of passion. She wanted him, and she needed him. But, more than that, she loved him. Hopelessly, senselessly, completely.

Why, how, when—none of those things mattered. All that mattered was Mac. Even with her eyes tightly closed and her face pressed against his hard chest, she could see him. His restrained smile that would flash with rare warmth when she walked into the room; his turbulent blue eyes that were often filled with such sadness that she wanted to weep; his magnificent body that bore scars of courage and honor.

She pulled herself out of his arms, framing his face with her hands. "Let's go to my room."

Mac turned his head to kiss her palm. "I thought you'd never ask," he joked softly with a throbbing note in his voice that made her nerve endings tingle.

Juliet smiled and slipped her arm around his waist. Side by side, they walked down the hall to her bedroom and through the open door. Mac led her to the bed, his hand tightly gripping hers. They stood in a puddle of sunlight coming through the narrow window a few feet away.

Her peripheral vision assured her that they were in her house, with her familiar things around her, but her eyes were focused intently on the face of the man who was going to make love to her.

What would he think? What would he say? Would he find her too inexperienced? Too eager? Not eager enough?

Juliet stood in silence, her body taut and quivering like a bowstring, her breath coming in shallow bursts as Mac threw his cane onto the end of the bed and took her in his arms.

She stretched, arching her body to fit against his wide chest. He was so big, so strong, so protective.

His hands drifted down her back, stroking, caressing, sending shivers spiraling down her spine. His lips were warm on the thin skin below her ear, his tongue raspy and enticing.

"I've been thinking about this ever since I saw you out on that pier shouting at the sky," Mac whispered against her neck, his breath tickling her and exciting her at the same time.

He took a deep breath, and Juliet felt the rise and fall of his chest as he cradled her against his body. His arms encircled her completely, holding her with firm pressure.

She felt the tension ease from her muscles as she surrendered to the need that had been building in her from the moment she'd first met Mac. Never before had she wanted to shed her inhibitions and give herself so freely to a man. Never before had she so desperately wanted to become part of a man. Never before had she been willing to risk her very soul.

"Oh, Mac," she whispered in a voice that was shaky but full of tenderness.

With a husky groan, he lifted her face and covered her trembling mouth with his, taking her lips with an explosive hunger that sent her spinning into a world of pure sensation, a bright new world where no other man had ever taken her before.

His hand slipped under the edge of her sweater to flatten against the tender skin of her back. Juliet shivered as he traced the hollow of her spine, moving outward toward the curve of her waist.

She raked her fingers through the crisp tangle of his wiry curls, scraping her short nails against his scalp as her need grew.

She returned his kiss blindly, without restraint, arching against him in growing demand. His lips were welded to hers, hot and hard, and his hand slid upward to cup her breast, the heat of his palm searing her skin beneath the lace of her bra. She inhaled sharply as Mac's fingers found the clasp, releasing the fullness of her breast into his hand.

"I need to see you," he whispered, moving away to tug the red sweater over her head. Her bra fell away, and Mac's eyes seemed to glow as he stared at her breasts, full and delicately rounded, the nipples hard and dark.

"Perfect," he murmured, bending his head to kiss each pink globe, anointing the nipples with the moist heat of his tongue.

Juliet moaned, whispering his name as he trailed kisses into the hollow between her breasts. Her skin felt warm beneath the firm pressure of his lips. His eyes were dark with craving as he lifted his head and looked at her.

"I need to see all of you," he said in a thick murmur. "Before I go out of my mind."

Blushing to her toes, Juliet swiftly kicked off her sneakers and shrugged out of her jeans and panties. She smiled at the swift intake of his breath and let the sweetness of his admiration fill her. Never in her life had she felt more feminine, more desirable, more cherished.

"Your turn," she murmured in fluid desire, lowering her eyes to his massive chest. With trembling hands she began unbuttoning his shirt. The soft flannel fell open, revealing his bronzed skin, which was covered with a downy thatch of curling chestnut hair.

Juliet traced the soft whorls with a tentative fingertip, smiling at the way his muscles contracted involuntarily as she played with the tiny male nipples hidden in the dark red pelt.

Mac inhaled swiftly, and he reached up to cup her head in his palm, pulling her face toward his until his lips met hers, insistent and seeking. His eyes were closed, his brows pulled together as the kiss ended, and he stood silently, expectantly, waiting.

Emboldened for the first time in her life, Juliet tugged his shirttails from his waistband and reached for the snap at the waist of his jeans. The sound of his zipper sliding down seemed to reverberate off the walls, bringing a hot flush to her cheeks.

Dear God, she breathed, suddenly astounded by her audacity. She'd been taught by her mother and society to be the passive partner, and she had never questioned that role. Until now.

Something primitive deep inside her had been released when Mac kissed her, something that was driving her beyond the bounds of reason.

"Wait," Mac commanded in a husky whisper, holding his hand over hers where it rested on the fly of his jeans. The slight pressure against his body made his hardness throb against her palm, and Juliet felt a heady rush of anticipation. "I'm not what you'd call pretty," he said almost defiantly, glancing down at his left side. "I'm more or less a mess."

Juliet hesitated, then raised questioning eyes to his as he captured her hand and removed it from his loins. There was an expression in his eyes that she'd never seen before, an expression of deep hunger and yearning overlaid by uncertainty. The taut lines of his face had deepened, giving him a look of vulnerability that tore into her with jagged force.

"Nobody's perfect," she whispered, letting him see in her eyes and on her face the love she felt inadequate to express.

"Sweet baby," he whispered. "I want to be perfect for you. I want *this* to be perfect—for both of us."

Joy burst from Juliet's heart, filling her with buoyant happiness until she felt weightless and free. "It will be perfect," she said in a voice that was nearly without sound.

Mac could hear a dozen emotions in that breathless whisper, emotions that he didn't dare analyze. He was afraid to say anything more, afraid that Juliet would suddenly stiffen in his arms and push him away. Afraid that this was just another dream of her.

With a groan of impatience, he reached down to strip back the covers, then quickly sat down on the side of the bed to undress.

Juliet inhaled sharply and let her eyes flow over his sunburnished skin. He was magnificent. His body had the strength of hard sinew and bone, the beauty of a primitive sculpture, the vitality of a jungle animal. Every taut inch of him radiated power and virility.

Not even the heavy brace protecting his knee or the awful puckered scars running from his thigh to his ankle detracted from the stunning magnificence of his bronzed body.

Mac hesitated as he began to unstrap his brace, his eyes, stormy and alive, fixed on Juliet's face as though gauging her reaction to his scarred flesh.

"Hurry up," she whispered, unable to keep the urgency from her voice, and he flushed as he deftly removed the brace and placed it on the floor beneath the bed.

"Come here," he ordered in a throaty growl, his eyes imprinting her naked body with molten intensity, and Juliet sank willingly into his arms, shivering with delectable anticipation as her thighs slid against his hair-roughened skin.

With a low groan, Mac moved, tugging her down to the mattress until they were lying side by side. His mouth sought hers, his breathing shallow and harsh in the quiet of the room. Juliet arched upward, clutching his shoulders in rising urgency. She pressed herself against him, feeling his arousal throbbing beneath the delta of her thighs.

He lifted his head, gazing down at her with eyes that looked almost black. His brows were knitted together as though in pain, and his breathing was ragged.

Juliet pressed her face into the hollow of his shoulder and inhaled the musky male scent of him. His body felt taut and powerful under her lips.

"You feel so good," he whispered, his hands sliding lower, the pads of his fingers barely touching her skin as he caressed the slight mound around her belly button.

Juliet inhaled sharply as his fingers moved lower to stroke the sensitive skin of her inner thighs. She whimpered in pleasure as his fingers began to venture higher with each slow stroke until his knuckles brushed against the soft curls at the tender spot where her thighs met.

"Easy, baby," he whispered as she moaned and arched against his hand. "We have lots of time."

Juliet was lost in a haze of pleasure, so lost that she barely heard his words of assurance. Her body was like a finely tuned violin, vibrating under his touch with achingly sweet notes that were soaring with such pure clarity of tone she wanted to weep.

She gripped his shoulders, pushing her breasts upward to meet his chest as his fingers rhythmically titillated her, probing and retreating, exciting a firestorm of sensations that threatened to swamp her.

She slid her hands lower, seeking, finding, caressing. Mac stiffened, then shuddered, moaning deep in his throat as she stroked him with a fevered need.

He groaned as though he were in pain, and Juliet froze. "Don't stop," he grated, his voice a throaty purr. "Don't..."

She arched upward, guiding him toward her. Mac followed her lead, thrusting slowly until they were touching, hardness against softness, oak against velvet, man against woman.

"Sweet," he whispered, probing with aching slowness until she thought she would faint.

And then Mac couldn't take any more. With a harsh cry, he moved, joining them together violently. Juliet gasped, loving the feel of him inside her. He moved slowly at first, then faster, his breath coming in harsh gasps as she met his thrusts with frantic movements. She was buffeted by pure ecstasy, drenched with sweet passion, driven beyond rational thought as release seized her, shaking her body with spasms of delirious pleasure. It was a cataclysm of sensation, an avalanche of bliss shooting through her body.

She cried out in exultation, her fingers cupping his hard buttocks spasmodically.

Mac faltered, then drove into her, a man out of control, his need exciting her even more. The sleigh bed shook from the force of his desire, and then he finished, his body shuddering with the final release.

He groaned harshly and then was still, his body collapsing next to hers, his face buried between her breasts. His breathing was labored in the silent room, and his body was covered with a dewy layer of sweat that Juliet found decidedly sensual.

She snuggled next to him, her heartbeat gradually slowing from the frantic pounding Mac had excited in her. He lay motionless, spent, his eyes closed. One arm was thrown across her belly, his hand possessively cupping her breast, while the other encircled her head.

Juliet felt a great heaviness envelop her, pulling her down into sleep. She felt so good. So very good. Her eyes drifted closed, then jerked open as the telephone jangled next to her ear.

Mac jerked awake, his body stiffening, and Juliet's eyes darted toward the phone. Maybe it's Rex, she thought, mixed emotions shaking her.

"Damn," Mac groaned, breathing harshly as he rolled away and reached for the receiver. "At least they waited until now."

Juliet felt the haze of passion slip from her, replaced by worry. Mac lifted the receiver and passed it to her. "Hello," she said cautiously, sitting up against the headboard.

It wasn't the hospital. It was Peter, and he was furious. She was late.

Reality crashed around her as she watched the curiosity playing over Mac's relaxed features. In her anxiety over Rex and her preoccupation with Mac, she'd forgotten all about her appointment to meet Peter at four.

As she listened to his castigating words, she began to shake. How was she ever going to explain this to Mac?

Juliet pushed her hair away from her cheeks and tried to concentrate on Peter's voice. She couldn't afford to think about Mac's feelings right now. The only thing she could do now was placate Peter.

"Look, I'll call you back in twenty minutes," she said abruptly, interrupting Peter's tirade. She hung up before he could object and gave Mac a bright smile.

Mac sat up and pushed the pillow behind his back, watching her with eyes that had turned inward again. His smile was warm, but there was a rigid set to his shoulders that seemed to contradict his expression, and Juliet's breathing faltered.

"Are you okay?" he asked in the slow drawl that invariably sent little spurts of pleasure through her system. "Was it the hospital?"

"No, just a...a friend." She twisted her fingers together under the coverlet and shifted her eyes to the vista beyond the window.

"Peter?" His tone was bland, even disinterested, but Juliet could sense his underlying anger.

"No, it was...my aerobics instructor. She's in a bind and asked if I could teach her class tonight." Juliet dropped her eyes. She hated to lie, but she had no choice.

Mac's lashes dipped swiftly, then rose to reveal expressionless eyes. "I take it you said yes."

Juliet nodded. Tension snaked down her spine, tightening the muscles of her back until she felt as though she were caught in a giant vise.

"I...I have to shower and change." She gestured vaguely toward the door. "Would you...like to join me?"

"I don't suppose you have a bathtub. I've had to give up showers. It's hard to get clean when you're standing on one leg."

He sounded so serious, but there was a glint of humor in his eyes, and Juliet smiled self-consciously. "I have a tub, but the stopper doesn't work."

Mac's mouth lifted in a lopsided grin, and his hand came out to smooth her hair away from her neck before tracing the line of her jaw with his thumb.

"Then I guess I'll have to pass. This time."

The air around them seemed to change, growing denser as she sat motionless, her body clamoring for his soothing touch. It would be so easy to lean forward and feel his strong arms close around her again.

She summoned a smile, covering his hand with hers. "I have to get ready," she said softly, fighting against the need that was growing in her again.

Mac brushed his lips against hers. "Mind if I make a call while you're in the shower? I need to see about having a phone installed in my place."

"Of course," Juliet responded with automatic courtesy, moving quickly away from him.

A sick feeling settled into the pit of her stomach as she collected clean underwear from her dresser drawer and left the bedroom. Dear God, what else? she wondered dejectedly. The lies were getting her in deeper and deeper, so deep she might never find her way out.

Mac waited until he heard the shower running in the bathroom on the opposite side of the bedroom wall before he picked up the phone. He punched out a number in a savage rhythm, his face creased into harsh lines, his eyes glacial.

The voice on the other end of the line repeated the number Mac had just dialed.

"This is McKinley," he barked. "I need an agent right away. There's someone I want tailed."

An hour later Juliet emerged from her cottage, her purse over her shoulder, her briefcase in her hand. The sun was setting behind her, and the sky was tinged with orange.

Mac had been gone when she'd returned from the shower, and she'd felt a pang of relief. She needed time to repair the rips in her composure before she faced him again.

She waved to the cab driver double-parked in front of the cottage, and the man casually waved back. The garage had promised her car for sometime Monday, but until then she had to rely on taxis.

"Hey, what's with the briefcase?" Mac's voice caught her off guard, and she turned toward him in surprise. He was seated on the grass in front of his cottage doing sit-ups, his cane and a towel beside him. "I thought you were going to your exercise class tonight."

He was dressed in gray sweatpants and a blue sweatshirt with U.S.N.A. emblazoned across the front. The sleeves had been cut off above the elbows, leaving a ragged fringe of threads, and the top had been enlarged to accommodate his muscular neck. It was apparent from the sweat stains darkening the fleece that he'd been exercising for some time.

"I am," she hedged, walking over to the spot where he sat gazing up at her. "I, uh, forgot my gym bag when I left the office yesterday." She patted the slim attaché case and gave him a bright grin. "This was handy, so I just shoved my things inside." Thank God I wore my sneakers, she breathed silently.

She caught Mac's quick look of skepticism as he glanced at the case. "Must be a pretty skimpy outfit," he said with a lazy purr of interest. "How 'bout me coming along? Just to keep you company?" He wiped his damp forehead with the towel and grinned up at her.

Juliet choked back the words of instant protest and pretended to consider his suggestion. "I'd like that," she said with a little laugh, "but I belong to a private club. No visitors allowed."

Breakers crashed against the rocks at the foot of the cliff, and gulls called in strident protest overhead as Mac digested her words.

Juliet was conscious of the heady scent of seaweed on the breeze as she tried to maintain her smiling facade. The last thing she wanted to do was to hurt Mac.

She thought he was going to protest, but he merely shrugged and rested his arms on his flexed knees. "So when am I going to see you again?"

Juliet fought against the instant surge of excitement pushing her heart rate into triple time. "I don't know," she said with perfect honesty. Tonight she had to spend with Peter, and tomorrow she had errands to run and work to do at home.

Wariness shadowed Mac's damp face. "Are you angry because we made love?"

She clutched the handle of her briefcase tightly and shook her head. "No, not angry." She was conscious of his eyes fixed intently on her face. Something in the angle of his head told her that he was not as self-possessed as he seemed. "I have no regrets, Mac." Her eyes softened into guileless sincerity as she gave him a sad smile. "But it can't happen again. It would be a mistake—for both of us."

One thick brow arched in question as he continued to watch her. "Why would it be a mistake, if it's what we both want?"

Juliet cast an anxious glance over her shoulder at the waiting taxi. She was already late; a few more minutes wouldn't matter.

"Because my life isn't my own right now, Mac. Because I can't handle a casual affair under the best of circumstances. Because—" she threw an impatient hand in the air "—because of a thousand reasons."

Mac grinned. "Is that all? I thought maybe I'd come on too strong too soon and scared you." The dry humor in his voice brought a reluctant smile to her face.

"You do scare me," she said in a sober vein.

Mac chuckled. "So when can I see you again?"

Juliet gaped at him. "You're not going to give up, are you?"

"Nope."

She sneaked another look at the cab. "I have to go. I'll be late."

"Sure. I'll see you later."

She nodded, suddenly reluctant to leave. There was something compelling about this man, something that drew her from the dark pit of her loneliness into the bright sunlight. It was more than physical, although the sight of him sitting there, disheveled and perspiring, had set her senses jangling.

Beneath the soft fleece she could see the hard outline of his body, rugged and powerful and sleek with sculptured muscle. All she had to do was stretch out her hand and ...

A horn blew an impatient tattoo, and Juliet winced. "Uh, that's my cab."

"Have fun," Mac drawled, resting his chin on his arms and watching her with enigmatic eyes.

"I'll try." She fluttered her fingers in farewell and hurried toward the waiting cab. Her heart was slamming painfully against her ribs as she climbed into the back seat and smiled her thanks at the driver, who shut her door firmly before trotting around to slide under the wheel.

As they drove away, Juliet risked a quick glance toward Mac's bungalow. He was sitting in the same place, his arms folded over his knees, staring straight ahead. And then, as she watched, he hunched his big shoulders and dropped his head as though he were in pain.

Juliet felt her depression deepen. Nothing was ever as easy as it seemed—for anyone.

"She's been inside for almost twenty minutes." The lanky agent for the Naval Investigative Services slid his fingers over the steering wheel and nodded toward the salmon-colored two-story house across the wide street.

Dusk had fallen, and the streetlights were coming on all over the city, orange pinpricks of light contrasting with the cinnamon sky.

"Any idea who's in there with her?" Mac stretched his legs out in front of him and tried to get comfortable in the cramped passenger seat of the agent's brown sedan. His own rental car was parked around the corner, hidden from view behind a large van.

Lieutenant Shawn Beatty, one of Commander Cahill's best investigators, had been on duty when Mac had called, and he'd tailed Juliet from her cottage to this address in one of the older sections of the city, where the houses were predominantly Spanish in style and the residents drove expensive cars sporting yacht club emblems on their bumpers.

Mac, alerted by the beeper built into the back of his watch, had arrived only a few minutes ago. He'd changed into a dark blue running suit and wore a baseball cap pulled low over his forehead. If anyone spotted him, he would appear to be a local resident, out for a stroll before dinner.

Beatty squinted his pale blue eyes against the gloom and consulted his notes. "A woman met her at the door. Caucasian, age fifty, fifty-five, approximately five-two, a hundred thirty pounds, gray hair, worn in some kind of a bun on the top of her head."

Mac grunted an acknowledgment. "Did they say any-thing?"

"I think so, but the wind's from the wrong direction. I couldn't hear."

Mac nodded and started to ask about the area, but the ear-splitting sound of a commercial jet climbing overhead drowned out his voice.

He winced and waited until the noise from the screaming engines faded. "Good Lord, how do these people stand this noise?" he asked with a scowl.

"Beats me," Beatty answered. "Maybe they're so deaf they don't notice it anymore." He grinned, then shrugged apolo-getically as Mac gave him a hard stare. "Sorry, sir," the lieu-tenant mumbled, clearing his throat.

He'd heard all about this guy McKinley from Commander Cahill, but he hadn't believed the hype—until he'd met the man. Dangerous, that was what Cahill had called him, and Beatty agreed.

The guy had the look. It was in those strange blue eyes of his. There was a coldness there, a lethal stillness in the back of the black pupils that chilled Beatty in spite of his experience. He would never have that look, not in a lifetime as an intelligence officer. But then, that was why he was only a field agent in-stead of a member of Hendricks' elite like Captain McKinley.

"I'm going to see if I can find an open window," Mac said in crisp tones. He needed information, and he would have to risk discovery to get it. "You get in touch with Cahill and have him contact D.C. with this address. Tell the records depart-ment that I want everything they have on the person or per-sons currently in residence."

"Yes, sir." Beatty reached for the transmitter as Mac opened the door and swung his legs out, pulling himself up stiffly. He crossed the street at the corner and began limping toward the large house, his eyes sweeping the surrounding area without really seeming to.

As he came abreast of the residence, he slowed, giving the house and its neighbors a swift but thorough inspection. All three homes were the same distance from the street, and each was different in design but not in style.

Making a swift calculation, he stopped and pulled a notebook from his back pocket, as though checking an address. He glanced up, making another complete inspection of the area. The street was quiet.

He tucked the notebook into his pocket and began heading up the walk leading to the front porch. His eyes were riveted on the large arched window where light streamed through the curtains to illuminate the yellow and orange blossoms of a large lantana bush planted in front of the house.

There was no sign of the inhabitants as he followed the path toward the backyard. The gate creaked loudly under his touch, and he froze. The faint sound of a television newscast reached his ears, along with the rapidly increasing sound of another plane screaming overhead.

Using the roar of the airliner as cover, he pushed through the gate and hurried along the walk. He stopped at the edge of the house and peered cautiously around the corner, his cane balanced easily in his hand.

Light streamed through French doors, illuminating the brick patio, and he could see shadows moving against the white fabric covering the square panes.

He approached cautiously, moving with careful slowness over the uneven brick. He flattened his back against the rough stucco and inched closer to the doors.

The sound of male laughter drifted through the glass, and Mac froze, straining to hear. His heart pounded as Juliet's voice cut through the laughter with a terse comment. The words she spoke were indistinguishable. All except one: Peter.

Mac's eyes glittered with a cold, determined light as he silently cursed the man behind the name. He was the one who had turned her, he was the one who was passing on the information to Hydra. Who else could he be?

Mac held his breath, trying to make out the gist of the conversation as the three people in the room argued. Random phrases, jumbled words, fragmented sentences reached his ear, and his expression darkened. They were discussing a cover story—for a female operative named Marta.

Damn, damn, damn, he breathed silently, closing his eyes. Was Marta Juliet's code name? Or were they talking about another operative? He would have to check out with Hendricks as soon as possible.

Mac glanced up as another plane roared overhead, obliterating the words coming from inside the house. He leaned against the wall and tried to regulate his labored breathing. He was sweating profusely, even though the temperature was in the sixties.

The sound of the plane faded, and he opened his eyes. A burst of feminine laughter reached his ears, and he stiffened. Someone had moved closer to the doors, one of the women, and her voice was clearly audible through the glass.

The words were heavily accented, and Mac flinched. The speaker was Russian; he would bet his stripes on it.

"Don't be so hard on poor Juliet, darling," the woman chided with a laugh. "Making up code words is your job." She moved away from the door then, and Mac's shoulders slumped.

He leaned forward cautiously, trying to get a clear look of the interior. Through the gauzy material, he could make out the blurred form of a woman seated at a desk, her slim back erect, her head bent. It was Juliet.

Sweet baby, why? Mac asked silently, clenching his teeth until his jaw hurt.

He wanted to break through those doors and haul her out of there, away from danger, away from the slimy pit she'd gotten herself mired in. He gripped the head of his cane as though it were Juliet's fragile neck.

Just then a door opened in one of the neighboring houses, and a woman spoke. "Outside, Woofie. Go on. Scoot."

The door slammed, and a dog began whining. Mac grimaced and edged away from the side of the house. He'd heard enough.

Mac was drunk.

On his way back to his cottage he'd stopped at a liquor store to call Hendricks, and when he was finished, he'd bought a bottle of cognac to keep him company through the night.

He was sitting in the tiny living room of his bungalow in the dark, his eyes trained on the lighted window of Juliet's bedroom.

She'd been home for nearly an hour, and the light was still on. It was a few minutes past midnight, but Mac was wide awake in spite of the brandy.

Hendricks had been elated at the progress he'd made, promising to expedite the identification of Peter as soon as possible—although the fact that it was the weekend made it somewhat more difficult.

The admiral had been effusive in his praise, but Mac had taken no pleasure in his superior's words. He was fighting an internal battle that was tearing him apart.

In spite of the evidence, he couldn't bring himself to accept the fact that they'd been right to suspect Juliet. His gut told him she was innocent, no matter how damning the facts. His head, however, told him that he was a fool.

Mac sighed and tossed down a generous slug of the brandy. He was drinking from a water glass, something that would have scandalized the Virginia aristocracy back home.

His lips quirked in self-mockery. He'd done a lot of things in his years with Naval Intelligence that would shock the home folks, things that even *he* didn't like to think about.

He tipped his head back, trying to relieve the tightness in his shoulder muscles. The worn armchair was too narrow in the back and too short in the seat, but it was still the only semicomfortable place to sit.

He sighed and reached for another cigar. He'd bought a box along with the cognac, and he'd smoked three already. He'd given up cigarettes during his time in Bethesda, and the cigars were a luxury he allowed himself only when he was particularly tense.

He lighted the cigar and blew the smoke toward the window. His head ached, and his tongue felt fuzzy, but his mind refused the numbing effects of the potent alcohol. The brandy had only served to sharpen his thoughts, which were anything but soothing.

The next few days were going to be pure hell. The net was closing, with Juliet the prey, and there wasn't a thing he could do about it.

He'd accepted that she'd done it for her brother, to pay for the treatment Rex so desperately needed. A part of him could accept that, even admire her motive—in a way. But he could never excuse her treachery.

Mac grunted and drained the glass. The liquor burned a path to his stomach, reminding him that he hadn't eaten since the picnic with Juliet.

She hadn't been playing a game this afternoon. He was sure of it. The woman who'd welcomed him to her bed was the real Juliet.

Mac's fist clenched around the empty glass.

So she was sweet and kind and dear.

So she had a way of driving a man crazy with wanting her.

None of that mattered when measured against the damning fact that a dedicated man could die because of her treachery.

"Why the hell should I care what happens to her?" he growled into the darkness, wincing as he sat up too quickly. Absently he rubbed his leg, rhythmically massaging away the dull ache.

There was no use kidding himself. He cared. More than he wanted to admit.

He stared across the grass at Juliet's blank window. The curtains were drawn against the night, but Mac's mind slipped past the opaque barrier.

He could still see her as she had been this afternoon, lying next to him, her perfect breasts rosy and sweet against his lips.

He felt his body stir. In spite of the pint of brandy coursing through his veins, he wanted her. In a few strides he could be there with her, lying next to her in that antique bed of hers.

Suddenly, with a violent curse, Mac threw his glass against the wall.

It didn't help.

* * *

Juliet finished the glass of warm milk and tried to find a comfortable position. She was so tired, but she couldn't close her eyes.

She'd tried reading, but that only made her eyes hurt. She'd tried the milk, but the warm liquid had merely soothed her tight throat, not her thoughts. The sleeping pills she'd gotten from the doctor after Rex's accident were in the medicine chest, but they made her so groggy the next day she could barely function.

She turned her head and glanced at the attaché case on the old steamer trunk by the window. She was scared.

Peter was becoming unreasonable, demanding more and more of her. She was being pulled in all directions. By Peter, by her job, by Rex, and now by her love for Mac.

It wasn't fair.

She sighed and flopped onto her stomach, burying her face in her pillow. The mattress was hard and unyielding, and she groaned. She could still feel Mac, hot and hard inside her.

All during the troubled evening with Tasha and Peter, she'd been conscious of her own heightened sensitivity. She could still feel Mac's big hands caressing her skin, could still feel the raspy warmth of his tongue as he tasted her nipples.

She hugged her pillow, struggling against the yearning raging in her body. Inside, she was on fire, burning out of control. No matter what she did, no matter how fervently she told herself that an affair with Mac would be a risk she couldn't afford, she couldn't douse the flame that he had ignited in her.

Chapter 8

Juliet's feet pounded the tarmac in a steady rhythm. Her breath hissed in and out of her open mouth in ragged accompaniment, and her heart pumped blood to her extremities in urgent spurts.

She'd run to the end of the point, where the old Cabrillo lighthouse stood in solitary splendor on the highest spot in Point Loma, and had returned along the same route, a six mile round trip.

Her legs felt heavy, and her coordination was jerky as she stopped at the gate, jogging in place while the guard inspected her badge.

"On your way, Dr. Prentice," the grizzled veteran said with a grin as he slipped the yellow badge over her neck.

Juliet gave him a damp smile and moved down the road leading to Building 3. It was lunchtime, and the traffic was heavier than usual. She dodged between pedestrians, some of whom called out encouragement as she sped past.

As she topped the hill and started down, she lengthened her stride, pushing her body to the limit. She could feel the wind against her damp cheeks, could hear it rushing past her ears as she ran. The skin of her hands and feet tingled with the freshly oxygenated blood, and her cheeks were blooming with color.

As she came abreast of Building 3, she abruptly swerved to the left, stopping in front of a large square shed that was tacked onto the two-story frame structure like an afterthought. Inside were the various supplies used to care for the dolphins.

Jogging in place to let her muscles cool down, she spun the combination lock, then stepped inside. Toys used in training, along with a small locked chest containing medicine vials and pill bottles, were arranged on deep shelves along the wall facing the bay, and a large walk-in refrigerator occupied the far wall.

Without glancing around, Juliet hurriedly retrieved a large brown paper sack from the refrigerator and left the shed, locking the door behind her.

In the sack were some sandwiches, brought from home because she'd promised to run the mechanic back to the garage on her lunch hour after he'd returned her car.

On her way back to the base she'd stopped off at the hospital and paid the next installment on Rex's bill. She'd tried to see her brother, but he had been in therapy.

At least that's something, Juliet thought with forced optimism as she walked along the shore to the pier. At least he wasn't refusing to cooperate.

"Hi, guys," she called out in a cheery voice as the four dolphins, two in each tank, heralded her arrival with exuberant chatter.

Bubbles, the dominant female, swam to the side of the tank and rolled over onto her back, begging for a rub. Juliet laughed and squatted down, sending the animal into another series of clicks and squeaks.

"What a pretty girl," Juliet cooed in a fond tone as she began massaging the slick skin of the dolphin's exposed belly. The wet surface felt like warm rubber beneath her fingertips, smooth and resilient and strangely pleasurable.

Bubbles closed her eyes and stretched out to her full length of nearly five feet, fluttering her tail in a slow arc to keep her afloat.

Juliet smiled, but her smile suddenly turned to a startled frown as Bubbles surged out of her reach, clicking frantically.

From the other tank came the sound of disturbed chatter as the males circled in agitation. Juliet glanced around anxiously. Mac was standing only a few feet away, a rueful grin creasing his hard cheeks.

"I don't think they like me very much," he drawled as he came forward slowly, his eyes inspecting first one tank and then the other. "They always do that when I'm around." In his brown tweed jacket and blue button-down shirt he looked very conservative and devastatingly attractive.

Juliet giggled at the affronted expression on his face. "They're not used to strangers," she explained with a gesture toward the deserted area. "Everyone in the base knows that this is a restricted area. Nobody comes around much." She stood up and brushed the sand from the knees of her yellow running suit.

Mac reached her side and pointed his cane toward the tank to his left. "How come the dolphins in this tank are huddled at the far end while those two over there are leaping around like crazy?"

Juliet assumed a pedantic air. "Because these are females in this tank. They'd rather wait to see if there's truly a threat before they expend their energy on self-defense."

Mac cocked his head to the side and gave her an arch look. In the sunlight his hair was tipped with bronze, and his eyes were shadowed. "While the males swim around in circles wearing themselves out," he finished in dry tones.

Juliet dimpled. "Precisely. Nature is very consistent."

"Care to explain that, Dr. Prentice?" Mac teased, leaning over to brush an oleander blossom from her hair.

She loved the way he cocked his head to the side whenever he teased her. He seemed to shed some of his reserve then, as though he'd been keeping that side of his personality hidden for a long time.

"It's been my experience that the male of the species reacts first, then reasons later," she said in a slightly breathy tone.

He arched one brow in obvious skepticism. "Makes us guys sound pretty primitive, doesn't it?"

Juliet pulled the sweatband from her brow and shook her hair free. His eyes flickered as the silken tresses cascaded in tumbled waves over her shoulders.

"Maybe you'd prefer the term predictable," she countered, a challenging smile playing over her lips.

"Why do I think I've just been insulted?" he asked in a wry tone.

She laughed. "Don't take it personally," she said briskly, tossing her head. "There's definitely nothing predictable about you."

An unreadable surge of emotion flashed in Mac's eyes as she turned away and strode with long, graceful strides to the other tank, where the two males greeted her in heightened excitement.

Both dolphins swam immediately to the edge, their bodies half out of the water in greeting. Tidy rows of white cone-shaped teeth lined the pink interiors of their long snouts as they whistled and clicked a welcome.

"They look like they're smiling," Mac said in disbelief, eyeing the sharp teeth warily.

Juliet laughed. "Actually, for the most part, they're very good-natured, especially Dolphus." She leaned over to give the adolescent dolphin a rub on the top of his head.

Mac gingerly leaned on the raised lip of the tank and let his hand trail into the water. Poseidon immediately swam over to nuzzle his palm.

"He wants a rub, too," Juliet told Mac softly, her brow puckering in amazement. Poseidon had obviously formed an instant liking for the big human in street clothes, something she'd never seen happen with the occasional strangers who were authorized to visit the tanks.

Mac hesitated, then stretched out his hand to touch the top of the dark gray head bobbing just a few feet from his face.

"Be careful around his blowhole," Juliet cautioned gently. "That area's extremely sensitive."

"A dolphin erogenous zone?" he asked quizzically.

"Not exactly, but close."

Mac grinned and rubbed his hand over the animal's long hard snout. Poseidon clicked slowly as though in pleasure, then snorted through his blowhole as he surged upward to plant a wet kiss on Mac's cheek.

"What the hell?" Mac jerked backward, his cane raised in attack.

"Mac, *don't*!" Juliet grabbed his left arm and held on. Beneath her hand, his muscles tensed into steel bands, and she threw him a beseeching look.

Slowly he relaxed and lowered his arm. His eyes were accusing as he studied her face. "You knew he was going to do that, didn't you?" he asked in a hard voice. The skin of his cheeks had paled under his tan, and his free hand was braced against the lip of the tank.

Juliet flushed. "I had a pretty good idea," she admitted, dropping her hand. She glanced at the rippling surface, where Poseidon had dropped back into the water. "He likes to play."

Mac snorted. "Some play. I could have smashed his head in with this cane." He eyed the black walking stick with an enigmatic expression.

Juliet's own expression sobered. "I know. If I'd known you would react that way, I would have warned you." A trace of anger tinged her words. "Do you always respond like that to a gesture of affection?"

"From a fish; yes," he countered, the color coming back to his cheeks.

"Poseidon's a mammal, not a fish," she retorted tartly. "Even a computer person should know that."

As though summoned by her words, Poseidon broke the surface in a crashing leap and swam over to the side, his curving mouth open slightly as though in a hearty chuckle, his dark eyes filled with interest.

"What's he doing now?" Mac asked gingerly.

"Studying you. He's very curious about people."

"Oh yeah?" Some of the wariness left his eyes, to be replaced by a boyish look of interest.

Juliet nodded. "Dolphins have an intense interest in everything around them. That's why we have to keep varying our test routines so that they don't get bored." She touched the top of the chain-link tank. "If these guys really wanted to leave, they could. But they stay here because they like us, and because they're stimulated by what we do together." She tilted her head in affectionate amusement. "Unlike a lot of humans, dolphins seem to like learning new things."

Mac chuckled. "Have you ever lost any of your test subjects?"

"One, since I've been here, and we deliberately turned him loose. He was a maverick—a gentle maverick, but untrainable."

Mac reminded her of Nemo, Juliet realized with sudden insight. Nemo had been the smartest marine mammal she'd ever encountered—and the most exasperating. No matter how she tried to bend him to her will, he'd resisted, countering her conditioning with a stubborn rebellion that had left her kicking the pier in frustration.

She'd tried all the tricks she knew and some she'd invented, but nothing had worked. Nemo was friendly and gentle—even playfully frisky—when he was left to go his own way. But try to restrict his movements or force him into a planned behavior, and he would refuse. After months of failure, they'd finally released Nemo to the sea, and he'd left them as he'd come. Untamed, powerful and free.

She glanced up at Mac's hard features. No one would ever tame this man. He was as much a maverick as Nemo—and just as difficult to understand.

"Hey, what's wrong? You look . . . funny." Puzzlement replaced the amusement in his eyes.

"I'm just hungry." She held up the rumpled paper sack. "My lunch."

His gaze flickered to the brown bag. "I guess that's my cue to leave, huh?"

He looked so boyishly hurt that Juliet burst out laughing. "Yes, I hate to be watched when I gobble."

It was Mac's turn to laugh. "Okay, I'll take the hint. Besides, I have work to do." He glanced at his watch. "I was on my way back from the cafeteria when I saw you run by, and I wanted to stop over and ask you to take pity on a poor bachelor and have dinner with me tonight." He grinned. "Think of it as a sort of housewarming."

And then what? What happens after dinner? prodded a little voice somewhere in her brain.

Nothing will happen if I don't want it to, she answered with firm conviction. After all, Mac's a gentleman.

She gave him a pert look. "How do you like Mexican food?" she asked suddenly, cocking her head.

Mac looked startled. "In small doses. My stomach's used to fried chicken and grits."

"Tell you what. You bring the wine, and I'll make you the most terrific burritos you've ever had."

Mac looked pleased. "What time?"

Juliet's eyes darted away from his. "It'll have to be fairly late—say eight-thirty," she said with as much nonchalance as she could muster. "I—I have an exercise class tonight."

"Again? You're going to wear yourself out." His voice had lost its teasing lilt, and she hesitated. Something volatile was bottled up behind his civilized facade; she could sense it. But what?

"If that's too late, we could make it another time," she said quickly, eager to avoid explanations.

He hesitated, then reached over to give her a hard, one-armed hug. "No problem. I don't mind eating late as long as you're there with me." He glanced around swiftly, then leaned over to kiss her soundly on the lips.

Grinning devilishly at her stunned look, Mac turned and walked away from her, his steps lopsided but sure as he navigated the slick boards.

"The house is owned by a man named Roger Percival and is listed on his tax returns as rental property. We're trying to track him down now to determine the identity of his current tenant." The admiral's voice was sharp with impatience. "I'm sorry, Mac. I put a rush on it for you, but these things take time when you have to do them the hard way."

Mac leaned against the glass wall of the phone booth outside the convenience store a block from his cottage. "Yeah, I know. I wish I could just go up to the blasted door and pretend I'm taking some kind of survey or something."

Hendricks chuckled. "Sure, and the minute you leave, our pigeon flies."

Mac frowned. "What about Hydra? Anything new there?"

The admiral swore. "I must be getting old, Mac. I meant to tell you first thing. He's received another packet of information—just as explosive as the last one."

Mac added his oath to his superior's. "When?"

"Yesterday."

Sunday. And Saturday night Juliet had met with Peter. Mac gazed out at the sandy beach in front of him without really seeing it.

"There's more."

Mac shifted his weight and closed his eyes. "What else?" he asked tersely, afraid to hear. He was tired, his leg ached, and he wanted a drink.

"According to Hydra's contact, the informant, code name Medusa, is having second thoughts because of a new person on the staff." Hendricks' harsh bark of laughter was without humor. "You, Mac."

"Yeah, I guess."

"Sounds like we were right about Prentice, though. The name Medusa would seem to indicate a woman."

Mac looked down at his loafers. They were covered by a fine layer of sand from the dusty sidewalk. "Maybe," he said curtly. "But she's not the only woman with access to sensitive information. Dr. Feldman has spent a lot of nights working alone. She could easily slip material out with her."

There was a long silence. "Are you saying you think we're on the wrong track with Prentice?" There was an edge to the admiral's voice that brought a rush of heat to Mac's cheeks.

His wide chest lifted in a ragged sigh of defeat. "No, Carter. Cahill's man found out that she paid another two thousand dollars to the hospital. In cash. So the timing seems pretty damn conclusive.''

"What about this Dr. Feldman, then?'' the admiral persisted. "Could they be in it together?''

"Maybe, but I doubt it. What's the motive? I've been over her file a dozen times, and there's nothing there.

"The same goes for Kurtz. Beatty of NIS tells me the guy is Mr. Clean in his personal life. An elder in his church, the president of the P.T.A., a soccer coach. And the kid, Handleman, doesn't have access to the database.''

Hendricks grunted. "So it all comes down to the man named Peter. He's our missing link. If Hydra can identify him as Alexey, we'll have enough to arrest Prentice on suspicion.''

Mac voiced his agreement. "If you get anything more, call Cahill and he'll page me.'' He watched a bright orange jeep containing two burly lifeguards drive slowly along the edge of the water. Beyond the breakers, surfers straddled their boards, and closer to shore a man jogged through the wet sand, head down, legs pumping.

Mac's face tightened. "And, Carter, one more thing.''

"What's that?''

"Tell Cahill not to contact me until morning. I'm off-duty tonight.''

"Oh-ho. Sounds like you've got yourself a heavy date, my friend.''

Mac closed his eyes. "Yeah, something like that.''

"Anyone I know?''

Mac hesitated. "No, no one you know,'' he said, then broke the connection.

Limping heavily, he walked toward the gently sloping fishing pier jutting into the sea. There were only a few people there, and most of them were strolling aimlessly, enjoying the view of the surfers and the cliffs.

Mac stopped at the first empty bench he came to and sat down, smiling at a solemn-faced toddler in a stroller parked a few feet away, a little girl with big black eyes and straight black hair. Her mother and father were engrossed in their fishing, leaning over the railing in total absorption.

Mac leaned back and gazed at the jagged rocks below. The coastline was slowly eroding, sliding into the Pacific inch by inch. Like his resistance to Juliet Prentice.

She'd gotten to him, in spite of the barriers he'd built against involvement. Somehow she'd managed to find a hole in the mesh of his personal armor, enticing him with her lithe body and languorous walk, seducing him with her hidden vulnerability.

He needed to purge himself of Juliet, to free his mind from the endless thoughts of her that kept him trapped on a dizzying merry-go-round of desire and need that was slowly eating away at his peace of mind.

Tomorrow—or the next day at the latest—Naval Intelligence would have Peter's name, and perhaps, if they were lucky, Hydra's positive identification that the man was in fact Alexey.

A friendly judge would issue a writ allowing the house to be bugged, and the rest was inevitable. Juliet would be caught redhanded turning over the information, and Mac's job would be finished.

But tonight was his. His and Juliet's. And he intended to have this one night. No matter what price he had to pay later.

"Right on time." Juliet swung the door wide and stepped back to let Mac enter. As she closed the door behind him, her heart began thumping furiously in her chest. Now that he was here, she was suddenly very nervous.

"This is for you." With a gallant bow and a wicked grin, he presented her with an oval cellophane box with the name of an upscale florist etched in gold on the top.

"Oh, Mac. *Orchids!*" she exclaimed softly, her eyes widening with surprise and pleasure. His lips trembled into a dazed smile. "I've never seen a color like that. It reminds me of...of sunlight."

"It matches your hair," he drawled, lightly touching her shoulder-length tresses with his hand.

Juliet resisted the urge to rub her cheek against that hand just to feel the warmth of his touch.

He stepped back to inspect her from top to toe, his head cocked to one side, his eyes registering open approval. "You look lovely tonight, Juliet. Beautiful."

His husky drawl sent shivers of silent bliss through her body, making her instantly aware of every square inch of skin beneath the satiny texture of her teal blue lounging pajamas.

"You look very...formal," she said with a slight catch in her voice. Formal? The man looked gorgeous, and so sexy she could scarcely stand it.

He was wearing a dark blue three-piece suit with a striped silk tie and a pristine white shirt, and from the top of his expertly barbered head to the tip of his polished hand-sewn loafers, he radiated sophisticated sex appeal.

As though he could read her thoughts, his eyes darkened until they were the color of midnight. "I'd like you to wear the orchid in your hair, Juliet," he said softly, his drawl so husky that she scarcely recognized his voice.

Feeling flustered and excited at the same time, she fumbled with the box, opening the lid at last and taking out the delicate golden blossom. The petals were exquisitely soft and rich with tawny color, while the throat was a deep burgundy red. There was a clear plastic comb fastened to the stem with florist's tape.

Juliet's fingers shook as she tried to attach the blossom behind her ear, but she couldn't seem to get the comb to hold the orchid in place.

"Here, let me." He took the flower from her. "Hold this," he ordered, handing her his cane.

The ornate silver handle was warm from his hand and smooth against her palm, and the cane itself was surprisingly heavy, as though weighted at one end.

Mac's fingers threaded through her hair, his knuckles brushing against her cheek as he tucked the flower behind her ear.

His face was taut with concentration, each chiseled line only adding to his attractiveness. "A man's character is written on his face," Justin used to say, and Juliet believed him.

Mac's character was one of courage and kindness; she could see it. But there were secrets there, as well, secrets that had left deep lines but no clue to their origin—or their meaning. Juliet's curiosity was heightened, even as her sympathy was stirred. Mac had been through hell of some kind and emerged scarred but intact.

"There. You just have to know how," he muttered with smug satisfaction, and Juliet giggled.

"Are you saying you've done this before?" she teased, tilting her head to gaze up at him flirtatiously. One velvet soft petal rested against her temple, making her feel as delicate and cosseted as a South Seas princess.

Mac flushed and retrieved his cane, his fingers brushing over hers. A muscle twitched along the column of his throat as he shook his head. "This is the first time."

He stared down into her eyes, an arrested look tightening his face. Juliet's flirtatious grin faltered as the full impact of his gaze hit her.

It was as though he were memorizing her features one by one, his eyes becoming more turbulent with each second that passed.

Juliet clasped her hands tightly in front of her and held her breath. He was beginning to frighten her, and she didn't even know why.

And then, just when she knew she would have to move, to distance herself from that scorching gaze, Mac blinked, and the intensity left his face.

"Did the kid from the liquor store deliver the champagne?" he asked, glancing around the room.

Juliet pointed toward the ice bucket sitting next to two fluted glasses on a small rattan end table by the sofa. "Yes, about twenty minutes ago." She smiled ruefully. "I haven't had Dom Perignon since my sixteenth birthday." She walked over to the table and picked up a folded linen towel. Wrapping the bottle in the towel, she extended it toward Mac.

He limped over and took the bottle from her hand, opening it so deftly that he didn't spill a drop. He filled both glasses and replaced the bottle in the bucket. He handed one glass to Juliet and kept the other one for himself.

"To you," he murmured in a deeply resonant voice that sent shivers up Juliet's spine.

"And to you," she answered softly, looking into his eyes. She'd had second thoughts about this evening all day, and twice she'd decided to cancel, only to change her mind in the next breath. Now she was glad she'd decided to risk the time alone with him.

Mac waited until she tasted her champagne, then lifted his glass to her as though in a private toast before taking a sip.

Juliet stood motionless, sipping the dry champagne, mesmerized by his closeness. The skin stretching over his strong throat was so dark it appeared copper next to his crisp white shirt, and there was a tiny nick at the edge of his jaw, as though he'd cut himself shaving.

All of a sudden Juliet found herself wanting to press her lips against that tiny cut, healing him with the surging love she didn't want to feel.

"I had a feeling that champagne wasn't exactly the most appropriate beverage to go with—what did you call them? Burritos?" Mac told her with dry humor. "But I thought, what the hell, it couldn't hurt." His eyes flashed with reckless enjoyment, and Juliet felt excitement kindle deep inside her.

"'What the hell,'" she parroted impulsively, lifting her glass. She was swimming in mine-salted waters, she knew, but she'd always been a strong swimmer. If she got in over her head, she'd just paddle furiously toward shore.

Mac's mouth lifted at the corners, and his whole face seemed to relax. It was as though her carefree attitude had been contagious, and Juliet felt a heady surge of pride.

He needed to relax more often. He needed to have more fun, and then maybe some of the tension in his face would ease.

"Why don't we sit down?" she suggested. She took the chair, leaving the couch for Mac. He sat down and propped his cane against the rattan frame.

"That's a beautiful cane," Juliet told him admiringly. "It looks old."

"It is. It was a gift from King George the Third to Randolph Roarke, my great-great-et cetera grandfather in appreciation of his services as a, shall we say, privateer, when Virginia was still a colony." He picked up the cane and handed it to her.

Juliet's eyes sparkled with interest as she lightly touched the faint engraving. The spidery script spelled out the year 1767. "What happened to this illustrious ancestor of yours?" she asked curiously, handing back the cane.

Mac's lips turned down at the edges, as though he were trying hard not to smile. "The poor man was hanged for reasons that are never discussed in polite company."

Juliet burst out laughing, and Mac grinned. "Promise you won't tell on me."

"Scout's honor," she said, holding up her hand. "I'm as silent as a clam." She could see a tiny muscle moving in his throat, as though he'd been oddly affected by her silliness.

An awkward silence fell over the room, intensifying the muted sound of the surf pounding eighty feet below the cottage. In the distance, someone was playing Mozart, and nearby, a car engine roared to life.

Inside the small cottage, the atmosphere changed as the silence lengthened. The very air in the room felt charged with extra electrons, as though a storm were building overhead, but the sky was clear, and the air outside was still.

Juliet sneaked a peek at Mac. He was staring down at the liquid in his glass, his expression frozen, as though he were wrestling with some thorny problem. Tension radiated from the taut set of his shoulders, and his jaw was clenched.

He caught her eyes on him and smiled as he leaned back against the down-filled cushions. "Have you heard from Rex?" He sounded interested, even concerned, and Juliet relaxed. It must have been her imagination, or even a trick of the light, that had given the impression that Mac was fighting some powerful internal battle.

"No. I tried calling again, but the switchboard said he wasn't accepting calls." Juliet looked down at her hands, which were clasped together in her lap. "I have a feeling he's . . . punishing me."

"More likely he's punishing himself for driving too damn fast on a slippery road, Juliet. He's paying the price for his own stupidity, and that's a hard thing to face." He drained his glass and reached for the bottle. "I've been there myself."

"You're talking about your leg, aren't you?" she asked softly, lifting her eyes to search his face.

"Yeah. I tried to blame a hell of a lot of people before I finally realized I was the one who smashed up my life." He refilled her glass as she stared at him in surprise.

"What happened?"

"I thought I knew better than my superiors and insisted on doing things my way. I got myself captured because of it," he said harshly, replacing the bottle in the bucket with a solid thump. He picked up his glass and drank.

"You were captured? By the Vietcong?"

His hesitation was barely noticeable. "I was captured, yes. Fortunately, I...escaped." His lips quirked, as though in amusement at some bitter private joke. "Sorry. I didn't mean to tell you that. It's not...relevant." He grimaced. "How'd we get on this depressing subject, anyway?"

"You were trying to make me feel better about Rex," she said with a faint smile that belied the sudden lump in her throat. With a hand that trembled, she reached out to touch his arm. She could feel his muscles contract, hardening under her fingertips.

"It's nice to have someone who understands, someone to talk to when things pile up." She sighed. "Life can get very... complicated, sometimes."

"So uncomplicate it. It's never too late to change direction, Juliet." He smiled only with his lips.

"I wish I could, but change isn't possible right now. I have too many...obligations." She dropped her hand from his arm and reached for her glass. Her fingers wrapped tightly around the fragile stem, as if to remind her of the delicate line she had to walk.

Mac's head came up slowly, and his eyes lifted to hers. His expression grew cold. "Change is always possible," he said, his words dropping flat and hard between them, "but you need to make the choice."

For an instant Juliet felt disoriented, as though she were caught in an airless space between reality and fantasy. Even the familiar furnishings that surrounded her seemed alien, as though she somehow didn't belong here any longer. She frowned in puzzlement. "I don't know what you mean. Are you talking about Rex?"

Mac ran his thumb around the rim of his glass. "I'm talking about you. Your life." He hesitated, then met her puzzled gaze squarely. "I care what happens to you."

He was telling the truth. Juliet could feel it deep inside. He was also worried about her. She could see the concern etched into his bronzed face.

Her soul soared. He cares about me, she told herself in growing wonder. Me. Juliet.

She could feel her lips soften into a smile. The joy of being a woman, protected and desired by a supremely masculine man, was more intoxicating than the premium champagne Mac had brought.

For tonight she was the one being cared for. For a few hours she could discard her tough shell and be the intensely feminine woman hidden inside the pragmatic scientist. With Mac, she could be herself.

"I'm glad you suggested dinner," she told him with open sincerity. "I needed a night like this."

Dusky color ran along his jaw and into his cheeks, and Juliet had the strongest feeling that he was going to kiss her. Her heart began to pound in delicious anticipation, but the moment passed in silence, and the web of intimacy drawing them together slowly dissolved into the silence.

Mac took a healthy gulp of champagne and glanced toward the kitchen. "Something smells awful good out there," he said.

Juliet felt her rosy glow wobble slightly as she forced a smile and stood up. "If that isn't a hint, I don't know what is. Come on. It's all ready. You can pour us some more champagne while I toss the salad."

Mac's face tightened as he struggled out of the deep cushions and pushed himself to his feet. "Sounds like a deal. Tonight I'm all yours," he drawled with lazy meaning.

Chapter 9

You're one great cook, Juliet. Is there anything you can't do?'' Mac's eyes met hers over the flickering tapers in the middle of the table.

"Actually, I'm practically perfect," she countered with a smile. "Except when it comes to that computer of yours. I don't think I'll ever understand how it works."

"No? What's the problem?"

Juliet kept her smile in place. "No problem. I just . . . lost a file. Remember how I told you it would do that to me?"

"Vaguely." Mac pushed his empty plate away and rested his elbows on the glass tabletop.

"Well, is there any way to get it back? Once it's been deleted, I mean?" She played with her napkin, unable to look at him. She had to know.

"Actually, there is, but that's a little beyond my skills. I could probably find someone to help you, though." His drawl was a silky thread of sound, without inflection, and very quiet. "Was it anything important?"

Juliet forced a laugh. "No, not really." Relief made her want to giggle. She'd deleted her personal file, but she'd been terrified that it wasn't really gone. "I was just...wondering, that's all."

"Well, now you know." Mac leaned back and flexed his shoulders, stretching the tightly woven worsted of his vest across his lean torso.

Juliet's eyes lowered to the V where the striped tie disappeared beneath the wool. All during dinner she'd been visualizing that broad chest beneath the conservative suit exposed and naked and gleaming in the candlelight.

And over dessert she'd caught herself remembering what it had been like to run her fingers over that powerful body from head to toe, exploring the rugged lines and craggy angles inch by inch.

She dropped her eyes to her plate. She was hooked on the man, totally and completely. Once they'd made love, her defenses had crumbled, blasted away by the force of their shared passion.

Her throat tightened convulsively as she loosened his tie and unbuttoned his collar. His finger skimmed the neckline of the shirt, pulling the material away from his muscular neck. Desire rocketed through her, and she fought down an urge to press a kiss against that strong brown throat.

She took a drink of water and forced her mind into safer channels. "So you think our new system will arrive soon."

"In about a month, if everything goes as planned."

Juliet frowned. "That sounds like a contradiction in terms."

"It does?"

"Sure. I doubt that the government really plans *anything*. Or, if there really is a person with the big picture, he's on an extended vacation." She grimaced. "In the five years I've worked for the NRC, nothing has ever gone as planned."

"Come on," Mac said with a wry grin. "Things must go right occasionally."

Juliet pretended to ponder. "Hmm, let's see. Two years ago we had a serious breach of security, and the NIS was right on top of it."

An alert look of interest replaced the lazy gleam in his eyes. "Oh yeah? That sounds intriguing."

A wicked grin spread over Juliet's delicate features. "It was really exciting, I have to admit." She tilted her head to the side and gave him a conspiratorial look. "Promise you won't tell?"

Mac assumed a solemn stare. "Cross my heart." As he reinforced the words with the appropriate gesture, Juliet's gaze fastened on the lean tautness of his belly beneath the navy blue fabric. The dark material seemed to add several inches to his broad chest, making him appear even larger than he was.

Juliet leaned closer until the candle flame warmed her skin. "It was the middle of winter, and high tide was about four in the morning. The next day, when Felicity and I arrived at the tanks to feed the dolphins, we discovered that we had an extra mouth to fill."

Mac frowned. "Another dolphin?"

"Yes. A male. Gorgeous fellow, he was. He was in with the females." Her eyes sparkled. "He was very persistent. We tried everything to get him to leave, but he had, um, romance on his mind and was determined to stay."

"Good man," Mac muttered, and Juliet threw him a haughty look.

"Not exactly. You can imagine what a stir it caused in our little dolphin community to have a randy male hanging around."

Mac chuckled. "So what did you do?"

"What else? We called security, and they called NIS. You should have seen these big burly types trying to figure out how to remove six hundred pounds of slippery, determined dolphin."

Mac was openly laughing, and Juliet felt warm all over. He seemed like a different person when he laughed like that. Warm and boyish and devastatingly attractive.

"We finally called Sea World, and they took our Lothario off to a new home." She paused, then added gleefully, "The last I heard, he'd fathered four babies."

Mac shook his head. "That's not a true story," he drawled with an accusing look. "You made it up."

Juliet shook her head. "It's true." She laughed at the look of disbelief on his face. As she watched, his expression slowly changed until he was looking at her with naked hunger, Shining in his eyes. His gaze bored into her, asking questions she wasn't ready to answer.

"How about coffee?" she asked in a strangled voice. "It's ready." Abruptly she stood up, painfully banging her knee against the table leg in her haste.

"Coffee's fine." His drawl gave the polite words an intimate twist that raised bumps of excitement on her skin.

"Do you mind if I take off my coat?" he asked politely as she reached into the cabinet for the cups.

"Of course not." Juliet began to feel overheated, and she glanced toward the window over the sink. Would he think she was crazy if she opened it? Just because it was in the low fifties outside didn't mean they shouldn't have fresh air.

Her back to the table, she heard the telltale click of Mac's knee brace as he stood up. She heard the rustle of fabric against fabric, and then the scrape of chair legs against the terra-cotta floor as he pushed the chair back under the table.

She blinked and tried to concentrate on her task, but the glass pot jerked suddenly, and she spilled coffee on the counter. Hoping Mac hadn't noticed, she grabbed a towel and mopped up the mess. It was hard to think about coffee when her mind was filled with a tawny gold image of his naked body, hard and fit and ready for her.

"Forget the coffee." The husky command was next to her ear, and his hand brushed against her shoulder as he turned her to face him. "I don't want to wait any longer." He laid his cane on the counter and pulled her hard against him.

His arms encircled her, pulling her onto her toes and trapping her against his chest. She could feel the tiled edge of the counter pressing into her spine as he held her captive, his body molded against hers.

His lips claimed hers, hot and possessive and captivatingly firm, branding her with a primitive force that was impossible to resist.

It was a long, searching, tender kiss, one that spread warmth all through her. He raised his head and looked deeply into her eyes, as though seeking her approval, and then, with a husky groan, his mouth took hers again. His lips had the spicy taste of her homemade salsa, tangy and hot.

Juliet returned his kiss eagerly, enraptured by the driving need she could feel in him. Her body strained against him, her muscles taut, yet feeling like warm elastic beneath her skin.

Her hands pushed upward, twining against his neck as she clung to him, wanting the delicious pleasure to go on and on.

Growling deep in his throat, Mac broke off the kiss and buried his face in the curve of her neck. She could feel his warm, moist breath on her skin as he struggled to contain his breathing.

"I promised myself I wouldn't rush you tonight," he whispered against her ear. "I don't want you running away from me."

Juliet felt him shudder as he released his tight grip on her, allowing her to slide down his body until her feet rested on the tile.

His body reacted immediately, bulging hard against her midriff, and Juliet held her breath. Would he take her here? Now? In the middle of her kitchen?

It was obvious that he wanted her.

Their eyes locked, and Juliet felt as though she were being pulled inside his soul. His need was hers, his desire a passionate call to the very essence of her femininity.

Juliet felt smothered by that look and closed her eyes. She pressed her cheek against his broad chest, crushing the orchid against her temple. She could hear his heart pounding beneath the soft material of his vest, surging with the same savage strength as the waves crashing against the cliffs outside her window.

Tonight she wanted to be with Mac, to be held in his arms, to be loved for herself alone.

For so long she'd postponed her own needs in order to care for those she loved. For so long she'd been strong and practical and sensible.

Just once, for tonight, she wanted to feel young and desirable and carefree. One more time, she wanted to make love with the man she loved. One more time, she wanted to see his eyes glow just for her, as though he really cared. She didn't care whether he was acting or not. It didn't matter. Not if she could have him one last time all to herself.

"Maybe I want you to rush me," she murmured against his shoulder. "Maybe I like that fierce side of your nature."

Moving slowly, she took a sliding step backward and reached up to remove the orchid from her hair. Her eyes locked with his as she lifted the fragile blossom to her lips and kissed the ruby throat. Mac watched intently, mesmerized by the provocatively inviting picture she made.

She was different tonight. Softer, and heartbreakingly beautiful, especially with the candlelight gleaming in her eyes, yet there was a reckless air about her that had his blood steaming.

She was ready for him tonight. No, she was *eager* for him tonight, a lovely, cuddly kitten with the soul of a wildcat, lying in wait just for him. Mac had never been so aroused by a woman in his life.

His heart began to pound in his ears, and his breath came harder and harder as he watched her remove the pins from her hair. The honey-drenched thickness drifted down around her face like a satin-spun cloud, caressing her dewy cheeks with whisper-soft waves of sunny color.

Mac reached out for her, needing to feel her pressed against him. His hands roamed over her back, tracing the curving lines of her lithe body in absorbed fascination. The sleek material of her top was cool and slippery under his palms, mimicking the satin smoothness of the tanned skin beneath.

Juliet moved against him, molding herself against him, sliding her arms over his shoulders and linking her hands at the back of his neck.

Mac pressed his face into her thick hair, breathing deeply of its flowery scent. He closed his eyes and rubbed his cheek against hers, careful not to abrade her delicate skin. She was so fragile, so intensely feminine, that he was afraid to unleash the full extent of his need.

He pressed a kiss against her temple, feeling her tremble as his lips grazed her skin, and he felt his restraint slipping. He crushed her to him, raining kisses on her eyes, her cheeks, her lips.

He raised his head and gave her a searching look. His eyes were half closed, his face softened with need. "You're so beautiful, so very beautiful." His voice was a husky river of sound, flowing over the words of praise in a lazy swell. "I want you so damn much."

Tumbling feelings cascaded through Juliet's straining body, brushing her cheeks with pink and widening her eyes, which glowed with the inner fire of her desire.

"I...oh, Mac, I want you, too," she whispered in desperation, clutching his neck with shaking fingers. All her doubts were gone. Nothing mattered but Mac, and the delicious things he was doing to her.

"Baby," he murmured in his soft drawl, tracing her lips with a blunt forefinger. "I need you."

Juliet felt the tears pressing against her lids. The three words seemed wrenched from him, and although they weren't the words she longed to hear, they were enough.

"Then what are we waiting for?" she asked in a sultry voice, boldly handing him his cane.

Mac's eyes glittered in the dim light as he slipped his arm around her shoulder. "I wish I could sweep you off your feet and carry you to your bed."

"You've already swept me off my feet," she answered with a soft look. "I don't think I can take much more."

Mac's husky laugh rumbled along the hall as they made their way to her room. The bedside lamp was lit, casting a circle of light next to the bed, and the curtains were drawn.

He held her hand as he led her to the bed and tossed his cane onto the foot of the mattress. "Tonight you're mine," he drawled in a throaty growl, pulling her into his arms. "Only mine."

Juliet trembled with the intensity of his words, thrilling to the savage possessiveness underlying his slurring drawl.

"And you're mine," she whispered through lips that had gone dry with desire.

"Yes," he hissed against her hair, his body quickening into an ache of arousal.

Urgently he began to trail kisses along her temple, feathering past her cheeks to her lips. She smiled under his soft kiss, her lips brushing his, and his blood ignited. His fingers tangled in her long hair as his lips began devouring hers. His tongue probed her mouth, seeking, plundering, tasting the nectar that was so sweetly hers.

Blood pounding in his temples, he poured the days and nights of longing for her into this kiss, feeling the heat rising in him, filling him, urging him toward the edge of his control.

She moaned softly, her chest rising and falling as though she couldn't breathe, and he eased his grip long enough to slip his hands beneath the loosely draped top. Her skin was warm and soft, covering the gentle curve of her waist with bewitching firmness.

She was a golden dream, an enchantress from the sea, a mystical creature fashioned from his hungry soul. She was everything he'd ever wanted in a woman—warm and loving, and full of life and fun. Her bubbling laughter filled his heart with hope; her sparkling eyes erased the ugly pictures from his past; her perfect body soothed the imperfections of his own.

He couldn't wait. He had to see her. Now. Ending the kiss, Mac braced himself on his good leg and eased away from her in order to pull the pajama top over her head in one quick movement.

Mac's eyes flowed over her exposed skin, a reverent smile creasing his hard cheeks. Her bra was a tiny scrap of flesh-colored lace, barely covering the swell of her firm white breasts. His hand trembled as he released the clasp and slid the silky material over her shoulders.

Juliet felt herself sinking deeper and deeper into a warm pink cloud of euphoria as Mac groaned and leaned down to trail kisses along the curving tan line above her breasts. He anointed first one nipple and then the other with moist kisses. The heat of desire pushed the tiny buds into stiffened points, and tendrils of aching need spread along her midriff.

His big hands circled her waist, pushing beneath the elastic waistband of her pajama pants. His eyes glittered with blue fire as he slid the cool satin over her hips and down her thighs.

The material drifted to the floor, and Mac stood motionless, his hands on her waist. His fingers pressed intimately against her skin, the tips nearly meeting at her spine, and she shivered, longing to feel those callused fingers stroking her thighs.

"You're unbelievable," he said in a thickened voice. "No wonder I can't think straight when I'm around you." His hands lingered on the curve of her hips before dipping into the waistband of her panties. Swiftly, the silk underwear joined the shimmering puddle of satin at her feet.

Juliet kicked off her shoes and stepped out of the pajama pants. She stood tall and proud before him, bathing in the glowing look of homage she could see warming his eyes.

Her lashes dipped modestly in a sultry smile spread over her face. Excitement built to a fever pitch inside her as she reached for his tie. Even with her help, it took him longer to get undressed, and Juliet watched impatiently as he peeled off his shirt and shed the rest of his clothes.

Together, they toppled over onto the mattress, and Mac's body twisted over hers. The curling mat of hair on his chest teased her breasts as he gazed down at her, resting his weight on his elbows, trapping her beneath him.

She could feel him move, could hear the sound of metal jangling against the floor as he dropped his brace, and then he was pulling her hard against him, rolling them both to the middle of the bed, his chest crushed against her breasts, his legs entwined with hers.

His massive thighs pressed against the curve of hers, bringing a rush of heat to every inch of her skin as his body swelled with powerful arousal.

Juliet writhed against him, frantic to feel him inside her. But Mac held her down, his face pressed against the curve of her neck, his lips anointing her collarbone with sizzling heat, moving lower to the shadowed hollow between her breasts.

His breath was hot against her skin, fanning a flame of need as he pressed kisses over her midriff and along the slight swell of her belly. His tongue curled around her navel, making her feverish with desire.

"Now," she begged. "Take me now."

"Shh," he whispered, moving lower, his lips trailing kisses along the tender skin of her thighs. Juliet felt as though she were filled with surging white heat, achingly near to bursting.

And then he buried his face between her thighs, kissing her so exquisitely that she whimpered with need.

"Baby," he murmured against the velvet delta beneath his lips. "My sweet Juliet."

Juliet dug her fingers into his shoulders pulling him toward her, arching upward to find him hard and willing.

Their voices mingled in unison as they gasped at the swift joining, their bodies eagerly meeting, their muscles straining, their breathing hissing in urgent chorus. The music of the surf surged around them, echoing the pulsating rhythm of their need.

Juliet went perfectly still, savoring the exquisite pleasure of the moment, but his body began to move against hers, urging her into a slow, undulating rhythm, that made her writhe in frustrated ecstasy. She wanted the sweet pleasure to last forever.

Suddenly, Mac groaned, the sound a feral growl deep in his throat, and his eyes grew dark and savage. His face tightened with urgency, and the gentle motion of his hips turned into a driving, surging rhythm, that ignited an explosion of desperate tension deep inside her.

A screaming ache tore through her, dampening her body and tightening her muscles until she couldn't bear the exquisite pain another instant. Totally out of control, she sank her teeth into his shoulder, sobbing out his name.

Mac groaned again, and his body heaved in one last desperate thrust, tipping Juliet over into a world of purest, deepest sensation.

Nothing mattered but this sweet, swirling rapture. It was blissful fulfillment, this joy that cushioned her. And Mac had taken her there.

Mac moved to lie on his side, his body still joined with hers. He cradled her against him and Juliet could smell the passion-born sweat burnishing his skin. The hair on his chest was matted in tight damp ringlets around his nipples, and a thin trickle of moisture bisected the broad expanse.

He lay with his eyes closed, his lips slightly parted, the lines of his face relaxed. His large hand lazily stroked the curve of her spine, gentling the tremors of lingering passion.

One heavy thigh was thrown over hers, and she could feel the rough texture of the hair covering his long legs.

She had never felt so complete, so contented. She wanted to stay in his arms forever, but that could never be. This was stolen time, time belonging to them alone.

She sighed, and Mac opened his eyes. For an instant she thought she could see agony in his sapphire gaze, but in the next instant his expression changed, and he was smiling. "Are you all right?" he asked in gentle concern, smoothing damp tendrils of honey-colored hair away from her cheek.

"I'm wonderful," she whispered with a smile in her voice. "Wonderful."

"I'll say," he drawled, a crooked grin slashing his cheeks with intimate humor.

Juliet giggled and slapped his arm with a gentle hand. "You're impossible."

"And you're a little hellcat," he said with a rueful glance at his shoulder.

Juliet paled. "Did I do that?" she asked in a shaky voice as she pressed her fingers to the already darkening bruise.

"Must have. I don't see anyone else here."

Juliet started to apologize, but her apology was swallowed by his kiss. His lips were hard on hers, but his hold was gentle. Like Mac himself, she thought in a daze of happiness. Hard and gentle, rough and smooth, remote and passionate.

The kiss ended, and he cradled her against his chest. She lay basking in the warmth of his body, listening to the comforting sound of his quiet breathing.

His chest rose and fell beneath her ear in regular cadence, moving in tandem with the beat of his heart and the pounding of the surf.

"Stay here tonight," she whispered, holding her breath.

"If you want me," he answered in a deep rumble, bringing a contented smile to her face.

"I want you."

She could feel a deep sigh whisper from him as he shifted to a more comfortable position. She reached down to pull the comforter over them.

The sound of his cane clattering to the floor startled her, and she could feel him stiffen instantly. "It's just that sexy cane of yours," she teased, covering their damp bodies with the thick cotton. "I think it rolled under the bed."

His smile was drowsy as he nodded and pulled her down next to him. "We'll worry about that tomorrow." He reached over to switch off the lamp.

Diffused light from the street lamp outside streamed through the coarse drapes covering the window, patterning the mat with an elongated rectangle.

Juliet smiled and snuggled down next to Mac. She didn't intend to sleep. She had less than eight hours to spend alone with the man she loved, and she wasn't going to waste a second.

Mac stared at the ceiling, his eyes stinging with tiredness. Juliet was curled up next to him, her back pressing against his side, her cheek resting on his arm.

Her breathing was a soft whisper in the dark room, her warmth a tangible reminder of his dangerous indiscretion. He shouldn't be here with her, in her bed, defenseless. The risk was all too real.

Mac scowled as his leg began to cramp, and he slowly stretched, easing the tightness. Most nights he wrapped his knee in a heating pad to ease the throbbing muscles. But tonight the pain was worth it. Just to have Juliet in his arms was worth any price.

He rubbed the weariness from his stubbled cheeks and slowly turned his head toward the corner of the room where he'd glimpsed her closed briefcase resting on an old-fashioned metal trunk.

In the hazy gray light, the trunk was a dark square against the pale wall. Mac estimated that only ten feet or so separated him from the briefcase. He had only to strap on his brace and cross the room, and he would have the answers he needed.

But he couldn't do it. In the first place, he didn't have a search warrant, and he didn't dare compromise the case. And in the second place, he didn't really want to know.

The truth was a deadly twisting snake, ready to sink its fangs into him, killing the glorious fantasy of Juliet he carried in his head.

It was worse now. Now that he'd made love to her, he wanted her even more. His need for her went to the bone, writhing inside him in a curling spiral of naked desire that had him lying there fully aroused once more.

Mac's face twisted in derision. He'd done it again. He'd allowed himself to care, and his body would carry the memory of hers for the rest of his life.

Frustration churned inside him as he turned his head and buried his face in the fragrant silk of her hair. For the first time since he'd found out he would keep his leg, he wanted to cry.

The brightly lighted bus station was nearly empty. Fluorescent tubes hissed overhead as the gray-haired security guard chatted with a thin, tired-looking woman behind the ticket window.

A man in casual clothes entered by the side door and stood blinking in the light. The guard broke off his conversation to glance at the newcomer. The man smiled and gestured toward the coffee machine, and the guard relaxed.

The tourist walked to the coffee machine and inserted his money. He stood sipping, reading a brightly colored brochure that detailed San Diego's nightlife.

He finished his coffee, glanced at the clock over the ticket window and strolled over to the bank of pay phones at the rear of the station.

He inserted a quarter and punched out a number.

"It's Dimitri," he murmured against the receiver when Alexey answered on the first ring. "Medusa wants to quit."

"Terminate her. Immediately."

The pleasant-faced tourist with the cold eyes hung up without saying another word. His orders were clear.

Juliet awakened to the sound of heavy breathing. She stretched languidly, wincing at the unfamiliar aches in her muscles. She was sore inside and out, indelibly branded by Mac's turbulent lovemaking. She felt gloriously rested and happy to be alive.

The first fingers of dawn were pushing away the gray as a mockingbird began serenading the new day from his home in a nearby tree. She was lying on her side, her knees pulled to her chest. Part of her was cold, but a delicious warmth blanketed her back.

Mac.

He was still here, asleep next to her. It was his breathing she could hear sighing into the awakening dawn.

She stiffened, then glanced at the clock. It was a few minutes after five. In spite of her resolve, she'd fallen asleep.

Slowly she inched across the mattress until she could turn over without disturbing Mac. He was lying on his back, one arm flung out to the side, the other resting on his left thigh. The comforter lay bunched around his knees, as though he'd kicked it off in the night, and his skin seemed very dark against the pale yellow sheet.

Juliet's eyes trailed down his body, pausing at his loins for a heart-stopping moment before skipping downward to his misshapen knee. Scars crisscrossed his skin, visible even in the dim light. His legs and hips were much lighter than the rest of his body, as though he didn't expose that part of him to the sun.

Juliet felt a surge of pity as she remembered the taut look of vulnerability on his face as he'd removed his brace in her presence for the first time. He'd been worried about her reaction. She'd seen it in his eyes.

Mac sighed in his sleep, and his face twisted as though in pain. A thin film of sweat covered his brow, and he stirred restlessly against the rumpled pillow.

Juliet bit her lip. Should she wake him? Or let him sleep? She glanced at the clock again. In less than half an hour she had to get up or risk being late to work.

Rising onto her elbow, she gazed down into his face. He looked tired, more tired than he'd looked last night after they made love, as though his slumber had been anything but restful, and dark red stubble roughened his cheeks, giving him a slightly dangerous look that she found oddly appealing.

In the growing light she studied his taut features. There was strength in the chiseled planes of his face, determination in the jutting hardness of his jaw, and a boyish charm in the thick crescent lashes resting on his tanned cheeks. But it was the sensitive curve to his mouth that she loved most.

She could still feel those soft lips pressing against hers. With butterfly gentleness she traced the line of his mouth with her finger, smiling as his lips parted, then curved into a sighing smile.

Juliet became bolder, exploring his body with her eyes and her hands. He was sculptured muscle and steel sinew, bronzed by the sun and forged from adversity.

She inched closer, her eyes studying the white network of scars. How it must have hurt, that terrible injury that left him partially crippled. Juliet dipped her head and kissed the puckered flesh, her lips lingering on his warm skin.

Mac sighed, and she jerked away, her heart pounding. His lashes fluttered, and he opened his eyes. His body stiffened instantly, and he stared at her in dark suspicion before the sleep left his eyes.

"Good morning," she whispered, loving the drowsy look of wary delight on his face when she leaned over to brush her lips over his.

Mac cleared his throat and bunched the pillow beneath his head. "Good morning." He reached out to touch her cheek. "What time is it?"

"A little past five."

His lashes drooped, then lifted to expose a roguish gleam. "What time do you have to get up?"

From the corner of her eye Juliet could see his body begin to stir. Her pulse accelerated until the blood was galloping through her veins at a frantic pace.

"Right now," she said with a teasing smile playing over her lips.

"Like hell," Mac muttered, hauling her against his chest. Juliet giggled and pretended to struggle. "Be still, woman," he drawled with morning huskiness, "and tell me how much time we have."

Juliet felt suffused in warmth. "Twenty minutes," she whispered, burrowing her face into the warm hollow of his shoulder.

The purpling teeth marks were visible remnants of their passion, reminding her of the soaring rapture he'd given her, and she dropped a kiss to the spot.

Mac groaned and rolled over, pressing her into the hard mattress. "Let's not waste any time, then," he murmured against her lips.

Juliet sighed and clung to him in helpless rapture. She could feel his body harden against hers, throbbing eagerly. Her thighs opened in welcome, but Mac held back, his hands moving gently over her body, stroking, searching, exciting her nerve endings in a slow massage of adoration.

Juliet could feel her need building with each skillful stroke of his hand. She twisted her head on the pillow, lost in the delightful sensations buffeting her. Her body thrashed beneath him, begging for him to fill the delicious ache growing deep inside her.

"Easy, baby," he whispered, pressing a kiss to her softly moaning lips. "I want to make it right for you."

He began to kiss her then, worshiping her body with his mouth. Juliet writhed in helpless pleasure, feeling her body come alive inch by inch as he loved her.

Through passion-dimmed eyes, Juliet devoured him, loving the coarse thickness of his hair, adoring the powerful slant of his naked shoulders as he buried his face in the delta of her thighs.

She could hardly breathe for the wanting building deep inside. She whispered his name, her voice emerging from her parted lips as more of a sob than a plea.

Mac stiffened, then groaned as he moved to make them one.

As Juliet was lifted on the crest of a soaring wave, she heard the echo of her sobbing cry. She had called him Roarke.

Chapter 10

Something's wrong with Bubbles." Juliet leaned over Greg's shoulder to study the dolphin's eyes. There was a suggestion of a dull glaze over the dark brown irises, giving the female an odd expression of unhappiness. As Juliet and Greg watched, she rolled over and began swimming slowly around the tank, clicking loudly in a random pattern Juliet had never heard before.

Greg tossed the last mackerel into Lady's waiting mouth and swished out the bucket with bay water. "She seemed fine when I started feeding them," he said with a worried frown.

Juliet pursed her lips in thought. "Maybe it's indigestion." She glanced sharply at Greg. "You checked the fish for spoilage?"

Her assistant looked hurt. "Of course I did. Just like I always do. It was fine." He hesitated. "We're out of vitamins, though."

"I thought there was nearly a week's supply."

Greg shrugged. "The bottle was empty."

"Oh, terrific." Juliet sighed. "How did that happen?"

"Beats me." Greg scratched his head, his bony fingers raking the coarse hair into spiked clumps.

Juliet stood up and rested her hands on her hips. Only three hours ago she'd awakened from a wonderful sleep, her back pressed against Mac's warmth, her body sated and throbbing with a delicious ache. It was hard to concentrate on a minor distraction when she was purring inside.

Greg mistook her preoccupied look for one of annoyance, and he gave her a grin of commiseration. "Maybe you and I should have called in sick this morning, too."

Juliet laughed, hugging her secret to her like a warm pillow. "Maybe we should have," she said with a wry grin as she glanced down at the dial of her diver's watch. It was nearly eight o'clock, time for the testing to begin.

Felicity was at home, nursing a case of the flu, and Fred, reluctant to work with an unfamiliar partner, had assigned Juliet and Greg to work with the females in the morning and the males in the afternoon.

"You'll have to drive over to supply and get some more tablets," she told Greg with a grimace. "We can't change procedure. Otherwise the results could be suspect." She grinned. "Besides, the delay might give Bubbles a chance to get over her sulks."

Greg nodded and began loping down the pier. "Back in twenty minutes," he called over his shoulder, and Juliet waved in acknowledgment.

Nothing could upset her this morning, not even an annoying delay. The day was too beautiful. And she was in love. Wonderfully, gloriously in love.

"Time to play, ladies," Juliet called to the two animals as she slipped out of her sneakers and dropped over the lip into the tank.

The water was cold, chilling the skin of her exposed hands and feet, and her face tingled as the sudden change of temperature brought a rush of blood to her cheeks. But not even the bracing cold could spoil the warm glow of contentment that had cocooned her from the moment she'd left Mac's arms.

A smile curved her lips as she floated on her back and watched the popcorn clouds above her head. The sky was a brilliant blue, and the sun was warm on her face.

The choppy waves lifted her gently as she turned her head and gazed toward the shore. A flash of red at the window of her office caught her eye, and she squinted against the sun, her smile broadening as she recognized Mac's massive shoulders and broad chest.

Just a few hours ago she'd pillowed her head on that hard chest. Her fingers had stroked the soft chestnut hair that was now hidden beneath the cashmere of his V-necked sweater. Beneath her thighs she'd felt the latent power of those long legs now sheathed in faded denim.

Excitement swept over her. They'd come to work separately, and they would go home separately, but after work they would be together.

Their time was so short. Soon Mac would be finished with his work, and then he would be gone. It would be hard to continue a long distance relationship, maybe even impossible, but Juliet was determined to give it a try. She couldn't let him go without a fight.

Mac hadn't said anything to indicate how he felt about that, but she was filled with optimism. How could he have made love to her so gloriously this morning if all he'd felt was lust?

Juliet reached out to stroke Lady's sleek head, her smile fading as she watched Mac move away from the window. He'd become a part of her in those few tempestuous hours of ecstasy they'd shared. His soul had touched hers, filling up all the empty spaces that had hurt for so long.

She bowed her head and let the breeze flow through her hair. She'd seen love in his eyes last night, even if he hadn't said the words. She would be patient. Mac was worth the wait.

Lady chattered noisily next to her ear, and Juliet reached out to give her a hug. As her arm encircled the slick body, the dolphin leaped forward. Juliet took a deep breath and tightened her grip. Lady sounded, pulling Juliet beneath the choppy water in a rush of motion.

Surface noises faded, replaced by the eerie clicking voices of the two dolphins. Water rushed past her ears, blurring the sounds into a bubbling white noise.

In one swoop they reached the rocky bottom and curved upward, aiming for the glistening surface above. Juliet tightened her grip on the stiff dorsal fin and closed her eyes. She loved the sensation of speed, exulting in the rush of water against her body. Her nerve endings tingled, giving her an exhilarating feeling of freedom.

As her head broke the surface, she turned her face to the sun. The scent of kelp and brine was strong in her nostrils as she shook the water from her lashes and pushed her streaming bangs away from her forehead.

A sudden splash sounded behind her, and water cascaded over her head. Juliet sputtered and spun around to see the cause of the disturbance.

Bubbles was weaving in frantic, drunken circles in the middle of the tank, her snout raised, her eyes white. Her cries were shrill, undulating in a wild pattern of discordant sounds that signaled panic in the complex dolphin lexicon.

Something was dreadfully wrong.

Juliet started to climb from the tank, then froze as Bubbles shot out of the water in a rising arc, her snout pointed directly at Juliet, who flung herself to one side. The dolphin came crashing down only inches from her, sending sheets of foaming spray over the pier.

Juliet coughed as the saltwater stung her throat, and tried to escape Bubbles' thrusting snout. Her heart began pounding, and her breathing came in audible gasps.

Lady began clicking in agitation, her tail slapping the water in warning. She swam closer to Juliet, trying valiantly to fend off the slashing attack of the much larger Bubbles.

Juliet glanced around in rising panic. She had to get out of the tank, but Bubbles was between her and the pier. The rest of the tank had no exit, only thick pipe supports that had jagged twists of metal encircling them, preventing her from getting a handhold.

Bubbles lunged again, and Juliet dove beneath the water. The dolphin crashed down on top of her, and Juliet felt a slashing sting of pain as Bubbles' teeth grazed her shoulder, slicing into her skin with the ease of a scalpel. Pain doubled her over as she clawed to the surface, fighting against the sickening nausea that was cramping her stomach.

Bubbles was trying to kill her, using her battering snout and murderously sharp teeth to slice her to bits, just as the dolphin's free-swimming cousins assaulted much larger killer whales in the open sea.

Juliet was no match for six hundred pounds of frenzied sea mammal, especially in the confines of the tank. Somehow she had to get away from those slashing teeth.

She quickly filled her lungs with air and dove toward the bottom, twisting her head to watch Bubbles and Lady battling on the surface. As she reached the bottom, she had a vivid image of Mac's face, his blue eyes half closed in desire, his arms open and beckoning to her. Her lungs burned as she tried to keep from panicking. She couldn't die now, not when she had so much to live for.

The water churned around her as Bubbles leaped high into the air, building momentum until she cut through the surface and began heading straight for the bottom, her glazed eyes fixed blindly on Juliet, her mouth open in a snarling grimace.

The spiked bottom of the steel mesh tore into Juliet's hand as she tried to burrow under the wall of the tank, and she beat her fist against the hard rock in frustration. It was no use; there was no escape.

She blinked in horror as a red haze began clouding her vision. Her lungs began to burn, and a smothering constriction tightened her chest. Bubbles was between her and the surface, and Juliet was running out of air.

Mac hung up the phone and stared across the room. He'd just spoken to Hendricks; and the admiral had given him the okay to search Juliet's house.

He'd been wrestling with his decision since he'd left her bed a little more than an hour ago; unfortunately he had no choice. He had only six days left until his deadline, and so far, the man named Peter had not been identified. The briefcase in Juliet's bedroom was the only tangible possibility they had.

Mac pushed himself to his feet, wincing at the sudden twinge of pain in his shoulder. His chest heaved with a heavy sigh as he pictured the dainty marks of Juliet's small teeth imprinted above his collarbone. His flesh would heal, but what about the rest of him?

The bitter taste of frustration rose in his throat, and pain twisted the muscles of his face. Damn you, Juliet, he thought in silent rage. Get out of my head.

He limped over to the desk to retrieve his jacket. Maybe once this case was wrapped up, he would take a month's leave. He could use some time to himself, time to get his thinking untangled and his emotions on an even keel again.

He sighed and glanced toward the window. More than anything else in the world, he wanted to be down there with Juliet, teasing her into that laugh that made him feel like a boy again. He longed to see her eyes warm and then glow just for him. It was almost a physical ache, just one more pain to endure.

He limped closer. He needed one last look, one final memory. The next time he saw Juliet, he would have the proof he needed. He was sure of it. And then the pretense would be over.

The window was open, and the sea breeze was cool. In the tank, Juliet was playing with the dolphins.

Mac leaned closer, a taut smile playing over a faint smile. She was underwater, swimming toward the surface, playing tag with the huge creatures. She was laughing....

Mac froze. That wasn't laughter he heard. That was a desperate cry for help. A scream. Juliet was in trouble.

He bit off a crude expletive, his eyes sweeping the area around the tank in a frantic search for Greg. Juliet was alone.

Mac felt the raw taste of terror push through his throat as he inhaled sharply, and his heart began to pound as he watched the large charcoal dolphin lunge toward Juliet's twisting body. Juliet threw up her hands, trying to fend off the angry creature. Her wet suit was torn, one sleeve hanging loose around her wrist, and there were dark red stains spreading down the front of the pale blue fabric.

Fighting a feeling of helpless frustration, Mac limped with awkward haste toward the door, cursing as his stiff left leg impeded his progress. In the corridor he shouted for Kurtz, but there was no answer. He hesitated for a split second, glancing toward the fire escape.

Could he make it? Or would he fall and mess up his leg for good? He gritted his teeth and took a deep breath. He had no choice. The elevator was far too slow.

On the landing he hesitated briefly, then dropped his cane and began running down the steps, his hand sliding along the railing for support.

Splinters ripped into his palm, and shards of white hot pain tore through his leg, bringing tears to his eyes, but he couldn't stop. Not when Juliet was in danger.

Steeling himself against the clawing pain, he ran at full speed across the thick grass, his gait awkwardly ragged, adrenaline giving him the kind of strength he'd thought he'd lost forever. His breath came in harsh gasps as he reached the end of the short pier.

The water on the rough boards caused him to slow his steps, and he swore in hoarse frustration. If he fell, he would never be able to get up.

The noise from the tank had reached a shrill crescendo. All four dolphins were shrieking now, and Juliet, desperately dodging Bubbles' slashing teeth, was yelling commands that had no effect.

Mac reached the tank, but she was just out of his reach, trying to hide behind the smaller of the females. Blood was everywhere. On her face, on the dolphins, spreading around them in a dark red pool.

Mac sucked in harsh gasps of air, and his mind raced. He couldn't go into the tank. He would never be able to get her out.

He cupped his hands around his mouth and shouted her name above the din. "Over here," he yelled, gesturing frantically as she looked up at him, her face a mask of fear. Blood dripped from a gash on her forehead and ran down her cheek to saturate her wet suit.

Mac forced himself to concentrate. He'd faced tighter situations than this and won.

Closing his ears to the frantic din, Mac scanned the pier, looking for something to use as a weapon as he urged Juliet closer to the edge, but there was nothing. Only a large galvanized bucket and a pair of bright pink sneakers.

Fighting to keep his balance, he reached down and picked up the bucket. He took hasty aim and threw it at the female's head.

The bucket hit Bubbles on the bulging knob of her skull, just above the blowhole, and she squealed in pain, tossing her head from side to side in anguished protest.

"Now!" Mac yelled, and Juliet took a deep breath, diving underwater to come up on the other side of the dazed dolphin.

Lady, bleeding from the snout, butted Bubbles away long enough for Juliet to reach the edge of the enclosure. Mac braced his good leg against the lip of the tank and reached for her, using the strength in his arms and back to pull her from the tank by her forearms.

Momentum carried him backward; his knee twisted, and then his leg slid out from under him. He crashed heavily to the pier, pulling Juliet down on top of him. His arms folded over her, crushing her to his chest.

She sobbed in relief, water streaming from her hair to wet Mac's white face. His features were twisted, and his breathing was harsh and labored.

"It's...okay," he muttered through clenched teeth. "You're safe."

Juliet framed his face with her hands and rained kisses on his face. She could feel the rapid rise and fall of his chest as he sucked in air through his partly opened mouth.

"Mac," she whispered brokenly, sobbing. "I love you, I love you."

Mac's chest heaved, and he moaned. "No," he whispered harshly, tossing his head from side to side as though he couldn't bear to hear the words. "Don't...don't."

"Shh, don't talk," Juliet urged, trying to swallow her sobs as she buried her face in the hollow of his shoulder. His breathing was raspy, and his muscles were tensed into hard knots.

She began to shake. "I thought I was going to die," she whispered against his throat. "I was so s-scared."

Mac tightened his grip on her trembling body and groaned. "Me, too," he whispered, fighting the viselike spasms gripping his knee. He rubbed his cheek against her wet hair and tried to control his ragged breathing.

Juliet closed her eyes. Her muscles felt rubbery, and her stomach was heaving with adrenaline reaction. Her head began to buzz. Sounds seemed to come from a great distance, distorted and disjointed. She could hear the sound of a siren and then, abruptly, voices raised in concern. Beneath her body the pier vibrated with the sound of clattering footsteps coming toward her.

"*Juliet!* Are you all right?" Maria reached her side and bent down. In her hand she carried Mac's cane. "I saw Mac running down the hill, and then I saw what was happening in the tank, so I called the ambulance. I didn't know what else to do."

Two paramedics in blue crouched next to Mac's prone form, and Juliet reluctantly tried to roll off him. But his arms held her fast.

"Mac, it's the paramedics," she whispered as calmly as she could. "They need to take a look at you." She caressed his face with fingers that shook violently.

But Mac didn't move. His eyes were closed, and his face was gray and drawn and damp with sweat. His arms remained locked around her, as though he couldn't bear to let her go.

"He's fainted," the younger of the two firemen said with a grimace. "He can't hear you."

Between the two of them, the men managed to pry Mac's arms loose. Juliet inched backward, afraid to hurt him, and one of the men helped her to her feet.

The two firemen exchanged looks, and Juliet frowned. "What's wrong?" she asked anxiously.

He nodded toward Mac, and Juliet felt the tears well in her eyes as she noticed the torn flesh of his palm.

"Splinters," one paramedic explained, examining Mac's hand.

"Superficial," commented the other. "There must be something else."

Juliet swayed violently, and the sunlit scene began to dim as the blood rushed from her head. One of the paramedics put his arm around her, while the other broke open a small ampule and held it under her nose.

The pungent odor of ammonia assaulted her nostrils, clearing her head, and she stiffened. "Please," she whispered, pressing her fist hard against her churning stomach. "I . . . I'm okay. Take care of Mac." Her shoulder was beginning to ache, and her entire arm felt numb.

The paramedic slowly released her, watching her closely as she stood unsupported. Quickly, with an economy of motion, the man inspected her injuries.

Juliet winced at his touch, and the paramedic muttered an apology. "You're going to need stitches," he told her as he gently wiped the blood from her forehead, then pressed a thick pad of gauze against the tear in her left shoulder.

Juliet felt light-headed as she quickly told the men about Mac's crippled leg. "It just folded up under him."

"Here, keep pressure on this," the paramedic ordered tersely, pressing her right hand against the pad.

Juliet nodded and tried to control her breathing. She swallowed a sob as the paramedic quickly slit Mac's jeans up to the middle of his thigh, exposing his scarred leg.

Maria gasped, and Juliet winced. "God, that looks terrible," the secretary whispered with a horrified look, and Juliet's eyes filled with tears.

His knee was beginning to balloon around the upper cuff of his brace, the skin taut and white from the fluid filling the joint.

Swearing under his breath, the paramedic carefully removed the brace and tossed it aside. Mac moaned as skillful fingers gently probed the area. His lashes fluttered, and his eyes opened to a slit. He tried to move, but strong hands held him fast.

The pain was excruciating, radiating in scorching hot waves through his entire leg, and for a few hazy seconds he didn't know where he was. His heart started to pound, and a clammy coldness dampened his skin.

Terror washed over him, and he struggled against the restraining hand. Where was Juliet? Was she all right?

"Let me go," he muttered, clenching his muscles.

"Mac, *please*! It's okay. Please stop fighting. You'll hurt yourself." The voice had a sweet urgency, soft and soothing, and filled with love. Fighting the smothering gray fog, he struggled toward the light, searching for that wonderful sweetness.

"Juliet?" he whispered, looking for her. He blinked, and the film cleared from his eyes. He was lying on his back above San Diego Bay, with the hard boards of the pier pressing into his spine and the breeze from the sea chilling his skin.

"I'm here, darling," Juliet whispered, bending over to caress his damp face. "Right here."

Mac raised his left hand and touched the blood on her forehead. "Are you okay?" he whispered. Nausea squeezed his stomach, and he closed his eyes at the sudden spasm.

"Yes, I . . . I'm fine." Her voice was shaky and seemed to come from a great distance.

Mac blinked in the brightness and shielded his eyes with his left hand. "Good," he muttered, trying to force some strength into his voice. "I'm glad."

"His vital signs are strong," the paramedic reported into his portable radio. "His knee feels intact, but he needs X rays." The second man began packing Mac's knee in ice, wrapping several Ace bandages around the cold packs to keep them in place.

The radio crackled, and Juliet could hear the order to transport Mac to the base infirmary. Reluctantly she moved out of the way, her eyes fixed on his strained features.

As one of the paramedics went to get the stretcher, Fred Kurtz came puffing down the pier. His round face was pink with exertion, and there was a wild look of fear in his eyes.

"What happened?" he asked Juliet in a hoarse voice.

She gave him a weary look. "Bubbles tried to kill me. If it hadn't been for Mac, she would have succeeded," she said with absolute certainty, and Fred blanched. Juliet quickly explained the sequence of events, and the tears began running down her face again.

For once the director was speechless. He stared at the tank in stark confusion. Bubbles was slowly crisscrossing the tank, while Lady cowered by the pier. Some of the crazed mania seemed to have left the larger dolphin's eyes, and her movements were less frantic, though not quite normal.

Juliet ignored Fred as she watched the paramedics lift Mac onto the stretcher. One of the paramedics bent to retrieve Mac's brace, and Maria silently handed the man Mac's black cane.

Juliet kept her hand on Mac's still form as she walked beside the gurney to the ambulance.

Tears nearly blinded her, and she dashed them away with a shaking hand. Because of her, Mac had risked further injury to his crippled leg, racing down those rickety stairs and across thirty yards of grass to get to her in time. If he had suffered permanent damage, she would never forgive herself.

Juliet heard a noise and opened her eyes to find the emergency room nurse leaning over her, a concerned look on her lined middle-aged face.

"Dr. Prentice, is your shoulder giving you pain? You looked as though you'd passed out on us."

Juliet managed a smile. "I'm fine, thanks. Just resting." She was seated on a couch in the waiting room of the infirmary, resting her head against the wall behind her. She'd been thinking about Mac.

It seemed like hours since they'd taken him to X ray. She'd had her shoulder sutured, her other cuts dressed and bandaged, and still he hadn't reappeared.

"How is he?" she asked the friendly nurse in an urgent entreaty. "His leg?"

"He'll be fine. A few days in bed, and he'll be as good as new."

Juliet murmured a silent prayer of thanks and gave the woman a blinding smile of gratitude.

The nurse looked startled, then brightened. "We've put him to bed. The doctor wants to keep him overnight—for observation." She pointed toward the end of the lobby. "Through the green doors, first room on the left."

The ward was large and dimly lit, with four beds, two of which were occupied. There were four lockers, four chairs and four walls of unrelieved white sameness. Juliet shivered at the drab institutional feeling and let the heavy door swing shut behind her.

Mac was in the bed nearest the door, half-lying, half-sitting, his left leg resting on a nest of pillows, his knee packed in ice.

He was wearing a loose-fitting hospital gown with tiny blue flowers on it.

He looked up as she entered, his face tightening as she gave him a bright smile.

"What in the world have you got on?" he muttered, taking in the starched white coat and blue hospital booties the nurse had found for her to wear.

Juliet pirouetted, trying to ignore the churning in the pit of her stomach. Seeing him lying there, his face as pale as the sheets, was making her sick all over again.

"Like it?" she said with deliberate flirtatiousness. "I understand it's the latest thing in daytime wear."

"Very chic," Mac muttered, his eyes shadowed and distant.

Juliet moved forward to run her unsteady fingers over the cotton gown stretching across his broad chest. "I like the nightshirt," she teased. "It's very sexy."

Mac scowled in drowsy indignation and glanced toward the burly, deeply tanned man in the next bed. The man was watching them with twinkling black eyes above seamed cheeks.

Juliet flushed, and the man chuckled. "Don't mind me, ma'am. I'm mostly deaf in one ear anyways." He grinned and turned onto his side, pulling the covers over his shoulder.

Juliet felt suddenly awkward and ill-at-ease as she rested her hip against the high side of the bed. "How do you feel?" she asked in a quiet voice, watching Mac's face carefully for a sign. The words were inadequate and banal, but now, confronted by his withdrawn mood, she was afraid to say the words that were in her heart.

"I'm sleepy," he drawled in a muted voice that was one tone above a whisper. "They gave me some kind of damn shot so they could x-ray my knee, and I have a feeling I'm down for the count."

He licked his lips and watched her with brooding eyes that held a glimmer of pain in their sapphire depths. At that moment Juliet would have given everything she owned to know what he was thinking.

"I won't stay, then," she whispered, captivated by the sleepy-eyed way he was looking at her. He seemed to be fighting some internal battle—like an adorable little boy, too tired to stay awake and too ornery to go to sleep.

"Stay," Mac murmured, capturing her hand with his. It was his left hand, the one that wasn't bandaged. His grip was surprisingly strong, and Juliet curled her fingers around his broad palm in willing acquiescence.

"Are you okay?" His eyes were narrowed in concentration as he looked up into her face.

"Mostly. I have some cuts and bruises, and I have to stay out of the water for a couple of weeks, but I'm going to be fine." Her voice began to shake, and tears cascaded down her face. "Thanks to you."

Mac swallowed hard and wiped the tears from her face with the swollen fingers of his right hand. "What the hell happened, anyway?" he asked with slurred vehemence. "It looked to me like that damn fish was deliberately trying to kill you."

"It looked that way to me, too," Juliet said in a tremulous whisper, letting him tug her closer. "Another few seconds, and I think she would have." She didn't want to talk. All she wanted to do was crawl up next to Mac and cradle his body next to hers. But he seemed so . . . remote.

"Is that usual?" Mac shifted uneasily on the pillow. His thick chestnut hair was rumpled, and his face was drawn, the paleness of his skin emphasizing the harsh lines bracketing his mouth.

"No, not with these animals, anyway," she said with a sigh.

"So what went wrong?"

"I'm not sure." Juliet fought down the terrifying memory of her ordeal in the tank and tried to concentrate. "It couldn't have been the food supplements, because we're out of them." She waved her hand. "Maybe Bubbles was upset because she expected Felicity and not me to be in the tank, or maybe she has some kind of a virus. I just don't know."

She shuddered and tried not to think of those razor-sharp teeth slashing into her tender skin. "I just know I don't *ever* want to go through an experience like that again."

Mac's lashes drooped, then jerked up as he tried to focus. "Neither do I," he said laconically. His voice faded into a deep rumble as he fought sleep. He looked so tired all of a sudden, as though all the strength had drained from him.

Juliet longed to kiss the furrows from his forehead, longed to lay her cheek against his and whisper all the words of love that were pent up inside her. Her throat hurt from the need to say the words.

"Don't scowl," she teased, watching his struggle to stay awake. "I'm fine, really I am. Please don't worry about me."

Juliet flinched at the savage clenching of his jaw. "It's too late for that," he muttered as though to himself. His eyes drifted closed, and he sighed, his features growing slack and defenseless.

He groaned and muttered in his sleep, his hand tightening convulsively on hers. It was the same hand that had caressed her with tenderness only a few hours earlier.

Juliet smiled reminiscently and smoothed the thin cover over his body, her eyes measuring the lean length of him inch by inch. He looked formidable, even at rest.

Her eyes misted over. He was so precious, this big brave man who kept everything inside. She reached out a trembling hand to smooth the taut V from between his brows.

His forehead was warm and slightly damp, and her fingers lingered against his skin. "Sleep well, my darling," she whispered soundlessly, brushing her lips against his. "Everything's going to be just fine."

Chapter 11

He was running.

The wind was hard at his back, urging him forward, and the sun shone brightly overhead.

The muscles of his legs moved with oiled grace as he raced with a powerful rhythm toward the sun-dappled spot where she stood, her arms held out to him in welcome.

She was smiling, her brown eyes glowing with sweet fire, her delicate features wreathed in seductive golden light. She was waiting....

He reached out his hand, stretching toward her slender form, straining for her touch, but the harder he struggled, the farther away she seemed.

He ran faster, his lungs straining, but a thick cold mist began rising from the ground, enveloping her in its icy tendrils. She was disappearing, sucked into the ugly gray fog, and he couldn't save her.

The coldness tugged at his straining body, pulling him farther and farther away from her. He was falling into a pit, his legs bound by the thick tendrils of the fog. He twisted in anguish, but the mist held him captive. He had lost her...lost her...lost her....

* * *

Mac groaned and opened his eyes, his heart pounding so ferociously that he could almost hear it in the eerie silence of the drab white room.

The dream began to fade, sinking into memory and leaving behind the anguished taste of bitter loss. It had been so real. Too real.

He scowled and tried to sit up. Pain rocketed through him, and he sank back against the pillow, his teeth clenched tightly against the sickening churning in his stomach.

Suddenly he was back in Bethesda, back in the orthopedic ward, his leg immobilized, his mind filled with tortured thoughts. The walls seemed to move, closing in on him, and he couldn't breathe. His chest heaved violently, and sweat dotted his forehead.

An image of Juliet, her soft lips pressed tenderly against the scars on his knee, pushed into his mind, and the panic began to recede. He took a deep breath and stared at the ceiling.

The lights were on, and the room felt cold. He could feel the starched sheets against the bare skin of his legs, could smell the sharp medicinal odor that seemed to permeate the air.

He stirred restlessly, lowering his chin to stare down at his battered knee. This time he almost welcomed the discomfort. Maybe the throbbing heat would drive her image out of his mind. Maybe the ache would help him live with what he had to do to her.

He turned his head on the pillow and looked toward the next bed. His roommate was sitting on the edge of the high mattress, a tray of food in front of him on the bed table.

"You okay, fella?" the man asked as he caught Mac's eyes on him. "You want I should get the nurse for you?"

"No thanks." Mac wiped the sweat from his face with the edge of the sheet and glanced at the telephone on the table between the beds. "I have a call to make first."

The clock over the door said five past six. Nine o'clock in the East. He'd been sleeping off and on for almost eight hours.

He scowled in impatience as he punched out the number. He had to talk to Hendricks. Maybe they could work a deal, hammer out some kind of plea bargain with the feds. Anything to take some of the heat off Juliet. Anything to keep her from spending the next thirty years in prison.

The admiral answered on the first ring. "Mac, where the hell have you been? I've been calling the number you gave me all afternoon, but there's been no answer." His irritation snaked down the line to echo loudly in Mac's ear.

"It's a long story, Carter. I got to a phone as soon as I could. Listen, I need to run something by you before—"

Hendricks interrupted. "Before you do that, Mac, I have something for you. I have a positive ID on your man Peter." He sighed deeply, and Mac stiffened, glancing uneasily at his roommate's craggy face. The man was listening, all right. Intently. Mac could only hope that Hendricks would realize from his choice of words that he wasn't calling on a secure line.

"I'm listening," he said in a flat voice.

Hendricks coughed. "We blew it, Mac. We've been on the wrong track. Juliet Prentice is innocent."

Mac couldn't move. He clutched the receiver in a violent grip that hurt his palm, and his throat squeezed shut. It was hard to breathe.

"I...don't understand," he enunciated with deliberate care. He filled his lungs, exhaling slowly. He wanted to shout with joy. Juliet was innocent!

"Peter's last name is DuBois. He's a former vice admiral, a high-ranking member of a special counterinsurgency force we were operating in the early days of Vietnam. He's writing a spy novel loosely based on his experiences with a Soviet agent who later defected and became his wife."

Mac groaned silently. "The woman with the accent."

"Exactly." Hendricks paused. "I spoke with Admiral DuBois myself, more than four hours ago. He explained that Prentice is his ghostwriter, and that he'd sworn her to secrecy on the advice of his literary agent, who thought a book written by a former admiral had more appeal than one written by a civilian."

"I don't understand," Mac said slowly, his brow furrowing as he concentrated. "Juliet's not a writer."

"Apparently she wrote her dissertation about an experiment DuBois and others conducted with dolphins during the

Korean War. Something to do with dolphins detecting mines. She sent him a copy when it was finished, and he was very impressed.''

Mac sighed. There was no way they could have known, no way they could have anticipated a coincidence like this.

The admiral's tone sharpened. ''The man's a blasted egomaniac, Mac. He all but blackmailed Dr. Prentice into working like a slave, making her come to his house at all hours whenever he had a brainstorm.''

''By threatening to tell her boss that she was moonlighting,'' Mac guessed in a low voice.

''Precisely,'' the admiral grated. ''Her security clearance was at stake.''

''And she also needed the money DuBois paid her, so she was stuck right smack in the middle.''

''Yup. The poor woman must have been going out of her mind.''

Mac closed his eyes and breathed a quick prayer of thanks. Juliet wouldn't go to prison. Or would she?

''What about the money, Carter? How will IRS feel about it?''

Hendricks chuckled. ''As long as the payments are included in this year's return, they'll be satisfied.''

He took a deep breath. They were right back at square one, and time was running out. In a week Hydra would leave for Vienna. Mac had to find the traitor, or Hydra would have to be retired.

''Any ideas, Mac?'' Hendricks sounded as cool as ever, but Mac recognized a hard wall of urgency behind the question.

His mind rapidly replayed the events of the last few weeks, skipping through the days rapidly before skidding to a halt at something Juliet had said that morning, something important that had slipped through his sleep-fogged mind without registering. Until now.

His jaw clenched, and his eyes narrowed. ''I have an idea,'' he told the admiral with grim resolution. ''Give me a couple of hours, and I'll get back to you.''

''Right. I'll be waiting.''

Mac hung up and stared at the phone. He had a sudden need to see Juliet.

And say what? That you're glad she's not the spy you thought she was? That even though the evidence branded her a traitor, you still wanted her? That you risked compromising the case because you needed to get her out of your head?

Mac's throat tightened. He didn't want her to know that he'd suspected her, that he was anything but the good guy she thought he was. He didn't want her to hate him.

Mac shoved the painful thoughts from his mind as he eased himself into a sitting position and began unwrapping his knee. He had to get out of here.

Juliet squinted and tried to make sense of the figures marching in amber lines across the black screen. Her mind was tired, too tired to handle the complexities of the data. She should have stayed home and rested, as the doctor had ordered, but her thoughts had nearly driven her crazy. It had been pure torture, lying there alone in her bed, with the scent of Mac's musky after-shave lingering on her pillow.

Work was her solace, her trusted panacea for loneliness. Sitting here at her terminal, alone except for the janitor, she felt distanced from her worries. Here she could sink into the tedium of paperwork, forgetting for a brief time the tumbling uncertainties of her life.

Her mind drifted, counting back almost twelve hours to those terrifying moments before Mac had pulled her from the tank. Her ruined wet suit was in the trash can at home, the imprint of Mac's bleeding hand starkly outlined on the thermal material.

Her eyes filled with tears as she looked out the window into the fog-shrouded night. From this angle she couldn't see the infirmary, but it was there, only a short walk away.

When she'd called at five, the nurse had told her that the swelling was down in Mac's knee and that he was still asleep.

"Oh, Mac, I wish I could be with you," she whispered into the empty room. Sighing deeply, she reached for her coffee cup. It was empty. She glanced down the hall. Terry usually brought a Thermos of coffee. Perhaps he had some to spare.

She wiggled her toes and stood up, stretching gingerly to loosen the knotted muscles of her neck and back. She'd been hunched over the terminal for more than two hours, and the trauma in the tank was beginning to take its toll. She grimaced and flexed her shoulders beneath the soft top of her yellow running suit, wincing as the sutures tugged at her skin. She would finish with this file and call it a night.

Her sneakers were silent on the shiny linoleum as she walked down the hall in search of the janitor. His bucket and mop were outside Felicity's office, but Terry himself was nowhere to be seen.

Juliet quashed a shiver of unease as she felt the hollow emptiness of the old building settle around her. She'd always felt safe here at night, knowing that the burly janitor was only a shout away. But tonight the silence felt unfriendly, as though the morning's terror had bled into the very air she breathed.

Oh boy! Talk about post-trauma jitters, she thought with dry humor as she walked down the hall. What a wimp she was. There wasn't a thing in the creaky old building that could hurt her.

She sidestepped Terry's bucket and poked her head into Felicity's office. Her colleague was seated at her terminal, peering at a graph rapidly forming on the screen.

"Felicity! I didn't know you were here." Juliet started to smile in welcome, only to blink in confusion as she realized that Felicity was looking at her with a stricken expression on her perfect face.

Terry Burton was standing at Felicity's elbow, his tiny radio in two pieces in his hands, and he was in the process of fitting a small diskette into a special compartment built into the back.

"I thought you said she'd gone home," Felicity cried in rising alarm.

"I thought she had," Terry answered in clipped tones, his eyes narrowing to threatening slits.

Juliet's mind raced in a direct line, straight to the chilling certainty that Terry and Felicity were stealing the test data. She had to get out of there. *Now.*

She backed out of the doorway and whirled to run, but she stumbled over the bucket, losing her footing, and Terry caught her before she could get away.

An ugly glint silvered his eyes as he twisted his hand around her ponytail and yanked hard, twisting her head to the side.

Tears sprang to Juliet's eyes as a red fury clouded her vision. Her fingers curved into claws, she tried to reach his obscenely grinning face, but the janitor was too quick for her. Moving with agile ease, he clasped her arm and twisted it behind her back.

Juliet cried out in pain as he marched her toward the desk, where Felicity sat in wide-eyed silence, her meticulously manicured hand pressed to her open mouth.

"Don't hurt her, Terry," Felicity pleaded, her amber eyes glowing with fear. "I don't want anyone hurt."

"It's too late for that, Felicity. She's seen too much." A vicious sneer twisted his lips as he shoved Juliet against the hard edge of the desk.

"But if we're leaving tonight, it won't matter." Felicity's voice took on a note of panic. "We can...we can hide her someplace." She looked around with wild eyes. "Downstairs. In the storage locker. No one will find her there till tomorrow, when Greg feeds the dolphins." She avoided Juliet's eyes. "Please, Terry."

The burly janitor shook his head in angry impatience. "We need time to get out of the country. We can't risk having her found." An evil grin creased his sunburned cheeks. "Besides, I have an idea what we can do with dear Dr. Prentice."

"What?"

"We'll let her take the blame." He trained his cold eyes directly on Juliet, two controlled circles of hate. He was a stranger, a dangerous, calculating man who bore little resemblance to the lazy, easygoing surfer Juliet had come to like. This man would kill without a second thought.

Her heart raced out of control, and her breath came in quick, shallow gasps. She was terrified, as terrified as she'd been in the tank when she'd known she was going to die.

Her head began to buzz, and spots danced in front of her eyes. Felicity's pleading voice began to fade, and Juliet's head flopped forward.

"Oh no you don't, doc. You're not going to faint on me now. I need you." Burton's hand smacked Juliet's cheek, bringing her head up with a snap.

Her skin burned where he'd hit her, and her head began to throb. She pressed trembling fingers against her tender skin and stared up at him in shock.

This is not happening, she thought in frozen detachment. Not to me. I won't let it happen.

"Poor Dr. Prentice," Burton said with acid sarcasm. "She'll be found tomorrow morning in her office, a cyanide capsule crushed between her teeth, a suicide note on her desk."

"Suicide?" Felicity had gone pale.

His sun-bleached brow lifted in arch amusement. "The spy's best friend. A neat touch, don't you think?"

"Juliet, I'm so sorry." Felicity's voice broke, and she dropped her gaze.

"Why, Felicity?" Juliet pleaded, her mind beginning to function again. She had to keep the other woman talking, had to buy some time. Security had to check the building at least once during the night.

"Why not!" Felicity's demeanor changed instantly as her eyes grew hot with anger. A mottled flush replaced the pallor of her unblemished cheeks. "I should have been named director, not that jerk Kurtz. I was the one who set up the procedures. I was the one who fought for money when the budget was cut." Her glossy lips curled in derision. "But I was only a woman. They couldn't make me manager. Oh no. Not those chauvinistic, air-brained idiots in Washington. They wanted one of their own."

Her chest heaved as she took an irate breath. "Well, that's what they got, all right. One of their own. Just as inept and as stupid as they are." The laugh that escaped her was devoid of humor and tinged with hysteria. "But I'll show them. In Russia I'll be the one in charge. Everyone will look up to me."

"Better hurry with that graph," Burton interjected impatiently. "We don't have much time." With deliberate roughness, the man grasped Juliet's arm and jerked her toward the door.

As he pushed her toward her office, Juliet fought against the terror weakening her knees. She couldn't give in to her fear. She had to think, had to outsmart this man who intended to kill her. It was her only chance.

In her office, Burton directed her to her desk and shoved her into the chair. He pulled a sheet of stationery bearing her name from her desk drawer and handed her a pen. ''Here. Write what I tell you, and no tricks.''

As she pulled the paper toward her, Juliet's mind fastened on Mac. She wanted to bask in the glow of his wonderfully changeable blue eyes, longed to hear his husky laugh one more time. Just one more time.

Terry began to dictate, and Juliet wrote, each second seeming like an eternity. The pen scratched out the incriminating words slowly, carefully, and she felt her control slipping with each curving stroke.

Mac gritted his teeth against the queasiness and leaned heavily on his cane. His leg felt like wet spaghetti, and the palm of his right hand was swollen and stiff.

He stood beneath the portico of the infirmary, alone in a patch of yellow light that splashed into the fog through the double glass doors.

He was cold inside and out. His jacket was still draped over the chair in Juliet's office, and the thin sweater provided little protection from the rising chill.

Inside, he was deadly calm. Adrenaline pumped with surging constancy through his veins, fueling the steady anger simmering in his brain.

If Juliet was innocent, there was only one logical suspect who could be Medusa—Felicity Feldman. And Felicity was going to tell him what he needed to know. Tonight. Even if he had to shake the information out of her.

He straightened as the sound of a car engine throbbed through the fog, followed by twin shafts of light as a young Navy corpsman brought the blue sedan to a stop beneath the portico. He left the engine running and the lights on.

"Thanks, son," Mac drawled with a grim smile as the seaman slid from the driver's seat, leaving the door open.

"No problem, sir. I needed the exercise." The corpsman watched with a pleasant smile. He watched with anxious eyes as Mac threw his cane onto the passenger's side and maneuvered himself with awkward stiffness into the driver's seat.

Mac's face was a frozen mask, and sweat glistened on his brow as he slammed the door and rested his forehead on the steering wheel. He should have taken the pill the nurse had offered, but he'd wanted to have a clear head when he confronted Felicity. Now, however, as he fought the nausea, he wished he hadn't been quite so bullheaded. He couldn't afford to pass out.

He drove slowly, his wipers monotonously dredging the mist from the windshield. The fog thinned as the car climbed the hill, disappearing completely in patches as he neared the parking lot below Building 3.

Mac slowed automatically as his narrowed gaze swept the deserted lot. Two cars remained. His mouth went dry as he recognized Juliet's. The other car was a red BMW, parked at the far end of the lot, next to the janitor's big Harley.

Mac braked and drummed his fingers on the wheel as he tried to place the second car. He'd seen one like it before, not too long ago.

But where?

The blood drained from his face in a rush as his brain made the connection. Felicity had a car like that. He'd seen it the night they'd met for a drink when he'd escorted her to the parking lot outside the bar.

His gaze shifted to the building on the right. Lights blazed from the second floor windows. His eyes found Juliet's office, and he inhaled with audible relief. She was seated at her terminal, her head bent over the keyboard. She was working late, probably making up for the time she'd lost that morning.

His lips thinned as he shifted his gaze to Felicity's office. Her window was blank, the blinds drawn.

Mac's mind raced. He didn't want to talk with Felicity while Juliet was present. He needed the element of surprise when he confronted the self-confident Dr. Feldman. And besides, he didn't want to get Juliet involved.

He sighed and rested his hands on the wheel. It was more than that. He didn't want Juliet to know who he was. Not until he'd had time to prepare her.

He glanced toward the deserted lot. He would park in the shadows and wait until one of them left. And then he'd get the answers he needed.

Juliet put down the pen and sat staring at the neatly written words. "Very nice," Terry said with a cold smile.

She felt her skin crawl with revulsion as he slid his fingers along the line of her jaw in an obscene caress. His touch lingered on her face, and his breath quickened. "It would almost be worth my time to take you here and now, one last indulgence in the life of Terry Burton before he disappears forever."

Juliet fought down a sob. Frantically she searched her mind for a way to keep him talking. She was so frightened that she was shaking uncontrollably, and her palms were wet.

"Who is Terry Burton?" she asked, forcing a flattering interest into her voice. "I mean really."

"An orphaned vagrant who was dumped into the Pacific one foggy night over ten years ago," the man called Terry said with a sneer. "His only mistake was having a marked resemblance to a man named Dimitri Korsov who needed a name and a history that would fool even the FBI. It was a simple matter to write to Sacramento for a copy of Burton's birth certificate, and the switch was completed." His hand tangled in her hair, and Juliet forced herself to remain perfectly still.

"I'm impressed," she said with a shaky laugh.

Burton's brows arched in arrogant pride. "It was pathetically easy. The FBI never questioned a thing."

"But why go to all that trouble?"

"Don't be stupid, Juliet, darling. I've been trained since I was twelve for a mission of this importance, and when I return to the motherland, I shall be a hero."

Juliet felt her spirits plummet. Even in the preliminary stages, her research would be invaluable to the Russians, who, she'd been told, had only just begun a similar project. What had taken Project Ping Pong twelve years to accomplish, the Soviets could now do in a matter of months.

"Terry, listen—"

"Dimitri," he growled with silky menace. "It's been a long time since a beautiful woman said my name."

Juliet swallowed. "Dimitri, I—" She gasped as his hand tightened around her neck.

"Time's up, my lovely Juliet," he said in a growling purr of regret. His thumb massaged the fragile skin under her ear.

She closed her eyes and breathed a quick prayer. Then a calm determination settled over her.

No matter what, she wasn't going to swallow the cyanide. If she died, it would be fighting, and in the bloody aftermath, her note would be meaningless. It was the only legacy she could leave Rex. And Mac.

Dimitri increased the pressure of his fingers, forcing her to raise her face toward his.

"A kiss before dying, my darling," he whispered with an insulting leer. "I want you to die with the taste of a real man on your lips." His eyes flickered toward the suede jacket hanging on the back of Mac's chair, and Juliet stiffened. "Oh yes, I've seen how you look at him when you think no one is there to see you." His laugh was harsh. "You deserve better than a cripple, my darling Juliet."

Juliet felt her cheeks flame with fury. "You're the one who's crippled, Terry, or Dimitri, or whoever you are. Crippled in your soul and in your obscene mind. I feel sorry for you."

His face contorted in cold rage. "We'll see who feels sorry for whom."

He reached into the breast pocket of his khaki shirt and removed a ballpoint pen. His eyes bored into hers as he removed his hand from her throat to twist the pen in half.

A pink capsule fell into his hand, and he began to smile. "Open up, darling," he said with a sneer.

Mac, Juliet whispered soundlessly as she locked her jaw and shook her head in proud defiance, I love you.

* * *

A cold chill shivered through Mac's body as he realized how close he'd come to being late. If his leg hadn't begun to throb, if the cold hadn't penetrated his thin sweater, if he hadn't grown impatient sitting in the car... He couldn't think about that now. Not when Juliet was in such danger.

Silently, he shifted his weight to his right leg and prayed that he wouldn't stumble. He balanced his cane in his left hand, testing the feel. His right hand was so swollen that he could barely make a fist, and he gritted his teeth in frustration. If he missed, Juliet would die.

An icy calm came over him, steadying his galloping nerves. His eyes bored into the back of the janitor's head, gauging the distance.

Suddenly the man stiffened, alerted perhaps by some sixth sense, and he started to reach for Juliet's throat.

Mac moved, swinging the weighted cane in a steady arc toward the man's temple. Burton started to duck away, but it was too late. The silver handle slammed into his head with all the force Mac's powerful body could put into it, knocking the burly Soviet agent backward over Juliet's desk. He hung there limply, his skin purpling rapidly, his jaw slack, and then, with infinite slowness, he toppled over onto the floor.

The sickening thud as the muscular surfer's body hit the linoleum echoed hollowly through the silent building.

Juliet stared at the Russian in stunned silence. He lay in a crumpled heap, his sunburned face smashed against the side of the desk.

Her life came roaring back to her, vibrant and precious and filled with light. She jumped up and ran straight into Mac's arms, laughing and crying at the same time. He shuddered as he closed his arms around her and held her so tightly that she could scarcely breathe.

"Hold me," she begged in a shaky voice, her legs trembling so hard that she thought she would fall. "Don't let me go."

Mac groaned and buried his face in the perfumed mass of her tousled hair. It had been so close, so damned close. If he hadn't grown impatient, if his leg hadn't cramped in the narrow space, he might still be sitting down there in the car while Juliet was up here—dying.

Another tremor passed through his body, and he forced the horrible thought from his mind. No matter how close it had been, he'd gotten here in time, and Juliet was safe.

"Oh M-Mac, it was so aw—awful." She twisted her fingers into the wool of his sweater and tried to pull herself inside his sheltering warmth. She could feel him shaking almost as badly as she was.

"Terry...Felicity...twice—twice in one day...I was so scared." Her mind refused to focus clearly as she stammered out a nearly incoherent account of Terry's plans and Felicity's duplicity.

"Shh, it's all over now," Mac whispered as he stroked her hair with a gentle hand.

Juliet pressed her face into the hollow of his shoulder and hugged him tightly. He felt so solid and so dear, and she needed him so desperately, for all the days of her life.

Mac's hand moved lower to caress her back in gentle, soothing circles. "You're one terrific lady, you know that?" he drawled with a catch in his voice. "I heard you stand up to that creep, and I was so proud of you."

Juliet started to sob. "I thought...I'd never...see you again."

Mac stiffened, and his hand stilled. And then he was crushing her to him, his face pressed into the perfumed silk of her hair. "Sweet baby," he whispered fiercely. "If that animal had hurt you, I would have killed him."

Juliet felt him shudder, and she wanted to shout with joy. He hadn't said "I love you," but why else would he be holding her so tightly? Why else would he have risked further injury to save her this afternoon?

Twice he'd been there when she desperately needed help. No, more than that. He'd been there for Rex, too, when she'd asked him.

God, she loved him. In fact, she loved him so much that she was afraid to say it aloud. Maybe he had the same superstitious fear, too. Maybe that was why he couldn't say the words.

Her heart filled with joy, and she lifted her face to silently ask for his kiss.

Mac groaned and dipped his head. She could smell the musky scent of sweat on his skin, and the heady male fragrance reminded her of the risks he'd taken on her behalf. She tightened her arms around him and moaned. Terry or Dimitri or whatever his name was, was a professional. In his inexperience, Mac could easily have been killed. For her. Tears of love and relief began coursing down her cheeks, wetting his lips and hers.

They were both shaken when the kiss ended. Mac stepped back and looked with searching concern into her brown eyes. His hand was shaking as he wiped her tears away. "I'd like to hold you like this all night, baby, but we have things to do."

Juliet wiped her eyes and nodded. Now that the danger had passed, she was beginning to feel limp.

"Can you call security?" he asked with an anxious frown as he eyed the connecting wall. "While I see what's happening with Felicity?"

Fear gripped Juliet, and she clung to Mac's arm tightly. "You'll be careful? I couldn't stand it if anything happened to you."

Mac's face twisted, and he swallowed hard. "I'll be careful." He leaned down to give her a hard kiss.

Juliet smiled with tender worry and stepped away just as Felicity came into the room.

The worried look on the other woman's face turned to shock when she saw Mac and then to horror as her gaze dropped to Terry's huddled body.

"Is he dead?" she whispered, clutching the radio to her midriff.

Irony twisted Mac's lips. "No. He'll live to stand trial for espionage—along with his accomplice. You, Dr. Feldman."

Mac picked up the capsule from the top of the desk where it had fallen out of the janitor's hand and edged toward the door, putting his body between Felicity and escape. The abused muscles of his leg were rapidly stiffening, making it difficult to walk. He didn't know how long he could manage to stay on his feet.

He glanced at Juliet, who was explaining to the person on the other end that she needed help immediately. A surge of possessive fear unlike anything he'd ever known rocked through him, and he wanted to go to her, to hold her so tightly that she would never get away. But first he had a job to do.

"You'd better sit down, Felicity," he told the woman with a curt nod toward the other chair. "Security will be here soon."

As though in a daze, the immaculately groomed scientist glided across the room, placed the radio under the desk, and sank into the swivel chair. She folded her hands in her lap and crossed her ankles, smiling vacantly at Mac as though she were holding court.

Mac's eyes narrowed. It was either shock or a damn good act. But which?

The sound of a distant siren split the darkness. "Security," Juliet said nervously, biting her lip and darting a quick look at the motionless man on the floor.

"This hasn't been a great day for you, has it?" Mac drawled with a tender look of commiseration. He was leaning against the wall, his left knee flexed to relieve the pressure.

His jeans had been pinned shut in several places, but Juliet could see a heavy Ace bandage beneath the brace.

"Are you all right?" she asked with a worried smile as she got up and moved to his side. "Maybe you should sit down."

Mac flinched. "Don't baby me," he said in a thick voice, his eyes filled with turbulent fire.

Juliet felt her lips start to tremble, and she silently berated herself for her tactless choice of words. Tears glistened on her lashes, and she turned away, only to be hauled into a powerful one-armed embrace.

"I didn't mean that," he growled in a frustrated rumble next to her ear. "I'm not used to your kind of caring."

Juliet twisted in his embrace until she could slip her arms around his neck. "I need you so much," she whispered, leaning against him.

He slid his arm around her waist and rested his cheek on the top of her head. Love welled inside her, filling her to overflowing, and she made a silent vow. When this was over, when they were alone, she was going to tell Mac just how much he'd come to mean to her. And she would tell him about Peter and the guilt that consumed her day and night.

Mac would understand, just as he'd understood about Rex. And he would be there for her. He would never betray her. She was sure of it.

The wail of the siren reached ear-splitting intensity, and then suddenly stopped, followed by a screech of brakes and the sound of doors slamming.

Footsteps pounded up the fire escape, and Juliet darted a quick glance toward Felicity. The woman was staring at the papers on Juliet's desk, her brow furrowed, her glossy lips pursed in thoughtful contemplation.

"Dr. Prentice?" The gruff call came from the hall, and Juliet jerked in reaction. The adrenaline was beginning to drain from her system, leaving her weak and jittery.

Mac gave her shoulder a squeeze and dropped his arm as he slid his back up the wall to push himself erect. He leaned heavily on the cane and waited, tension radiating from him.

"In here," she called, her voice high and thin.

"Coming," shouted a man's deep voice.

A strange look passed over Mac's face. "Juliet, listen, there's something—"

Three men appeared in the open doorway, crouching low, guns drawn. Juliet held her breath as they looked around, assessing the stiff tableau spread out in front of them. Seemingly satisfied that there was no danger, they straightened and holstered their guns.

Two of the men were dressed in civilian clothes, while the third, the shortest and broadest of the three, wore the two-toned blue uniform of the base security force.

He was a man Juliet knew only as Gallagher, a jovial ex-Marine with a salt-and-pepper flattop who'd been working nights for as long as she could remember.

Gallagher nodded in Juliet's direction. "Looks like you've had some excitement here," he said with a sketchy smile.

"Too much," she replied in a tired tone.

Gallagher nodded, and his gaze swung to Mac. His sunken black eyes narrowed. "You the guy who decked the janitor?" He gestured toward Burton with a beefy hand.

Mac nodded. "He was going to kill Dr. Prentice." He pulled the cyanide capsule from his back pocket and handed it to the guard. "With this."

Gallagher frowned in puzzlement as he rolled the deadly pill between the finger and thumb of his right hand before handing it to the shorter of the two civilians. "And just who are you, sir?" he asked brusquely, his hand resting lightly on his holstered revolver.

"His name is Roarke McKinley, Gallagher," Juliet spoke up before Mac could answer. "He's a consultant from Washington. He doesn't have anything to do with this."

The strain in Mac's face increased, as though he resented her words, and Juliet frowned. She'd only been trying to help. But Mac wasn't a man who asked for help, she reminded herself, sneaking a quick glance at his closed expression. He looked like a man caught in some kind of a trap.

The two civilians watched Juliet with remote eyes, their faces blank. The younger of the two, a lanky olive-skinned man with straight black hair and a cleft chin, looked vaguely familiar, but she couldn't place him. The other, balding and built like a fireplug, had a quiet air of command about him that reminded her in a curious way of Mac.

Gallagher's gaze swung back to Juliet. "This guy, Burton, he tried to kill you?"

Juliet nodded. "He was an agent of... of the KGB, I guess. Uh, I think his real name was Dimitri something. He said he was Russian, planted here years ago." As coherently as she could, she recounted the events of the evening. "I don't know how much information they managed to get." Her eyes drifted to Felicity. "You'll have to ask Dr. Feldman about that."

All eyes swung to Felicity. Juliet nearly gasped aloud as the woman seemed to change before her eyes. She assumed a haughty air, her entire demeanor becoming cool and composed, her expression disdainful. "Good try, Juliet," she said with a pitying smile. "But I'm afraid it just won't work."

She leaned over the desk and tapped a note in Juliet's writing with a scarlet nail. "They were in it together—Juliet and Terry," she said with an earnest smile in her sultry voice. "I was working late when I heard them talking. That...that man,

Terry or whoever he is, caught Juliet writing this note, and he was furious with her. Read it. You'll see what I mean."

Juliet stiffened. "That's a lie. I caught *them* in the act." Her stomach churned as she watched first indecision and then suspicion kindle in the eyes of the two civilians as each in turn read the note.

Gallagher seemed more skeptical. "Why didn't you leave when you found out what was going on, Dr. Feldman?" he asked in a gravelly tone.

"I was hiding," Felicity said, her face twisting as tears gushed from her eyes. "I was afraid." Her voice fell away at the end, and her shoulders drooped as she wrung her hands.

To Juliet, watching with stunned eyes, it was a chilling performance. She almost believed it herself. Shivering suddenly, she moved closer to Mac and gripped his arm for support.

Gallagher measured the two women with a thoughtful gaze. Finally he frowned and turned to the hard-faced civilian, the one with the receding hairline and the big shoulders.

"What do you think, Commander Cahill? This is really your baby."

Phil Cahill drew his dark brows together in an enigmatic frown, then slowly raised his gaze to Mac's face. "Maybe you'd better ask Captain McKinley. He's in charge of this investigation."

Chapter 12

Juliet stood motionless, afraid to move. Her world began to tilt in silent slow motion, and for a frightening few seconds she thought she was going to faint.

A spasm of movement beneath her palm reminded her that she was still clinging to Mac's arm, and she stared down blankly at her fingers.

Moving slowly to keep from shattering, she loosened her grip, curling her cold fingers into her palms as she summoned a mask of composure. "Is it true?" she asked evenly, marshaling every ounce of self-discipline she possessed to keep from screaming.

Mac's eyes held hers, unflinchingly direct. "Yes, it's true. I work for Naval Intelligence." His drawl had a flattened quality, as though the words had been forced from his throat only with reluctance.

"I see," Juliet said without inflection. She hung on to her control with resolute tenacity, her years of determined self-reliance giving her strength.

"I don't think you do," Mac said with a sigh of impatience as he moved to shield her from the eyes of the others in the room. He stumbled slightly, and his face reddened as he caught her anxious look.

Compassion filled Juliet, but she forced herself to ignore it. Maybe they would give him a medal for risking his leg in the line of duty, she thought with bleak humor. Above and beyond, or something like that.

"Look, I know we need to talk, but—" Mac shrugged, glancing pointedly around the room.

"There's nothing to talk about, Captain," Juliet said stiffly, wrapping her pride around her like medieval armor as she edged out of his reach. "I've been used before, remember?"

Mac's face went blank, and his eyes took on an opaque sheen. "I was afraid you'd react this way," he muttered in a gritty voice. He jerked his gaze away from her face and directed his attention to the squat man in the dark brown suit.

"I can't give you chapter and verse here, Phil, but I'll vouch for Dr. Prentice." Mac's hard gaze pinned Felicity. "As for Dr. Feldman, we have reason to believe she's very much involved."

Felicity gave him an incredulous look. "Why would you say that, Mac?" she whispered in a piteous voice. "I'm innocent, I swear."

Mac shook his head. "It won't wash, Felicity. Juliet saw you at the terminal, transposing the files to disk for Burton."

"Look in the radio," Juliet said, coming out of her self-imposed isolation long enough to glare at Felicity. "It's there, by her feet. And her fingerprints are all over it."

Lieutenant Beatty hurried to the desk before Felicity could get her hands on the tiny player. He kicked it away, then handed it carefully to Cahill, who found the hidden spring. The back flipped open, exposing two miniature disks.

Felicity's pose of innocence fell away, and naked hatred blazed from her eyes as she glared at Mac. "I knew you were trouble. I *warned* Terry, but he wouldn't listen. I should have—"

"*Shut up, you stupid bitch!*" The man on the floor struggled to a sitting position, his face bloodless and twisted with murderous warning. A thin trickle of blood snaked down his swollen cheek, and he brushed it away with an impatient hand.

"Don't ever call me that again," Felicity ordered in a seething voice, a glittering light in her thickly fringed eyes. "I'm not stupid."

Mac gave Felicity a hard look. "Aren't you? Then why did you risk everything for a man who intended to kill you?"

Felicity gaped at him. "What?"

"You were the one who was supposed to be killed this morning," Mac told her, glancing toward the man on the floor. "Your buddy here had it all worked out—except you crossed him up and stayed home." His eyes raked her with icy anger. "I don't know what he used, but whatever it was, it made that big dolphin attack Juliet, who was in the tank instead of you."

Felicity swung her gaze to Burton, who met her disbelieving look with a bored shrug.

"Tonight," she said in a dull voice. "Tonight you were planning to kill *me*, too, weren't you? After we left here."

Burton remained silent, and Felicity began to cry.

Commander Cahill interrupted, reading both Burton and Felicity their rights in a clipped monotone. "Cuff 'em, Mr. Beatty," he ordered when he finished, and the younger man hastened to comply. Officer Gallagher assisted him, his face taut with contempt.

The commander glanced over his notes, then gave Juliet a thoughtful look. "If you're not too upset, ma'am, there are a few questions I'd like to ask."

Juliet stared at him. "Questions? What kind of questions?" Mac had asked questions, too. Dozens of them. But so cleverly that she'd been flattered instead of suspicious. What she'd seen as an almost mystical bonding between them had been instead a deliberate seduction on the part of a very clever and dedicated man.

She felt a deep pain slice through her at the memory of their lovemaking. It had been a sham. A farce. An obscenity.

A sob rose in her throat, but she refused to cry. Mac might have taken her body and her pride, but she was determined to keep her dignity.

Cahill was speaking again, and Juliet frowned, forcing herself to concentrate. "I'm sorry. What did you say?" It would be over soon, and then she could go home. She was beginning to feel terribly tired all of a sudden, so tired that her brain felt sluggish and her entire body ached.

Mac moved between Juliet and the commander, his broad back only a few inches from her face. His sweater was ripped at the neck, and there were flecks of white paint from the pier trapped in the burgundy cashmere.

"She's pretty upset, Phil," Mac said, his words more a command than an explanation. "I think we can wait until tomorrow for those questions."

"Yes, sir. Of course." Cahill closed his notebook and shoved it into his jacket pocket. "I'll radio for some men to seal off this area until the technical guys are done with it."

Cahill glanced over his shoulder at the others, who were bunched around the handcuffed janitor. "Anything else you need, Captain?" the commander asked, his blunt face impassive.

Mac's lips thinned. "Nothing you can give me."

Cahill nodded. "That's it, then. Good night, sir. Good night, ma'am."

Juliet and Mac stood side by side, watching in silence as Burton and Felicity were taken away. Felicity was white-faced but calm, her eyes focused on an inner scene only she could see.

The Soviet agent, on the other hand, seemed to be enjoying himself. "You'll never make it stick, suckers," he said with an arrogant sneer. "I'll be home in a month."

He was still jeering as they hauled him down the hall. Finally his voice faded into silence, and Juliet stared at the empty doorway. She felt naked and exposed—and frighteningly defenseless.

Her office seemed unfriendly, somehow, even evil, and she longed to go home. But first she needed answers.

"You knew someone was stealing secrets, didn't you?" she asked in an arid tone. "That's why you were here."

"Yes." Mac didn't like the hollow sound of her voice. There was no warmth, no gentle teasing, no spirit. Only distant courtesy. His stomach began to knot.

If only she would scream at him, call him all the names that he deserved, maybe then he could unload some of the guilt he felt, but she only looked at him with those wounded brown eyes that held no tears.

As soon as he'd heard Cahill's voice, he'd known that this moment had to come, known it and dreaded it. He knew how much she was hurting, how betrayed she must feel. He'd been there himself.

"I was the prime suspect from the beginning, wasn't I?" she asked with a chilling smile.

"Yes."

"I'd like to know why. I think you owe me that much, at least—after spending the night in my bed."

Mac flinched at the bitter mockery in her voice. "Juliet, don't," he pleaded.

"Don't what? Don't be upset? Don't be hurt?" Her voice rose as hysteria pulled at her. "Don't feel like a gullible fool? Is that what you mean?"

"You're not a fool," he said softly, touching her face with the back of his hand. "And you're not gullible. You're adorable and kind and sweet and—"

"Don't touch me!" She twisted away from him and crossed the room to stand at the window, arms crossed over her chest, her eyes fixed on the darkness outside. "I want to know why you suspected me," she said in a cold voice. She didn't look at him as she spoke.

Mac limped over to the chair where Felicity had sat and shrugged into his jacket. The office had become icy cold, and the pain in his leg was making him light-headed. He clenched his teeth and lowered his tired body into the chair. Better to sit down than fall at Juliet's feet, he admitted with grim self-mockery.

"It was the money for Rex's care," he told her with a heavy sigh. "There was no paper trail."

Juliet's chuckle was bitter. "I didn't know I was so clever."

"You're too damned clever. That's why it took us so long to figure out what you were really doing." Mac rubbed his hand along his jaw. He needed a shave, and his eyes felt gritty. He stifled a sigh. Never in an eternity could he have anticipated the way this day had turned out.

Juliet turned away from the window. "You know? About Peter? And his book?"

"Yes, I know. Now."

"Leave your address and I'll send you a copy." Her voice took on a brittle edge. "Oh, silly of me. Naval Intelligence is in the Pentagon, isn't it? I'll send it there." She stared at him, daring him to answer.

"Juliet, this isn't getting us anywhere," he said impatiently. "I know you're upset, but—"

"I'll get over it," she interrupted, looking around for her purse. She wanted to leave before the tears pressing against her lids overflowed and betrayed her.

Mac watched with unreadable eyes. Why doesn't he just leave? she thought in deepening anger as she retrieved her purse from her drawer. Surely he'd gotten everything he'd come for.

She took a step toward the door, only to be stopped by Mac's voice. "You said you loved me," he said in what sounded like an accusation. "This morning, out there on the pier. Or did I dream it?"

The anger fell away, leaving Juliet exposed and silently screaming in pain. "I loved the man I thought you were," she whispered through trembling lips. "The man I knew in my heart as Roarke, who was kind and decent and... and loving. A man who would never lie to me."

"Juliet, it's not what you think. I suspected you, yes, but I didn't want to believe it was you. I tried everything I could think of to prove that it wasn't, but the evidence just kept piling up." He was losing her; he could see it. But he couldn't give up. Not yet.

He ran a hand through his hair. "Sometimes innocent people get hurt, Juliet. It's no one's fault. It just...happens." His eyes met hers, his expression bleak. "I'm truly sorry if I hurt you. I just didn't have a choice."

Juliet wanted to go to him, to kiss away the deep valleys of fatigue aging his face, to tell him that it didn't matter. But it did.

"You did have a choice, Mac," she said in a sad voice that sliced with surgical precision at his rigid control. "Sunday and last night, in my bed, you could have stopped."

He squared his shoulders. "Would you believe me if I told you it was just you and me in your bed? Not the project and not the Navy? Just one man and one woman who shared something beautiful?"

"That's a laugh," she said with a disbelieving smile. "I think it's called pillow talk, isn't it, Mac? When an agent trades sex for information?"

"Think, Juliet," he ordered brusquely. "Did I try to pump you for information? Did I mention the project? Or ask a few discreet questions about Rex's hospital bills? I could have done it, done it so subtly you never would have noticed. But I didn't, did I?"

"I really thought you were different," she said with a sad quiver in her voice. "I told myself that I could trust you, that you were decent and kind. Not like Robert, who only wanted to sleep with me to get my research." Her mouth trembled. "I thought you just wanted *me*."

"I did. I *do*. I've wanted you from the first instant I saw you." His mouth slanted into a rueful expression. "If I weren't dead tired, I'd prove it to you right now, right here."

Her shoulders jerked with pain. "Don't, Mac," she whispered. "Please don't keep pretending."

He saw the curtain come down over her beautiful eyes, shutting him out. She stood like a lovingly fashioned statue, alone in her ethereal beauty, every curve of her slender body rejecting him.

He closed his eyes, and his broad chest lifted in a ragged sigh. When he lifted his lids again, it was as though a stranger sat before her. A hard man with remote eyes the color of the deepest ocean. A man whose face held lines that told stories of battles won and lost. A man who had no heart.

"You don't have the faintest idea what my job is like, Juliet. Or what I've had to do to get it done." The words uncoiled with steely menace, chilling her to the marrow. "But one of the things I've *never* done is sleep with a woman for any reason other than a personal one. I'm not that kind of man, but I can see you're not in any mood to believe me tonight."

Silence stretched between them, deepening with each second that passed.

"I want to believe you, but...I can't," she said finally, feeling as though she were drowning in her own pain.

Mac bowed his head. "Have it your way, Juliet," he drawled at last. "I'm too tired to fight you."

The muscles of his arms bulged as he pushed himself to his feet, leaning heavily for an instant on his cane as though to catch his breath.

She bit her lip to keep from crying out. In spite of his perfidy, he was still the bravest man she'd ever met.

"If you don't mind, I think I'll call it a night," he said with black irony. "Can I see you to your car?"

Juliet shook her head, tears welling in her eyes. A long look passed between them, poignant and sad and filled with raw pain.

"Try not to hate me too much," he said with abrupt finality, turning away. His back was ramrod straight as he limped out of the room. He didn't look back.

It was raining the next morning when Juliet arrived at the base. Fat black clouds, heavy and smothering, lay above Point Loma, blocking out the sun and turning the bay to a dreary gray.

She shook the raindrops from her umbrella and collapsed it with a sigh as she stepped into the elevator and pushed the Up button.

It seemed like an eternity since she'd taken that first ride with Mac in this same elevator. No, a lifetime, she corrected, staring at the closed doors. Her lifetime.

The doors opened, and she stepped out, only to come face to face with a huge black man wearing the combat fatigues of a Marine corporal.

"I need to see some ID, please, ma'am," he said politely, his eyes watchful and hard.

Her throat tightened as she remembered another time, another place, when she'd been the one examining a badge. She could still see the startled look in Mac's eyes as she'd repeated his beautiful name.

As the Marine handed back her ID with a curt word of thanks, Juliet wondered how many more times she would be reminded of Mac before this day was over.

"Juliet, I can't *believe* what happened." Maria hurried around the desk to give Juliet a hug. "Fred said Mac saved your life—again. This place is becoming more exciting than a spy novel."

Maria's black eyes were wide with questions, and Juliet felt her spirits sag. The last thing she wanted to do was relive last night's nightmare. She'd done enough of that during the tortuous hours that had passed for sleep after she'd left the base.

Giving the secretary a wan smile, she headed for the safety of her office, only to be confronted by another Marine.

"Sorry, ma'am. This area is off-limits."

"But that's my office," she protested, peering around his body.

"I have my orders, ma'am."

So that's the way it's going to be, she thought dejectedly, walking down the hall to Fred's corner office.

The sound of Greg's nervous laugh drew her toward the conference room, her steps slowing with reluctance as she reached the door.

The door was ajar, and through the slit she could see Fred standing by the window, his pipe in his hand, his fist thrust into his pants pocket.

Napoleon in wingtips, she thought with a mental shake of her head. Wanting to tell me my clearance has been revoked, and I'm out of a job. She lifted her chin, wet her lips and reached for the doorknob. If she had to go, she would go with all flags flying.

"Good morning," she chirped, giving Fred her best smile. "Lousy weather out there, isn't it?"

"*Juliet!* I didn't expect you so early," he said with a frown of concern. "Are you sure you're all right?"

"Right as can be," she said in a cheery voice. She sailed into the room and dropped her purse and umbrella into the nearest chair.

Greg, seated close to the door, bolted to his feet to give her a spontaneous bear hug. "I hope they hang the scum," he said with a fervent scowl. "No good Commie creep."

Juliet laughed and squeezed Greg's arm as he released her. Only then did she notice the third man in the room.

It was Mac.

She felt the blood drain from her face. She should have known he'd be here. His job wasn't quite finished. What did Peter call it? Mopping up, that was it.

"Good morning, Captain McKinley," she said with exquisite politeness, meeting his gaze squarely.

His sapphire eyes were narrowed at the corners, lines fanning into the tan of his temples, and he was looking at her without expression. "Dr. Prentice," he answered with equal courtesy as he slowly got to his feet. His face was drawn, his lips compressed. There was an air of command about him that made her stiffen her spine in self-defense.

He was in uniform, winter blues, meticulously tailored to fit his huge shoulders and narrow torso. Five rows of campaign medals were pinned above the left breast pocket, bright colorful bits of ribbons that contrasted starkly with the dark blue wool.

Juliet's eyes fell to the four gold stripes on his sleeves, the insignia of great power in the hierarchy of the military. The mark of success. And a brutal reminder of his true purpose in courting her.

"I saw the report on the news this morning," she told him. "Congratulations."

His lashes dipped a fraction. "Thanks."

"Was the project badly compromised?"

He shook his head. "We managed to intercept the courier before he delivered the films."

"Films?"

"Yes. Burton had a PC and a printer at his apartment where he printed out the information, then microfilmed it."

Juliet and Fred exchanged looks. "Sounds too simple," she commented in dry amazement.

"Security can't check everything." Mac's drawl sounded flat, even stilted, as though he were trying to contain his impatience.

Juliet nodded, then glanced at the director. "I guess I'm out of a job."

It was Mac who answered. "The Navy department understands that there were . . . extenuating circumstances. You can keep your job. *Both* your jobs, until Admiral DuBois' book is finished."

Juliet gaped at him. She had a feeling there was more behind the Navy's decision than he was telling her.

"Why don't we all sit down?" Fred said, bustling toward the head of the table. "Now that you're here, Juliet, Mac can give us all the details." He chuckled, a forced man-to-man growl.

Juliet's eyes clung to Mac's. She couldn't seem to look away. A dozen emotions buffeted her tense body, pushing and pulling at her until she wanted to scream.

The scrape of a chair leg shattered her concentration, and she blinked, glancing down at the polished surface of the table as she slipped into the chair across from Mac and focused her gaze on the white uniform cap lying on the table next to his cane.

Mac sat down and cleared his throat. He folded his hands together on the table in front of him, and Juliet winced at the raw scratches that reddened his palm in a wide swath.

"The man you know as Terry Burton is what is known as a 'mole,'" he began without preamble. "An agent of the KGB, rigorously schooled in American ways, language, culture, history, everything. As far as we've been able to determine in the short time we've had, he was sent here when he was seventeen, eighteen, something like that, and he's been living in California ever since." Mac paused, glancing at Juliet before continuing.

"As far as we've been able to piece together, the sole purpose of Burton's presence here was to infiltrate the NRC in some way, and once he'd done that, to turn one of the key researchers. I'm not sure if it was fate or luck that had him assigned to this building." He raked a hand through his clipped curls. "The rest, as they say, is history. Apparently, Felicity felt humiliated when Fred was brought in over her, the young janitor had a sympathetic ear, and it was just a matter of time.''

"But I still can't believe Felicity would do such a thing," Juliet burst out without thinking. "I mean, she seemed so...dedicated.''

Mac's expression tightened. "She was—to herself. Glory and recognition were more important than her country.''

"What about the dolphins?" Greg asked. "Did Terry have anything to do with Bubbles' attack on Juliet?''

Mac nodded toward Dr. Kurtz, who answered somberly, "From what the vet told me this morning, Bubbles had been given the equivalent of ten food supplement tablets, more than enough to cause temporary insanity. Burton must have administered the drug sometime in the early hours, before you arrived to feed the animals, Greg.'' He gave Juliet an apologetic look. "Burton must have heard us arguing about those vitamin tablets, or read one of your reports.'' He cleared his throat. "I'm truly sorry, Juliet, that I didn't listen to you.''

Juliet forced a smile. "It's okay, Fred. Just as long as we get a safe substitute out of it.''

"Bubbles seemed fine this morning," Greg interjected, grinning nervously across the table at Juliet. "Right, Captain McKinley?''

Mac nodded, his lips lifting in a faint smile. "She looked all right to me.''

He glanced around the table, his eyes coming to rest on Juliet's face. "There's one more thing I think you should know. All of you.'' His eyes swept the table, returning to Juliet's face. "A man's life was at stake here, a very valuable man. If the traitor hadn't been uncovered, it's quite conceivable that our man would have been killed—or at least neutralized—with very grievous results for the country's national security interests.''

Juliet felt her heart begin to pound. It was as though Mac were speaking only to her, as though he were pleading with her to understand. Or was she only imagining the throbbing note of raw feeling beneath the terse words?

She studied the gold leaves on the shiny black brim of his cap. She couldn't seem to think logically. Last night everything had seemed very clear, laid out in brutal black and white to taunt her. But this morning, here, now, with Mac looking so cold and distant and unrepentant, shades of gray were beginning to creep into her thoughts. She had to get away, had to find some time to think, without the fog of fatigue and hurt clouding her brain.

"Excuse me," she mumbled, stumbling to her feet. She grabbed her belongings and was out of the room before anyone could stop her.

"...so that's when I left. I've been walking on the beach in the rain most of the morning." Juliet stared down at the powdery black dregs in the bottom of the Styrofoam cup. The hospital coffee had been bitter and scalding hot, just what she'd needed to revive her flagging strength.

Rex watched her with thoughtful eyes. He was seated in his chair by the window, dressed in a gray running suit, with heavy white socks on his feet.

It was almost eleven-thirty, the time when he was supposed to be resting after his morning therapy, but when Juliet had arrived unexpectedly, looking pale and sad, he'd forgotten all about his fatigue. For the first time in his life, his sister needed *him*.

"Sounds like you made a real mess of things, big sister," he said in a matter-of-fact way. "Letting a cold-hearted fella like that take advantage of you. Guy should be castrated."

Juliet's head jerked up, and her jaw fell. "Don't be crude, Rex. I didn't come here for gutter talk."

Rex's face softened. "Just why did you come, Julie?"

"I told you. I need a little T.L.C. from my brother."

Rex shook his head. "I don't think so. I think you came here so I could tell you that you're right and Mac's wrong."

Juliet stood up and began pacing the small private room. "Surely you don't believe it was okay for him to...to sleep with me because it was part of his job."

"He told you it wasn't."

"He's lying," Juliet declared flatly, perching on the edge of the high bed.

"Is he?" He gave her a probing look. "How can you be so certain about that?"

"Sure, stick up for him," Juliet sputtered, feeling oddly disoriented. "Don't listen to me."

Rex propelled his chair closer. "I like Mac a lot, I admit it," he said in a forceful voice, "but I *love* you. That's why I hate to see you being so damned obstinate about this."

Juliet glared at her brother in outrage. "You should talk," she accused him with a hurt look. "How many phone calls of mine did you refuse to take these past few days?"

An embarrassed flush colored Rex's thin face. "You're right," he admitted with a crooked smile. "I've been a jerk, just like Mac said early this morning when he came to say good-bye."

Juliet's jaw dropped, and her eyes flashed. "He came to see you? And you didn't tell me."

Rex met her accusing stare with stiff defiance. "My friendship with Mac has nothing to do with you, Julie. Just as what happens between you two has nothing to do with me."

Juliet opened her mouth to protest, then shut it with a snap. Rex was right. No matter how much Mac had hurt her, he'd still been there for Rex when he'd needed an understanding friend.

Juliet stared at her brother, seeing the determined light in his eyes. A fresh deluge of tears shook her. Why couldn't she make herself hate Mac? Then maybe this wouldn't hurt so much.

She crumpled her cup and tossed it toward the trash basket by the bed. She missed and started to bend over when Rex stopped her. Leaning over, he scooped up the cup and dropped it into the basket, beaming up at her with twinkling eyes.

Juliet's grin was shaky as she plucked a tissue from the box on the nightstand and wiped her eyes. "I guess I'd better go," she said with a rueful frown. "Thank God I still have a job."

She slid off the bed and bent down to give her brother a hug. "I'm glad you're feeling better," she said softly.

Sadness touched Rex's face. "I'm sorry it didn't work out between you and Mac. I think you two could have had something really special."

"Me, too," Juliet whispered with a wistful note, squaring her shoulders. "But I guess we can't have everything in this life."

Twin lines of indecision furrowed Rex's brow for an instant before he took her hand. "Julie, there's something I need to tell you, something that I think you should know."

He dropped her hand and stared down at the floor, as though searching for words. "It's about Dad."

Juliet frowned. "What about him?"

"You won't like it," he warned, raising apprehensive green eyes to her face.

Juliet heaved a sigh. "You might as well tell me. This seems to be my week for trauma."

Rex managed a small grin. "Once, when I was visiting Dad and Ingrid in Palm Springs, a letter he'd written to you came back unopened, and I asked him why he kept sending them, especially after the rotten things you'd said to him that day at the house when he tried to explain his decision to divorce Mom."

Juliet felt a clammy uneasiness settle into her stomach at the memory of her years of estrangement from her father before she'd managed to work through the pain and anger she'd felt at his leaving. "And what did he say?"

The room was still very still as Rex answered. "He said that he loved you. And because he loved you, he'd forgiven you."

With that he squeezed her hand, whirled around and wheeled toward the door. "I'm late for lunch. Say hello to Mac for me—if you should happen to see him, that is."

Then he was gone, leaving Juliet staring after him, his words ringing loudly in her ears.

It was a few minutes past one when Juliet pulled up in front of her cottage. Before she returned to the base, she needed to change out of her damp clothes.

There was an official Navy vehicle parked in Mac's spot, with a man in an enlisted man's uniform seated in the driver's seat.

He nodded impersonally to Juliet as she passed, and she muttered a greeting in return. Mac must be in his bungalow, packing to leave.

Her steps dragged as she walked through the gate and up the walk to her front door. She should see him, should say good-bye, at least.

But the words were locked in her head, her thoughts a dark maze of troubled contradictions and jumbled questions. She'd thought about Rex's shocking revelation all the way home, but whenever she thought about forgiving Mac, a wave of chilling resistance swept over her. If only she didn't feel so humiliated . . .

She kept her eyes trained on her door as she fumbled in her purse for her key. Even if she did see him, even if she could bring herself to forgive him, what was left to say? I wish you hadn't hurt me? I wish you'd loved me? She shook off the sardonic thoughts and pushed open the door.

The house was quiet when she entered, too quiet. She shivered and dropped her purse on the small table by the door.

"Hello, Juliet. I was beginning to think you'd never get home." Mac was standing by the window, watching her with those fathomless eyes that seemed to bore more deeply into her soul every time he looked at her.

"How did you get in here?" she asked, her voice a mere thread of sound.

"That's a trade secret," he drawled with gentle humor, and Juliet felt a sad smile tug at her lips.

"I . . . forgot."

"Did you?"

In that simple question she could read hope and doubt. And sadness. She moved to the end of the couch and perched on the arm, keeping the room between them.

"Is that your car outside? The one that says, 'Official Business Only'?"

Mac's face creased into a grin. "Yeah. Promise you won't tell on me."

"Why should I?" she said in a stiff tone. "I'm sure this *is* official business for you, Mac. Just like everything else between us."

In an instant the humor was gone from his face, leaving his expression cold and furiously angry. "I'm going to say this one more time, and then I'm finished with it, Juliet. I did not, repeat, *did not* sleep with you because of my job. I slept with you because I wanted to, because you're the sexiest woman I've ever met, and because I was rapidly going out of my mind thinking about making love to you when I should have been thinking about the case." His eyes flashed with impatience. "I'm not some kind of stud who can just leap into bed with any available female, Juliet, no matter what you've decided."

"How do you know what I've decided?" she shot back, stung by his words. "Are you a mind reader as well as a phony?"

Mac uttered a rude obscenity as he took two steps toward her before stopping abruptly. "If you were a man, I'd deck you for saying that."

"Go ahead," she challenged recklessly, deliberately masking her pain with anger. "I dare you."

Mac's face flushed. "Don't push me, lady. Just don't push me." He looked like a man stretched to his limits, a man ready to explode.

"And don't *lie* to me," Juliet shot back heatedly. "I'm not totally naive."

Mac's nostrils flared as he inhaled slowly, his eyes glittering chips of icy anger. "I am not lying," he told her with staccato forcefulness. "And I wasn't lying about my feelings for you, though God knows why I was so tied up in knots over a woman who's so bloody narrow-minded."

Juliet's face twisted into an expression of anguish. *"Stop it,"* she shouted in a voice that broke. "Stop pretending!"

Mac's fist clenched around his cane, and his eyes flashed blue heat. *"I'm not pretending!"* he shouted back, making Juliet flinch. "I'm telling you the God's honest truth. I wanted you then, and I want you now." His lips quirked, and his voice dropped into a husky confession that seemed torn from him. "Making love to you was very special to me. It had nothing to do with the job or the Navy or, God forgive me, the country I love. I swear it." His lips twisted. "But I can see you don't believe me."

Juliet began to shake. "I want to believe you, Mac," she said in a quivering voice. "I do. But I'm afraid."

He crossed the room in three stiff strides, his face a harsh mask. "Feel me, Juliet," he challenged in a ragged voice, pulling her hard against his body. "Feel how much I want you. Why can't you believe in that?"

Juliet fought against the tears. The anger that had been her shield had been stripped away by his touch, leaving her defenseless against the truth. "Because it's not enough. I—I need love." She pressed her wet cheek against his shoulder and closed her eyes. He smelled of soap and cigar smoke, and the rough wool of his uniform was smooth against her skin.

Mac stiffened, and his arms tightened. "Isn't it enough that I care about you? That I was scared half to death when I saw you pinned against the side of the dolphin tank?" His big body shuddered against hers. "I've never felt so helpless in my life."

Mac sighed and leaned down to rest his forehead against Juliet's. Her skin felt cool against his, and smooth as silk.

He could still remember the feel of that tawny skin beneath his hands. She'd come alive for him, all vibrant curves and sweetly straining kisses. His body taunted him with the memory, exciting a need that was nearly overpowering.

Juliet tried to pull herself out of his arms, but Mac held her fast. "But you believed I was a traitor!" she cried in a tortured voice. "You actually thought I could . . . could do something so. . .so despicable." Her voice fell to an anguished thread. "How could you, Mac? How *could* you believe something like that?" That was the most terrible hurt of all, she realized with sudden insight. That he'd actually believed her guilty. Hot tears flooded her eyes and dotted her lashes, and she dashed them away with an impatient hand.

Mac moved restlessly, shifting his weight. He could hear the agony in her voice. But how could he explain something to her that he barely understood himself?

It was all so new, this insight that had come to him in the middle of the pain-tossed night. What if he was wrong? What if he was only feeling guilty? He needed more time to think it through, but his time had run out.

She'd already erected a formidable barrier of pride against him. Give her a month or a week or even a few days, and she would have made it insurmountable. And then nothing he said would reach her.

Mac grasped her arm and silently guided her to the front of the sofa. "Sit," he said gruffly. "And don't say anything. This isn't going to be easy, and I want to get through it without interruption. Okay?''

Juliet nodded, blinking up at him warily. He searched his mind, trying to decide where to begin. How could a sweet and loving woman like Juliet possibly understand the kind of life he'd led?

He retrieved his cane and limped over to stare out the window. His shoulders were squared beneath the tailored line of his uniform, and his head was held stiffly as he tried to ignore the need tormenting him to distraction.

"Eight years ago I was involved in a covert action in the Middle East. My job was to set up a network of informers sympathetic to the U.S. in a small but strategic sheikdom near Saudi Arabia.

"There was a woman there, the daughter of a minor government official. She'd been educated at Vassar and spoke perfect English. She was one of those who proved invaluable in making contacts with potential sympathizers."

Mac's heart began to pound as the memories began flooding over him. During the endless months in the naval hospital he'd systematically dismantled those memories and shoved them from his mind. Each time one would struggle up from his subconscious, he would shove it ruthlessly back down, out of conscious thought.

He took a deep breath. Only for Juliet would he put himself through this. Only to remove the terrible hurt from her eyes and from her heart. He owed her that, at the very least.

"Her name was Misrani. She was beautiful and smart and very sophisticated. I . . . fell in love with her."

His throat tightened, and he had to stop. Swallowing hard, he stared out at the sea. There was a soft murmur behind him, and he turned around.

"She's the one you told me about, isn't she? The one you wanted to marry?" Juliet's chest was so tight that she could scarcely breathe.

"Yes," he said with a smile that didn't quite succeed. Then he turned back to the sea. It was easier when he didn't have to watch the pity surge into her eyes.

"Misrani was a double agent, using me to get the names of our contacts in the other countries in the area." In a flat voice he told her about Misrani's betrayal and his capture.

"It took our people four days to find me, and another day to get me out. I was in pretty bad shape by that time." He cleared his throat. "That's why I could believe that you were guilty, Juliet. Why I could continue to believe it, even when I got to know you. I wanted to go with my gut instinct that you couldn't be guilty, in spite of the evidence, but I'd been so damned wrong about Misrani, that I just couldn't trust myself anymore."

Juliet stood up and walked to his side. She couldn't bear to see him standing there so alone. "What did they do to your leg?" she asked softly.

The muscles of his face tightened into stony resistance. "You don't want to know."

"Tell me."

He swallowed hard. "Colonel Hashemi, Misrani's superior, had been a blacksmith in his younger days. He was very . . . capable with a hammer."

Juliet tried to imagine what it must have been like, having his leg smashed inch by inch with the blunt end of a heavy hammer, but her mind refused to function.

"I told you that you didn't want to know," he said in a dry voice.

"What happened to him? This Colonel Hashemi, I mean?"

Mac hesitated. "A man named Carter Hendricks blew his head off."

Juliet blanched. "Good," she said in a strong voice. "I'm glad."

Mac's jaw dropped.

"I mean it," she said, lifting her chin in defiance, her eyes flashing velvet fire. "I'm glad he's dead."

Mac reached out to touch the lone tear quivering on her soft cheek. "Don't cry for me, Juliet," he said in a voice that he couldn't keep steady. "I don't want you to pity me. I've told you before—that's not what I want from you."

Her eyes searched his, doubt filling her gaze. "I'm not sure I know what you *do* want," she said quietly, holding her breath.

If he asked for her forgiveness she would give it willingly, because she loved him. Her father had been wiser than she'd known.

She exhaled slowly, feeling the anguish slip away, leaving her feeling oddly cleansed. She would hurt for a while, maybe for the rest of her life. But she would always have the memory of this one special man.

Mac stood frozen. He didn't know what he wanted. Not really. He only knew that the demons of loneliness and loss that drove him night and day disappeared when he was with her. That she could make him forget the pain in his leg and all the commonplace things he couldn't do anymore. That she excited him and fascinated him more than any other woman he'd ever met. That he would kill for one of her sweet smiles and the gentle touch of her hand.

His heart began galloping in his chest, and sweat dotted his brow. Fight or flight, he knew the drill. But which did he want to do?

Mac took a deep breath. He was terrified, more terrified than he'd ever been in his life. Nothing had seemed more frightening—not Vietcong bullets or terrorist torture.

He took a firm grip of his cane, squared his shoulders and looked her straight in the eye. "I want you to love me as much as I love you."

Silence greeted his terse declaration, and Mac stiffened. For the first time in his adult life he wanted to run and hide. He should have known better. Juliet was young and beautiful, with a perfect body. Why the hell should she want him?

"To...to what?" she asked finally, looking dazed, even dismayed, and he knew for certain that he'd made a terrible mistake.

"Forget it," he muttered, taking a jerky step away from her. "I knew it was a long shot."

He looked around for his cap. "Look, I have a plane to catch, so—"

"Oh no you don't," Juliet said in an emphatic but shaky voice. "Don't you dare walk out on me."

Mac blinked in confusion. She sounded angry, but her whole face was glowing, and there was a shimmering light in her eyes that he'd never seen before.

"Juliet, there's nothing else I . . ." He lifted a hand in a gesture of helpless confusion, and she reached out to guide that big rough hand to her face.

"You've told me what you want, and now it's my turn," she said in a gentle voice. "I want you, my darling Roarke."

She moved closer to press her body to his. She was dizzy with happiness, and her body was aching with need. Just the feeling of his palm against her skin was deliciously erotic, reminding her of how it could be.

Mac felt a constriction in his throat. "For how long?" he asked in a hoarse voice, curling his fingers around the delicate sweep of her jaw.

"How about if we start with forever, and then negotiate from there?" she answered softly, looking up at him with adoring eyes.

"I want it all," he whispered in the soft drawl she loved. "Marriage, a house, kids." His brow was furrowed with doubt, and Juliet reached out to smooth away the lines.

"The whole package," she said with an eager smile, caressing his hard face with her fingertips.

The smile started deep in the midnight pupils of his eyes, and spread to his lips, softening the austere tightness of his face as it blossomed into a lopsided grin.

"It won't be easy, loving me," he said in a rough whisper. "I've gone my own way for a long, long time. And sometimes I resent the things I can't do. Also, there's my job to consider. I'm not ready to quit, baby. Not yet." He had to lay it on the line for her; there had been too many lies between them.

She gave him an impatient look. "I'm not sure it's easy loving anyone. But I'm willing to take the risk—because I can't stand the thought of living the rest of my life without you."

Mac swallowed hard. "I want you to be sure, Juliet. Sure that you know what you're letting yourself in for." He rested his cheek against the top of her head for an instant, then leaned back to look into her eyes. "I want you desperately, but I can't promise you happily ever after. You need to know that. I'll do the best I can, but—"

Juliet put gentle fingers against his hard mouth. "I can read between the lines, darling. I'm not asking for promises or guarantees. All I'm asking for is your love. The rest we can handle when it happens."

He closed his eyes and crushed her to his chest. He felt something hard and cold give way inside him, letting the warmth that was Juliet's love rush in. His eyes filled with the tears that neither torture nor pain had been able to wring from him.

"Sweet baby," he whispered in the honeyed drawl Juliet loved so much. "I love you."

Her fingers trembled as she wiped the tears from his cheeks. He was hers, this hard-faced man with the tender heart. And she would cherish him all the days of her life.

Epilogue

It was a perfect wedding.''

Juliet rested her head on Mac's hard shoulder and played with the shiny gold band next to his Academy ring on the third finger of his left hand.

They were in the bedroom of their new home in Key West, close to the Navy research facility where Juliet was now assistant director of the dolphin training program.

"It was too bloody long," her new husband drawled in sleepy protest next to her ear. His hand rested possessively on her breast, and his body was stretched out in a relaxed sprawl next to hers. "I thought we'd never get out of there."

Juliet giggled. "You should have seen your face when the photographer asked for one more picture."

Mac groaned and nuzzled her temple. "You try standing for hours with a starched collar digging into your gullet."

She tilted her head so she could look into his eyes. "You looked so handsome in your uniform," she said with a dreamy smile. "All I could think about when I came down the aisle was how much I love you."

A wash of dusky color spread across his cheeks. "I was just trying not to embarrass myself," he said with a growl. "You kept me out of your bed for the entire week you were staying on the farm.''

"Is that why you're trying to make up for seven days all in one night?" she asked impishly, stretching her body with languid grace. It was almost dawn; they'd been in bed almost eight hours, but had only slept an hour or two.

"You're darned right I'm trying to make up for it," Mac exclaimed. "I've been one frustrated guy, having to leave you at the door to that blasted guest room every night. I don't know how I'm going to be able to stand it whenever I have to fly up to D.C."

Juliet chuckled softly. Mac's parents had been so sweet to her, welcoming Rex and her with an old-fashioned courtesy that had put her at ease at once.

They'd looked so proud as Mac took his place in front of the altar—proud and relieved.

Juliet smiled reminiscently. Her father would have loved the setting. The tiny stone church in the town of Roarkeville, Virginia, had a simple charm that was more beautiful to her than any cathedral, and the day itself had been one of those exquisite celebrations of nature, warm and fragrant with budding blossoms, the sky a deep cerulean backdrop for the riot of color that lined the road to the chapel.

The entire county had been invited to witness the marriage of Roarkeville's most elusive bachelor, and most had attended, filling the chapel and overflowing onto the green lawn outside.

Juliet had worn her mother's wedding dress, which had aged to a beautiful ivory satin, and Mac had worn his dress whites. His sister had been Juliet's only attendant, and Rex, recently released from the hospital and eager to return to college, had been Mac's best man.

At the reception, which had been held in the rose garden of the antebellum mansion where Mac had grown up, Juliet had been kissed and praised and congratulated until Mac had finally insisted that they had to leave or miss their plane to Florida.

Now Juliet rubbed her toes against the inside of her husband's calf, loving the feel of him. He would never be handicapped in her eyes, no matter how badly he limped. "I like Carter Hendricks very much," she said, stifling a yawn with one slender hand. "He's a lovely man."

Mac chuckled. "Don't ever tell Carter that. He thinks he's as tough as they come." He nuzzled her temple with his cheek. She smelled of roses.

"It was nice of him to let you work out of Key West," she murmured.

"Nice, hell. I told him it was that or nothing. Carter's a pragmatist."

"Oh yeah?" She tangled her fingers in the curly hair of his chest and tugged gently.

"Ouch, woman," he protested in a baritone growl, capturing her hand with his. "That hurts."

Juliet giggled. "I'm just...exploring," she teased. His body stirred, then surged to life against her belly. She purred silently, an intimate smile spreading over her face.

"Uh-uh," Mac drawled, raising her fingers to his mouth to take a nip. "You're trying to get me all worked up again."

"Do you mind?" She gave him a sultry look, eager to see his eyes sparkle with happiness when she teased him. Slowly, patiently, without seeming to, she was teaching him to play.

Mac's laughing eyes turned serious. Every time they made love, he found himself more vulnerable to her. At first he'd been wary of opening up to her, having been conditioned for so long to hold back, but the harder he tried to protect himself, the more he yearned for the shining love she offered.

He moved slightly, adjusting their bodies into a more comfortable position. "I guess I'll get used to having a wildcat temptress for a wife—after a while," he drawled with a laconic smile. "In the meantime, I guess I'll just have to do the best I can to keep you happy." His fingers traced her parted lips with reverent gentleness, and Juliet shivered with pleasure.

Little by little he was changing, letting go of the reserve that had distanced him from her in the beginning, even after he'd asked for her love.

He was still moody, especially when he was frustrated by the limitations his leg imposed, and sometimes he shut her out, but he was slowly learning to share himself with her.

She trailed her fingers down his hard body, feeling his muscles ripple under her fingertips as he reacted to her touch.

His chest heaved, and he closed his eyes, his face tight with pleasure. Juliet moved lower, pushing the sheet from his naked body, anointing his hard torso with tiny kisses.

His skin felt slightly rough under her lips and smelled of soap. She moved lower, finding the line of curling chestnut hair that trailed below his navel.

He shuddered under her caressing tongue, then groaned. His fingers tangled in her hair as he writhed beneath her.

"Sweet baby," he whispered in a choked voice, reaching for her.

Juliet raised her head and pressed him back against the rumpled sheets with gentle hands. "Let me show you how much I love you," she pleaded in a voice that vibrated with emotion.

Mac's face relaxed into a tender smile as he lay back on the pillow and closed his eyes. He'd come a long way since that cold and snowy day in February when he'd first seen the photo of Juliet Prentice.

My wife, he thought with infinite satisfaction. She was his love. His very life.

For as long as he lived, he would need her. And he would love her every day of that life, love and cherish and protect her. He would never walk alone again.

* * * * *

ATTRACTIVE, SPACE SAVING BOOK RACK

Display your most prized novels on this handsome and sturdy book rack. The hand-rubbed walnut finish will blend into your library decor with quiet elegance, providing a practical organizer for your favorite hard-or soft-covered books.

Only $9.95

Approximately 16" x 8" when assembled

Assembles in seconds!

To order, rush your name, address and zip code, along with a check or money order for $10.70* ($9.95 plus 75¢ postage and handling) payable to *Silhouette Books*.

Silhouette Books
Book Rack Offer
901 Fuhrmann Blvd.
P.O. Box 1396
Buffalo, NY 14269-1396

Offer not available in Canada.

BKR-2A

*New York and Iowa residents add appropriate sales tax.

Silhouette Intimate Moments

WHEN OPPOSITES
ATTRACT

Roberta Malcolm had spent her life on the Mescalero ranch. Then Hollywood—and Jed Pulaski—came to Mescalero, and suddenly everything changed.

Jed Pulaski had never met anyone like Rob Malcolm. Her forthright manner hid a woman who was beautiful, vibrant—and completely fascinating. But Jed knew their lives were as far apart as night from day, and only an all-consuming love could bring them together, forever, in the glory of dawn.

Look for Jed and Roberta's story in *That Malcolm Girl*, IM #253, Book Two of Parris Afton Bonds's Mescalero Trilogy, available next month only from Silhouette Intimate Moments. Then watch for Book Three, *That Mescalero Man* (December 1988), to complete the trilogy.

Silhouette Intimate Moments

COMING
NEXT MONTH

#253 THAT MALCOLM GIRL—Parris Afton Bonds

Rob Malcolm had been a rancher all her life, and her only dream was to have her own spread someday. Then Hollywood—and Jed Pulaski—came to Mescalero, and she fell in love with a man as different from her as night from day. Only time would tell if these two opposites could merge forever in the glory of the dawn.

#254 A SHIVER OF RAIN—Kay Bartlett

FBI Agent Luke Warren burst into Rachel's quiet life, insisting that her former husband had been a thief. Worse still, the sexy man planned to stick around until the stolen money was recovered. Soon Rachel found herself the target of the real thieves and of Luke's latest campaign—to win her heart.

#255 STAIRWAY TO THE MOON—Anna James

Ella Butler, widow of a famous rock star, was sick of publicity, and then she met Nick Manning, a prominent diplomat. His career placed him in the limelight, and she was certain they could never have a future together. But Nick would do anything to keep her—even climb a stairway to the moon.

#256 CHAIN LIGHTNING—Elizabeth Lowell

Mandy Blythe didn't want to be anywhere near the Great Barrier Reef. She didn't like the water, diving made her nervous—and she certainly didn't trust Damon Sutter. He was a womanizer, and the last man she could ever fall for. But the tropics were a different world—and paradise was only a heartbeat away.

AVAILABLE THIS MONTH: